A THE ARCHERS

Map of Ambridge

Archers Addicts Official Map of Ambridge © BBC 1994. Licensed by BBC Worldwide.
Published by Old House Books (Tel: 01647 440707)

THE OFFICIAL INSIDE STORY

ATHE ARCHERS

The Changing Face of Radio's
Longest Running Drama

VANESSA WHITBURN

The Archers

Virgin

For my mum, Eileen

Acknowledgements

My thanks particularly to Fiona Martin, Joanna Toye, Sue Ward, Camilla Fisher, Hedli Niklaus, Norman Painting, Liz Rigbey, Keri Davies, Brendan Martin, Sally Wainwright, Owen Bentley, Donald Steele, Justin Kelly, the cast, writers and production team of *The Archers* for their invaluable help, in so many ways, with this book.

I am also especially grateful to Mary Cutler, Louise Page, Graham Harvey, Mick Martin, Simon Frith, Caroline Harrington, Sam Boardman-Jacobs, Sally Wainwright and the estates of Edward J. Mason and Geoffrey Webb for giving me their kind permission to use extracts from their *Archers'* scripts.

This edition published in 1997
First published in 1996 by
Virgin Publishing Ltd
332 Ladbroke Grove
London W10 5AH

Picture Credits
Photograph behind all "Who's Who" © Romilly Lockyer c/o Image Bank
pp2–3 © Romilly Lockyer c/o Image Bank
p6 © Simon Wilkinson c/o Image Bank
All other photographs copyright © BBC

A catalogue record for this book is available from the British Library.

ISBN 0 7535 0107 4

Designed by Blackjacks Limited
Reproduction by Scanners
Printed in England by Jarrold, Thetford, Norfolk

Contents

Looking Back

chapter one

It all started on the evening of Whit Monday 1950 when 50,000 BBC Midlands Home Service listeners tuned into the strains of the now famous 'Barwick Green', which was to be the enduring signature tune of the *The Archers of Ambridge*, and the world's longest running radio drama serial was born - although to be strictly accurate, it wasn't *The Archers of Ambridge*, because the announcer at the time introduced the programme as 'The Archers of Wimberton Farm, on the fringe of the village of Ambridge'. Somewhere between the first five pilot episodes, which were transmitted only in the Midlands region, and the trial three-month run on the national network Light Programme the following year, Wimberton Farm became Brookfield Farm and the focus became not only the Archer family, with Dan and Doris at the head, but the village of Ambridge itself. All part, of course, of the creation and refining of detail which goes on as soon as any programme idea is bought by the commissioning powers that be.

From that moment onwards, continuing through 46 years to the present time, *Archers'* editors and production teams have striven, in their different ways, to guide the programme through the ups and downs of production fortunes, the highs and lows of audience appreciation, the vagaries of fashion and the pressures of real life events, to

Dan (Harry Oakes) and Doris Archer (Gwen Berryman) at the gate of Brookfield Farm.

provide a drama that is entertaining, enduring, informative, popular and, of course, thought provoking.

Looking back on the history of how the programme started, there is no doubt that BBC bosses approached the project with considerable caution. The idea for *The Archers* had come two years before it was first transmitted at a meeting between farming representatives and the BBC in Birmingham's Council Chamber. The War had just ended and to help get the country back on its feet, the representatives were talking about giving out essential, up-to-date, farming information in a popular way. A well-known Lincolnshire farmer, Henry Burtt of Dowsby, stood up and said 'What we need is a farming *Dick Barton*.' *Dick Barton* was, at the time, a hugely successful adventure serial based on an intrepid special agent who got himself in some exciting, if sometimes improbable, scrapes.

Godfrey Baseley, The Archers' *first editor.*

It is now a part of radio history that Godfrey Baseley, then a producer of gardening and agricultural programmes and later to become *The Archers* first editor, laughed with the rest of the people there at the silliness of the idea. But, unlike the rest of them, he didn't forget it. In fact, the idea kept popping into his head again and again until he felt impelled to follow it up. He knew, from his own experience, of the gentle excitement and interest which could be created around the everyday happenings on a farm or in a small country

Dick Barton *scriptwriters, Geoffrey Webb and Edward J. Mason, recruited by Godfrey for* The Archers.

village, and he had a notion that a skilful blending of such goings on with the more adventurous side of life might provide the ingredients for a new hit. Realising that he would need some skilled help with the drama side of things, he contacted the two *Dick Barton* scriptwriters, Geoffrey Webb and Edward J. Mason. He persuaded them to come on board. He then went on to secure approval for the five trial episodes from the then head of Midlands programmes, Denis Morris. Next he recruited a splendid young sound engineer in Tony Shryane, who was later to produce the programme for 28 years, under three successive editors and the small team set to work.

The trial episodes were very well received locally and led to the three-month nationwide run starting in January 1951. Success indeed, but London expected Godfrey to produce the programme for a mere £47 an episode and to continue his other job at the same time. Tony Shryane was given the additional role of junior producer and a clerk was employed at £6 per week.

Denis Morris, Midland Region Head of Programmes, with Tony Shryane and Norman Painting.

Godfrey wrote and recorded an introductory trail to the national programme, which went out before it started, in which listeners heard the editor himself, microphone in hand, wandering around Ambridge talking to the characters as if they were real people. He went into Brookfield to take tea with Doris Archer and discussed the merits of that 'new fangled nuisance, the wireless' with scurrilous Walter Gabriel. No wonder that, to this day, some listeners think Ambridge really does exist.

The trial national run was a great success, and within weeks the audience was two million. By Easter the serial had been moved to the prime spot of 6.45pm. By May the audience was four million, and needless to say, the idea that this was an experimental pilot with a limited life rapidly disappeared. Tony Shryane was elevated to producer and Godfrey Baseley wrote of his pride in the programme's dramatic success and, most importantly to him, the authenticity of its farming detail. He spoke also of the balance between the big stories and the 'straightforward story of the daily happenings in the countryside'.

In 1997, *plus ça change*. With the help of our agricultural story editor, Graham Harvey, we are still proud of the authenticity of our farming detail and we are still balancing the everyday story of country folk, the small anecdotal happenings that make up the day-to-day pattern of most of our characters' lives, with the bigger events; those huge, sometimes life-changing occurrences, the ripples of which spread wide around what Shakespeare,

Producer Tony Shryane gives notes to the cast.

Godfrey Baseley (right) talks to countryman Maurice Jones to get facts first hand.

putting it all into an even greater perspective, called our 'little lives'. And we are still tempering those many letters of praise and audience identification with those that criticise us for too much realism or too much violence or, inevitably, too much sex.

It is interesting, in this context, to look back at a memo from the fifties from a BBC boss after he heard a particularly smouldering scene on the sofa between Carol Grey and Toby Stobeman.

It reads:

It was faded out at a moment and after such scenes of heavy breathing and what you will, that could only lead one to suppose that Miss Grey had forgotten her mother's good advice – a supposition more than confirmed in the episode covering the following day during which Miss Grey did a good deal more sighing of a retrospective and reflective character and again left the more worldly listener in no doubt as to what had happened on the sofa.

And another which reads.

The Archers used to be for family listening. But recently it has become disgusting.

I remember some of the letters we got after Jennifer had her recent affair with ex-husband Roger Travers-Macy or when Caroline slept with the vicar, Robin Stokes. *Plus ça change* indeed.

But of course, though the concerns of listeners and higher authority, and our scrutiny of our storylines and scripts based on those concerns (more farming or less farming; more real life or less; more sex or less; more violence or less), continue and are, in essence, the same, they are not the same in detail. One generation's tolerance is different to another's; one generation's fashion is different to another's. The temperature of the times is always changing and the writers and producers of drama are in the middle of it all, seeking to respond sensitively to the evolving times, sometimes to follow and sometimes to lead. One listener's, nay one BBC boss's, 'daring and forward-looking storyline' is another's 'aberration and exaggeration'; one listener's 'exquisitely sensitive and moving moment' is another's 'self-indulgent bathos'; one listener's appreciation of 'a character's strong conviction', is another's example of the character's and therefore the programme maker's bias.

No wonder, then, that script meetings in 1997, when I sit down with the eleven writers, the agricultural story editor and five production team members each month, can be both exhilarating and exhausting affairs as we debate and manoeuvre. It is always a challenge to find our way through the mass of opinion and fact, to the guiding light of what, in the end, feels 'true' to our characters. It is finding that 'truth', through testing ideas and developing journeys for the characters, that is uppermost in our minds in our storyline meetings these days.

Taking a sweeping look back over 46 years of *The Archers*, the high and low points, one can see that the programme has definable eras and that those eras are, to a large extent, fashioned and led by the editor of the time.

In the fifties and early sixties, for example, there seemed to be a cunning blend of 'everyday story', action and melodrama which exactly fitted listeners' expectations. In 1954 the story of Dan and Doris negotiating to buy Brookfield after the death of Squire Lawson-Hope sits side by side with the visit of a Baroness Czorva on a mysterious errand to Mike Daly, a village resident who turns out to be a resting secret agent. Eventually the Baroness whisks Mike away from Ambridge and he is never seen again.

Secret agent, Mike Daly (John Franklyn).

Examples of melodrama are not hard to find in those early days and in 1959, while Dan Archer is deep in organising farm improvements, Charles Grenville's extravagant and jealous housekeeper, Madame Garonne, disappears too, only to be exposed in the *Borchester Echo* the following autumn as a diamond smuggler. There is plenty of action too: in 1961 vandalism first hits Ambridge when three teenagers on motorbikes start a fire in a hay-filled barn on the Grenville

The Ambridge church fête (1959): The mysterious Madame Garonne (Irene Prador, extreme left), Charles Grenville (Michael Shaw, centre), Mrs Turvey (Courtney Hope) and Dan Archer (Harry Oakes, extreme right).

estate. Walter Gabriel and Sally Johnson catch them in the act but in the ensuing scuffle Walter is kicked and left unconscious. Charles Grenville comes to the rescue and breaks one of the vandal's arms with a judo blow.

There is intrigue in 1962 when newly married Carol Grenville has a bundle of love letters from former beau John Tregorran stolen. Both she and John receive threatening phone calls demanding £200 for the letters but Carol decides to call the blackmailer's bluff and she admits all to her new husband. Eventually, by arrangement with the police, John Tregorran drops the money at a pre-arranged spot and P.C. Bryden catches the crooks, estate worker Harry White and his accomplice Chuck Ballard, red-handed.

Back to melodrama, and in 1965 handsome, dark-haired Roger Patillo, working as Laura Archer's chauffeur, admits that he has been using an assumed name. He isn't a foreigner after all. His real name is Roger Travers-Macy and he has assumed the name Patillo, taken from the villa in the South of France where he spent childhood holidays. He had a major row with his parents and had sought to disappear. Eventually true to his romantic and mysterious style, he meets, intrigues and marries Jennifer Archer. The key to *The Archers'* success was that such extravagant storylining, very much to the taste of the times, was well balanced with gentler stuff, with farming stories and with humour.

By the late sixties and early seventies, however, the programme was failing to keep up with the spirit of the times. The 'everyday story' got rather bland and the melodrama, by then rather out of fashion, got even bigger, less credible and certainly less to the audience's taste.

One of the best examples of the less likely was, undoubtedly, Nelson Gabriel's involvement with the great mailtrain robbery of 1967. Returning home alone from a cruise, Nelson apparently fakes his own death in a plane crash so that he can secretly link up with Charles Brown at Paunton Farm to plan and execute the robbery. It is a bungled attempt but the robbers do get away with some money and in 1968 Nelson is tracked down by Interpol and committed to trial at the Assizes. By March he has, however, got away with it, and is released in spite of fingerprints all over an empty Scotch bottle at Paunton Farm. Nelson always maintained to his father, Walter, that he had been framed, but the listeners never really knew the truth. However it seems, from the sketchy details available, both an unlikely release and an unlikely story.

Rosalind Adams · Clarrie Grundy

Rosalind has played Clarrie since 1988. The daughter of an actress, she studied at the Royal College of Music before becoming an actress herself and her first radio part was Tracy in Radio 2's *Wagonners' Walk*, in which she and Patricia Gallimore (Pat Archer) played flatmates. Her favourite job was creating the part of Annie in *The Norman Conquests* at Alan Ayckbourne's Theatre in the Round, Scarborough and her recent television work includes *Floggers, Hetty Wainthropp Investigates*, and *Nelson's Column.* Rosalind particularly enjoyed touring with other members of the cast in *Murder at Ambridge Hall* in 1993.

Eric Allan · Bert Fry

Eric Allan was born in Yorkshire, but his whole family moved to British Columbia when he was fifteen. His primary interest at this point was football, but he began to develop an interest in acting through amateur dramatic groups – there was no professional theatre in British Columbia. He joined a theatre company in Vancouver that moved around the province putting on plays in schools, and took part-time jobs to support himself while doing this. In his early twenties he decided to come back to England. He got a scholarship to RADA, and after graduation went into rep at the Phoenix Theatre in Leicester. After further work in rep around the country and a spell with the RSC in the late 1960s and early 1970s, he moved into television, playing the part of Frank Blakey in *Emmerdale Farm* for 18 months. This led to many more TV credits, including *Bergerac* and *The Sweeney.* Habitual Radio 4 listener and self-confessed *Archers'* fan, Eric joined the cast to play Bert Fry in 1997. He lives in Stroud with his wife. They have two grown-up children, a son and a daughter.

Gareth Armstrong 🍂 *Sean Myerson*

Gareth wanted to be an actor from the moment he saw Laurence Olivier in *Richard III* when he was eight years old. He read drama at Hull University and his first professional performance was at The Leeds Playhouse. Since then Gareth's extensive theatre work has included seasons at Leeds, Nottingham, Exeter, Bromley, Cardiff, Bristol and Birmingham, where favourite roles have been Oberon in *A Midsummer Night's Dream*, the Narrator in *Under Milk Wood*, Aimwell in *The Beaux Strategem* and Richard in *Richard III*. He has been a member of The Royal Shakespeare Company and appeared in the West End in Stoppard's *Dirty Linen*, Agatha Christie's *A Murder is Announced* and Noel Coward's *Easy Virtue*. Television appearances have included *Parnell*, *Witchcraft*, *Dr Who*, *EastEnders*, *London's Burning* and *One Foot in the Grave*. As a director, Gareth founded the Made in Wales Theatre Company and was Artistic Director at the Sherman Theatre in Cardiff for three years. Sean is Gareth's third role in *The Archers*. He played the original Mike Tucker in 1973 and was postman Harry Booker from 1973 to 1983.

Bob Arnold 🍂 *Tom Forrest*

Bob was born on Boxing Day 1910 in the Cotswolds village of Asthall in the Windrush Valley halfway between Minster Lovell and Burford. His father kept the local village pub and Bob left school at fourteen to work for a butcher in Burford. When he was only 22 he spent 15 months in hospital with a tubercular spine and when he came out the only job he could get was painting white lines on roads for Oxfordshire County Council. But Bob was well known around the Burford area as a singer and story teller, so when the BBC were making a radio programme called In the Cotswolds in 1937, he was a natural for it. His success on that programme led to other guest appearances and he soon found himself being billed as Bob Arnold, The Farmer's Boy. During the Second World War Bob served in the RAF and it was then that he met Dorothy who was to become his wife. After the War he returned to radio working in *Children's Hour* and on radio plays. When he first auditioned for *The Archers* in 1950, he was told he would never be cast because of his recognisable accent. Luckily there was a change of heart and four months later he was offered the role of Tom Forrest, a role he has been playing with great success ever since.

In 1972 when editor Godfrey Baseley retired and former Coronation Street producer Malcolm Lynch took over, the melodrama reached heroic proportions. In one week alone, notoriously, there was a plane crash, an attack on a local girl and the village bells collapsed! Often the melodramatic effect was created by the way the storylines were treated and paced rather than by the content of the ideas themselves.

In May 1973, for example, Jack Woolley is mugged by robbers and found seriously injured in the club lounge at Grey Gables. He is rushed to hospital where he remains unconscious for several days. Soon afterwards it is revealed that paintings and silver have been stolen but the robbers are never found and gossip soon dies down in the village.

The next substantial reference to the situation is in August when Jack's wife, Valerie, asks him for a divorce and he immediately collapses with a heart attack, presumably due to the stress some months earlier.

The melodramatic effect was largely created by the sudden importance given to the storyline one week, followed by a rather rushed wrapping up of thin events a few weeks later. In reality, the mugging of such a central member of Ambridge's community would have caused a considerably larger stir over a longer period of time and should have led seamlessly through to other stories.

When Charles Lefeaux arrived as editor in 1973, there was certainly a noticeable shift in the pace of the storylining and stories became more credible. But examples of melodrama could still be found and in 1975, whether as a result of mutiny in the writing ranks or simply because the programme was again trying to find its style, there was a disquieting sense that the bigger stories were beginning to be rather dangerously debunked by comedy, and listeners might have been forgiven for being confused as to what kind of story was being attempted. One of the best examples of this is when bandits set up a road-block and try to attack the post bus carrying Walter and Laura. Postman Harry Booker drives the bus over the fields to safety and events suddenly spiral into a comedy chase resulting in several broken false teeth!

Despite this example, there is no doubt that in the late seventies under Charles, the programme was stronger, with sustained stories which arose out of characters and a sequence of highly plausible situations, and which could be developed over several years.

Under William Smethurst, from 1978 to 1986, however, the programme did not tackle many long-running substantial storylines. William saw *The Archers* primarily as social comedy and developed the lighter anecdotal side of the programme, often deliberately at the expense of the more serious side. One notable example was the way the storyline involving the squatters who turn up in one of the Home Farm cottages in 1985 was handled. Although the inevitable rumours spread about drugs and spongers on society, there was no spin-off into the dilemmas created for the Aldridge family and for the village. The squatters are never featured, unlike the complex and sometimes contradictory characters, Lisa and Craig, in 1992. Jenny does not argue with Brian about possible courses of action in the way that Jill does with Phil, or Ruth with David, seven years later. Instead Brian, in a comic tour de force which dodges a million issues, simply puts paid to the problem by taking the roof off the cottage!

The author.

You can't really keep strong stories down for long, however, and by the mid 1980s they were again coming to the fore. One of the most ambitious, created by Anthony Parkin, involved the bankruptcy of small farmer Mike Tucker. This storyline, reflecting the tough times which farmers who had over-borrowed in the first flush of Thatcherism were having, provided a strong base from which subsequent editors, including myself, could develop interesting future lines as we pulled Mike back up from the scrap heap.

Editors Liz Rigbey and Ruth Patterson in the late eighties picked up on this deeper agenda and from Kathy Perks's affair with Dave Barry and the threatened break-up of her marriage to Sid, to Shula's IVF treatment; from David's tussles with his father Phil over who has a say in running the business at Brookfield to Sharon's homelessness, both Liz and Ruth developed the more serious side of the programme.

Since I took over as editor in 1991, I have sought to capitalise on this increased realism and most importantly, to sharpen the focus of the drama without losing the humour or the charm of the everyday story, which is the essential difference that helps to make *The Archers* unique.

The Big Stories

chapter two

A quick look through the storyline of the first few years shows just how dramatic and pacey it all was. Everything from Mrs Perkins's nephew, Bill Slater, dying from head injuries after a fight outside The Bull to a plane crash in Dan's five-acre field; from rioting saboteurs plotting to wreck an ironstone drilling site to the revelation that newcomer to the village, Irish thriller writer, Mike Daly, is not, as rumour has it, a Major in the Pay Corps who has been cashiered for embezzling funds, but a secret agent. There are kidnappings and fires and both Doris Archer and Jack Woolley are left unconscious, mugged by robbers. And, of course, Tom Forrest kills Bob Larkin, or does he? Eventually the charge against him is reduced to manslaughter but it is interesting to compare the way this big story, centred around one of the programme's most popular characters, was treated in 1952 with the way we treated the trial of another one of our most popular characters, Susan Carter, in 1994. The threat, I suppose, to poor Susan, accused of 'seeking to pervert the course of public justice' was less than that facing Tom Forrest should the charge of manslaughter have been upheld. But the complexity of the storyline and the twists and turns which the writers put our heroine through certainly caught the imagination of the press and public alike as well as the legal profession and the politicians. And somehow it all seemed much tougher, as we dealt in detail with the slow process of the law and heard how it impinged on Susan's life, than the story of Tom, which nevertheless, in the fifties, set listeners' hearts fluttering and journalists rushing for their typewriters.

Tom's saga begins in January 1957 when Bob Larkin, the brother of Brookfield farmworker, Ned Larkin, is visiting Ambridge from Dorset. Loveable Ned has invited his brother to stay, wanting him to meet a young local girl, Pru Harris. Ned thinks she will exercise a good influence on Bob. But Pru isn't interested in him at first, that is until he begins to turn on some of his irresistible charm. She refuses to go out with him but he

continues to press his suit. Eventually, beaten down by his persistence, she relents. In a very short space of time he manages to propose to her twice. But instinctively she refuses, waiting instead for the boy she really loves, Tom Forrest, to make a move. And Bob is a dubious lad, causing much trouble for his brother by stealing petrol from cars around the village. When a pair of gloves belonging to Ned is found soaked in petrol in a hedge, Ned has to endure the rumours that he is the thief, until his wife, Mabel, reveals that Bob borrowed the gloves. Later, it falls to Ned to persuade the police to drop the charges. In return Ned promises to pay back the money to all the people from whom his brother robbed.

Nowadays, I don't think the police would be persuaded so easily and the details of how that happened are all very sketchy in the script.

Ned Larkin (Bill Payne) and Tom Forrest (Bob Arnold) at The Bull being served by Jack (Denis Folwell) and Peggy Archer (Thelma Rogers).

In February, Tom, head-keeper on the Fairbrother estate, notices a sharp increase in poaching. Unable to stop it, he decides to watch overnight in long cover. But before he does so, he lets it be known that he will be away the day before in Fordingbridge doing some business in a game-rearing establishment. He hopes that the poachers might therefore believe that it is safe to poach that night. Around this time, Tom, being ribbed in The Bull about Bob's courtship of Pru, is heard to say that he'd bash Bob's face in if that man went near her again.

The fateful day of February 21st arrives and that morning, as we later hear at the trial, Tom is driven by his nephew Phil to the station where he boards a train ostensibly for Fordingbridge. Instead, he gets off at Merton Halt where Phil is waiting to collect him. Secretly Phil takes him back to a hut near the woods where Tom changes into working clothes and has something to eat. There Tom stays until eleven at night when Phil again joins him and together they set off to find the poachers. From eleven through the night they watch but nothing happens until about an hour and a half before dawn.

Then a shot from a four-ten shotgun echoes around the field. Tom and Phil are alert. Tom knows it is one of the men he is after because he had picked up his empty cartridge cases on previous nights. Now is their chance. Tom decides it is best for them to

Dan Archer (Harry Oakes), Tom Forrest (Bob Arnold) and Director General of the BBC (Sir Ian Jacob) look at a few of the many telegrams congratulating Tom on his engagement to Pru Harris (1958).

separate and make quickly, in a pincer movement, towards the place from where the shots have come. Then whoever finds the poacher will blow his whistle to summon the other. They go their separate ways.

Soon there is another shot and a pheasant drops from the sky in front of Tom. Out of the dusk comes the poacher and as he bends down to pick up the bird, Tom plucks up all his courage. 'What are you doing with that bird?' he shouts fiercely.

'Whassat?' replies the gruff voice.

'All right, you monkey, the game's up,' cries Tom.

But the poacher is not inclined to give up so readily. He punches Tom hard in the face and a struggle develops.

Tom tries to wrest the gun from the poacher's hands. He manages a few blasts from his whistle before it is roughly knocked from his mouth. Then he sees clearly, and for the first time, the man's face. 'By golly. I know you now, you rascal. 'Tis Bob Larkin.' And with that, they tumble together, crashing through the bush, undergrowth rustling and snapping all around them. Somewhere in the midst of the tumble, the shotgun goes off again.

Tom Forrest is on the look out.

Tom Forrest and Phil Archer find Bob Larkin is dead.

Phil approaches. 'Uncle Tom, Uncle Tom. Are you all right?'

He is. But Bob is dead. Phil calls the doctor and the police and later D.I. Browning arrives at the scene. The D.I., finding it impossible to work out how and when the gun had gone off and, with the only witness, Phil, being unable to say he'd seen the moment clearly, arrests Tom for murder.

All the time Tom is blabbing, talking nineteen to the dozen, afraid and, as the listener seems to have heard, innocent – an excellent use of radio since even the listener, I should think, could not have been sure. But one thing the listener did know was that Tom was provoked.

We later learn that Tom is remanded in custody. The details here are far sketchier than we would permit today. However, poor old Tom languishes in prison until the end of March, receiving poignant and often surprisingly buoyant visits from Dan and Pru as well as his friends and family.

Finally, he is committed at Borchester petty sessional court to be tried at Assizes on the charge of manslaughter. No doubt to every listener's relief, he is then allowed out on bail of £1000 put up by himself and his boss, George Fairbrother. Dear Dan and Doris take him in at Brookfield and many a tear-jerking scene occurs between then and July 4th when his trial begins – one of the most effective being when he sees Ned Larkin and assuages his guilt and Ned's grief.

Throughout, the police are nicely pitched. The D.I. is a suspicious and stern interrogator and as Dan says to his face, 'You're certainly not the fairy godmother, are you.'

And back comes the enigmatic reply: 'I might be ... at the end of it all.'

Dan (Harry Oakes) and Phil Archer (Norman Painting) look at a farming magazine.

It can be a tough farmer's life for Walter Gabriel (Chris Gittins).

Walter Gabriel, the Eddie Grundy of his time, is, of course, suspicious of police methods. 'Twist the words round to mean anything, they would. Never forgot the time they pinched me for drivin' with no lights in Felpersham once ... tied me up in knots they did and afore I could say "warble fly" I'd been fined a couple o' quid.' There is even the very modern worry from Walter of police corruption. 'Oh, if I said anything as was helpful they'd cross it out. 'Tis evidence against him as they'm after... get promotion if Tom goes down ...'

All in all though, the hand of the editor and the BBC's objectivity is evident with Dan, Phil and other key members of the community assuring the listener that 'the police are only doing their job' concerned to be efficient and effective. And as the storyline eventually proves, 'truth will out', and in contrast to the complexity of the fate of Susan Carter in 1994, justice is seen to be done.

And so it is, taken though we are, with Tom sitting quietly, 'paler than usual' in the dock, through every nook and cranny of the evidence: how the counsel for the prosecution tries to

suggest that Tom's anger against Bob for his interest in Pru fuels the intensity of the struggle and therefore the result; how Phil cannot have seen clearly what happened but did hear Tom call out Bob's name, thus proving that Tom recognised Bob; how Tom had previously been heard to utter threats against Bob in The Bull and other public places around the village. In the end, in a remarkable court coup by the jury and in a decision ratified by the judge, Tom is set free.

It is a decision made in some haste and in extraordinary circumstances. The jury, we are told, are extremely impressed by the honesty of Tom's face and his testimony. And when Phil Archer takes the stand and the prosecuting counsel attempt to suggest duplicity in Tom's instruction that they should split up in order to approach the poacher from both sides of the covert at once, Phil explains the sensible countryman's reason why Tom had made the decision and requests that the counsel's questions should, in future, be more intelligent. The court cannot resist laughter. That is enough for the foreman of the jury who leaps to his feet and asks, after consultation with the rest of the jury, for a recess to take advice from the judge.

When the court reconvenes they are told that the jury wish to hear no more evidence and Tom is set free. He returns to Ambridge in triumph to a reception organised by Walter Gabriel, resplendent with waving crowds and the Borchester silver band playing on the bridge near the River Am.

Quite how the foreman communicated so accurately with his fellow jurors in mid-trial was never really explained and neither, in any great detail, was the evidential basis for the final judgement. However, no doubt a very large number of listeners were relieved as poor old Tom was rightly exonerated.

In 1994 the outcome of the trial of Susan Carter was a far murkier, less satisfactory affair in its outcome and fans, journalists, the media, lawyers and even Michael Howard the Home Secretary joined in a debate, which Sir William Gilbert in the last century would certainly have recognised as they asked, 'Did the punishment fit the crime?'

We gave Susan Carter a six-month jail sentence for 'seeking to pervert the course of public justice'. The case centred on a very fine point of interpretation of the law and I, for one, thoroughly enjoyed the heated

Free Susan now, Archers fans demand in poster campaign

By R Barry O'Brien

IN a bizarre cocktail of fiction and reality, a fan of *The Archers* has started a campaign to have Susan Carter, one of the characters, freed from jail.

Ms Jenny Webb, 43, who has listened to the programme since childhood, felt it was not enough just to join the national tremor of outrage which has brought a spate of readers' letters to *The Daily Telegraph*.

She began producing "Free [Susan Carter] posters [in Ambridge] began [sentence] for h[er] escape [in] an ar[rest] lage [of]

Nov[w] How[ard] her l[egal] make [a] case [with] the [introduced] gran[ted] Susa[n] resp[onse] oth[ers]

A[t] Ker[n] hav[e] has [t] Ar[chers] sto[ry]

Campaigner: Ms

'Jailed': Charlotte Martin who plays Susan Carter

Justice plea by Home Secretary

Howard joins battle to free Ambridge One

By Express Reporter DAVID JARVIS

IT has aroused a brand of passion seldom associated with rural England. But such is the national outrage at the jailing of The Archers' Susan Carter that Home Secretary Michael Howard has joined the campaign to free her.

It was even speculated yesterday that the Radio Four show, as himself, to appe[ar]

Mr Howard, an avid fan of the world's lon[gest] many others because Susan received six mon[ths] brother elude the law.

"I don't think any judge would send a woman [with] children, to prison just before Christmas," he said.

Parish fetes and village carnivals were matters of distant memory yesterday as sleepy Ambridge became a focal point for the law-and-order debate.

Fiction

The controversy raged around the radio village's 1,000 imaginary inhabitants as they went about their [dai]ly business.

Mr [H]oward's intervention came as a nationwide Free The Ambridge One campaign gathered pace.

It is led by college lecturer Jenny Webb, 42, of Lydd, near Folkestone.

CONCERNED: Howar[d]

we'll get back to yo[u] came the uncertain rep[ly]

Following a week[end] end approach by Mr[s] Webb at his [...]

MARTYR: Susan, played by [actress] Charlotte Martin

Support grows to free Ambridge One from everyday country storyline

Andrew Culf Media Correspondent

AFTER the Birmingham Six and the Guildford Four, there comes the Ambridge One. The latest alleged miscarriage of justice file is about to thud on to the Home Secretary's desk — raising perplexing questions about sentencing policy.

"Free Susan Carter" posters have been printed in Romney Marsh, Kent, and a petition to Michael Howard calling for her release has been launched.

The mother of two was jailed for six months two days before Christmas for harbouring Clive Horrobin, her brother, on the run after an armed raid at a [...]

Susan Carter's imprisonment is the latest sensational storyline designed to pep up The Archers, Radio 4's 43-year-old everyday [...]

Jenny the Fre[e] paign, s[o] not just happenin[g] reflects [...] tion faci[ng] worryin[g]

Tyron paigner said: "W[e] ard will considere[d] for a ro[yal]

Roger Law S[ociety] commit[...]

Campaign to free 'the Ambridg[e]

A PRISON sentence that may have escaped your attention in the run-up to Christmas — it was handed down by an insignificant judge in an obscure part of the country to a rather dippy woman who harboured an armed robber (albeit her brother) — has stirred strong feelings within the agricultural community, *writes Charles Oulton*.

One group of countryfolk has now written to the Home Secretary, Michael Howard, demanding she be pardoned.

The case concerns one Susan Carter, 30, who has now served two weeks of a six-month sentence described by a penal reformer as the harshest and most unjustifiable decision he had encountered in nearly 25 years of listening.

When the judge chose to make Carter an example of the new toughness Michael Howard expects of the judiciary, he expected a *cause célèbre* — she is known to millions of people who listen to their radios every evening,

and on Sunday mornings — but the depth of public outrage has surprised even Mr Howard himself. The Home Secretary is currently taking sanctuary in America, where his advisers have so far been unable to brief him on the latest development.

When he returns to Britain, he will be handed a letter from a group of people describing themselves as "Archers" fans.

The letter, postmarked Lydd, near Ashford in Kent

Our lives are one big soap

THIS is Susan Carter The poor girl, mother of two youngster[s] was [...] s just [...] s for [...] after [...]r to [...]t in [...]she [...] e is [...] who [...] in [...] of [...] he [...]d [...]b-to [...] s [...]s [...]

■ SERIOUS: Sue Anderson

Call to free 'jailed' soap star

A PETITION calling for the release of a jailed radio soap character has been signed by Birmingham city councillors.

The petition asks the BBC to release Radio 4's *The Archers* character Susan Carter after she [...] months for [...]

THE AMBRIDGE O[NE]

Policy should be argued by Soap as well a[s ...]

[...]p washes life. That is what soap opera is [...]posed to earn its money from. It echoes [...] imitates and simplifies, and sells advert[ise]ments for soap powder, except on the [...]vertisement-free zone of the BBC, which [...]vertises nothing but its own products. *The* [...]*chers* radio programme, an everyday [...]ry of country folk that has run for the past [...] years, has once again trespassed into the [...]al world and created uproar.

Most radio is a medium that allows people [...]o have nothing to say to drone and twitter [...]way at people who are not listening. But [...]e *Archers*, which in theory deals with [...]llion miles from Birm[ingham...] of its remarkable long[...]ews sense. The prog[...] become more socially [...]ith adultery, abortion [...]l as cows, village bitch[...]

In a recent episode, [...]r of two, was jailed for [...]

The campaign [...] of the campaigne[...] fact, though the [...] makes it plausible [...] skill of catching [...] making them p[...] fiction. If h[e] lived [...] writing in [...]

The p[...]sulted th[e] sentence [...] was at [...] possibl[e ...] a serio[us] senten[ce ...]

Soapie fans seek pardon

LONDON - Outraged BBC radio listeners have launched a campaign against a jail sentence given to a fictitious woman character in the world's oldest soap opera.

Soap [...]
dramatising [...] and [...] abstract, unanswerable questio[ns ...] human condition, they bring the [...]rth. That is how tragedy bega[n ...]

The campaigners have asked the Home Secretary for her pardon and [...]wed they would appeal [...] the Queen for a royal [...]don if all else failed [...]listeners to the BBC [...]io's soap opera. The [...]iers, deluged the let[ters ...] pages of national [...]spapers after the [...]lar [...] character [...]n Carter was jailed [...] harbouring her [...]er who was on the [...] or armed robbery.

[...] hapless Carter [...] sentenced to six [...]s and her hos[...]aking brother was [...]ced to six years.

[...] sentence should [...]muted and she [...] be immediately [...]," said 43-year-[...]ny Webb, who [...] producing Free [...]arter Now pos[ters ...]er home town of [...]outhern Eng[...]en the story [...] to its 3.75 mil[...]eners just before [...]s

[...] and neigh[...]pported her [...] and she sent [...]s across [...]he [...]fellow addicts [...]ear-old radio [...]n the ficti[...]ng village of [...] — AFP

NEWS OF THE WORLD **ARCHERS CAMPAIGN**

FREE THE AMBRIDGE

FANS of radio serial The Archers have got up off their bum-ti-tum-ti-tum-ti-tums to protest about the greatest injustice ever to hit the fictional village of Ambridge . . . the jailing of mum Susan Carter over Christmas.

Now the News of the World is on the case too. With up to 7.5 million listeners, the series is more popular than Brookside. Susan Carter—played by Charlotte Martin, above—was jailed for six months after she was bullied into shielding her robber brother.

The issue has developed into a full-blown legal argument. What if Susan was a REAL person suffering such injustice?

Now it's time to show how YOU feel. Fill in the coupon on the right and return it to us now. Then we'll send them all to the highest judge in the land (as far as the Archers is concerned)—series editor Vanessa Whitburn.

She has the power to re-order scripts and have Susan released.

Storyline advisor and Law Society secretary Roger Ede said: "I wanted to get across how, in many cases, prison doesn't serve a useful purpose."

NEWS OF THE WORLD **FREE AMBRIDGE**

Dear Vanessa:

I think Susan Carter should be released from prison

Signed ....

SEND TO: Archers, News of the World, 1 Virginia St, London, E1 9XR

debate which followed outside the programme. It all started with Jenny Webb, a fan from Kent, producing posters demanding 'Free the Ambridge One'. Later there were badges and T-shirts carrying the same slogan. None could deny that a severe judge could have put Susan down but whether he should have, or would have, engaged the nation.

Eminent barristers argued in the press, eventually drawing out a detailed account of the research on which the judgement was based from our adviser and member of the Law Society, Roger Ede. Robert Kilroy-Silk took up the issue on his early morning TV programme and women who had been similarly imprisoned and had a tale to tell crossed swords with politicians who said it could never happen.

The press painted Jenny Webb as everything from a loony-lefty to a worried and responsible member of the community. Some papers tried to hi-jack her message to knock the show, saying we'd got our research wrong. Jenny's point, as she later told me, was precisely the opposite. She thought we'd got our research right and wanted to draw attention to the fact that many women are imprisoned too severely, usually by elderly male judges with little or no compassion.

Eventually Michael Howard himself said he felt the judgement was too harsh which left him in the surreal position of being personally asked to free Susan. I quivered in my wellington boots for a brief moment when I contemplated the enormous amount of hard work, re-writes, re-recordings, etc., should he have decided to do so. But the fear didn't last long – a legal precedent created from a fiction was something, I felt sure, of which even Mr Howard would fight shy. But how did we get to such an extraordinary position? Let me take you back.

Archers' fan Jenny Webb and Susan Carter (Charlotte Martin) celebrate Susan's release from jail.

In April 1993, Susan Carter's brother, Clive Horrobin, with an accomplice Bruno, mounts a raid on the village shop. They take Jack and Betty hostage and demand money from the till and the Post Office. Meanwhile, Kate and Debbie, having seen the men entering the shop, try to phone the police. But the phone box isn't working and Kate, to Debbie's horror, runs to let down the tyres of the getaway car. Courageous and plucky, it is nevertheless a stupid thing to do because the men see her through the shop window, leap out and drag both her and her sister inside. Holding them all hostage, Clive then phones his mate Derek to bring another getaway car to the scene. The tension of the situation is further increased by the fact that Jack, who already has a pacemaker, appears to have had a heart attack for which it is obvious he needs urgent medical help. Although Betty courageously stands up against Clive, whom she secretly recognises, and tries to phone the ambulance, Debbie stops her, fearing that even if only out of panic, Clive or Bruno may kill one of them.

Bank raid drama: Jack Woolley and Kate Aldridge.

Eventually Derek arrives and to Betty and Debbie's immense relief, the robbers leave and Betty is at last able to phone the ambulance. The shock has been profound for all concerned and Jack is hospitalised for a while but thankfully recovers. Meanwhile rumour spreads that Clive Horrobin was one of the raiders and the strain for Susan, Neil and the family is enormous.

On 26th April, Clive is arrested but his accomplice is still at large. By 18th May, Clive, under questioning, shops Derek and Bruno, but Bruno won't confess and Debbie and Betty have to attend an identity parade, a harrowing event for them both. Clive is remanded in custody to await trial but, a few months later, on the way to have his remand renewed, he manages to escape from a prison van. On 11th August, the police call on Susan to ask her to inform them if he makes contact with her. On 17th August, Susan's worst fears are confirmed. Clive arrives in the middle of the day at No.1 The Green and forces her to cash her child allowance. While she is out doing this, he searches the house, finds money put aside for the kids' August Bank Holiday treat and takes that as well. Susan is shaken by his visit but cannot bring herself to phone the police.

Betty is also traumatised by Clive's escape and keeps imagining that she sees him in Borchester or Felpersham and that he will come back to the shop to take his revenge on her for phoning the police. The news of Clive's

BETTY	(STANDING UP) I've had enough.
DEBBIE	Betty!
CLIVE	Sit down!
BETTY	I'm going over to that phone. Now. And I'm going to call an ambulance.
CLIVE	You're going to sit down.
BETTY	I'm going to call an ambulance.
CLIVE	You think this thing isn't loaded?
KATE	(FEEBLE) Don't. Betty. Don't.
CLIVE	Sit!
KATE:	Debbie. Make her stop.
CLIVE	Sit!!
DEBBIE	(QUIET) Betty ... (PAUSE)
CLIVE	(CALMER) That's right darling. You just get back there and sit down. Everybody just calm down. Then no-one gets hurt.

escape fuels gossip in the village. Poor Susan can hardly look villagers in the eye – she feels acutely responsible for her brother's actions, even though, as Neil keeps telling her, it is nothing to do with her.

At the beginning of September, Tom is burgled and the cashbox from the off-the-road riding goes missing at Home Farm. Susan blanches, fearing Clive's involvement, though both incidents, in this case, have nothing to do with him. From time to time her brother phones her, asking for money to be sent to him. Susan, recognising her position is a difficult one, and, torn between doing the right thing and concern for her brother, keeps her contact with Clive secret even from her husband, Neil. She simply begs Clive not to come back to Ambridge.

On 9th September, however, she returns from work at the estate office to find Clive inside the house, having stolen her spare key last time he was there. He's been living rough for three weeks and now wants to go to a friend in London who will help him. But he needs more money and help in dyeing his hair. Susan begs him to give himself up and even says that she has been so worried about him that she will ring the police herself.

Susan Carter
(Charlotte Martin).

But Clive tells her that he will get sent down for at least seven years and maybe more. Susan cannot bear the thought and Clive is quick to exploit her family feeling for him. She has to find more money, which she can ill afford, and fetch peroxide from the chemist.

Later, while she is dyeing Clive's hair and trying to persuade him to leave before the children arrive home, Neil returns unexpectedly early from work and, hearing voices in the bathroom, creeps softly up the stairs. He overhears Clive give the address at which he will stay in London. He also overhears Clive's tone change to a harder anger when Susan again asks him to give himself up. This is enough for Neil and he bursts into the room. Clive knocks him to the floor and hurtles down the stairs and away.

A sobbing Susan is comforted by Neil as she reveals that Clive has been there before. By September 12th, Neil, very worried by the hold that Clive has on his wife, surreptitiously and anonymously rings the police with the address he has overheard. On September 14th the police raid the address, but Clive is nowhere to be seen. Later, believing that Susan has informed on him, an angry Clive phones and threatens to 'take her with him' if he goes down. He tells her that he needs more money now that the heat is on and that he will phone her again to tell her where to bring it to him. Upset, Susan confides in Neil, but during the conversation she realises that her husband must have shopped Clive as he was the only person to know the address. Neil does not deny it, saying he did it for her and the children 'to get us out of this mess'. A coolness comes between them as Susan feels betrayed.

At work and at home, Susan is very jumpy, wondering when Clive will next call. When he finally does so, he is more aggressive than before. He says he will ring again the next day and Susan, fearful, unplugs her phone at home so she cannot take the call. During September, the situation drives a wedge between Susan and Neil as they cease to trust each other.

Meanwhile Neil goes cold calling at Hill Farm and meets farmer's wife, Maureen Travis. Maureen's husband Geoff is often away, since he supplements the family income from their small mixed farm by driving a haulage lorry. Neil has to make his sales pitch for animal feed direct to Maureen and it isn't long before chatty Mo is telling Neil all about her children, Becky and Daniel, who go to the same school as Neil's children, Emma and Christopher. Neil has to make several more calls to Mo to bring off his deal and as the strain continues between him and Susan, he increasingly needs a shoulder to cry on.

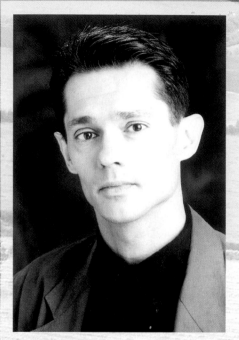

Yves Aubert 🍃 *Jean Paul*

Yves joined the cast of *The Archers* in 1988 as the French chef Jean-Paul. Not only were they both born in France, but Yves and Jean-Paul share the same surname. Yves is very much a European as his father was French, his mother Hungarian and Yves himself has spent many years living in England. His television work includes *Grange Hill, Bergerac, The Bill* and *Hercules Poirot*. He has numerous stage appearances to his credit and was most recently in a production of Moliere's *Le Bourgeois Gentilhomme* at Covent Garden. In his private life, Yves is an accomplished cook who enjoys entertaining and, like Jean-Paul, he maintains his own herb garden.

Sam Barriscale 🍃 *John Archer*

Sam was only thirteen when he joined the cast of *The Archers* as Pat and Tony's son, John. It was 1987 and since then he has also taken part in other radio drama including *The Brothers Karamazov* and *Adam Bede*. Sam's theatre credits include the National Youth Theatre and the RSC and on television he has been seen in *Casualty, The Bill* and for Screen One, *In Your Dreams*. On film he can be seen in *Judge Dredd* starring Sylvester Stallone. Home for Sam is a Grade II listed loft conversion in Worcester where he lives with his girlfriend, Jo.

Judy Bennett 🍂 *Shula Archer*

Judy joined the cast of *The Archers* in 1971 to play Shula and because she specialises in children's voices, she has also successfully played Shula's twin brother Kenton, her sister Elizabeth and even Adam Travers-Macy when they were growing up. Judy was educated at a Liverpool Convent Grammar School and gave her first public performance when she was fourteen playing St Bernadette at the festival in the City's Philharmonic Hall. After studying at the Guildford School of Music and Drama she got her first job as an assistant stage manager and understudy in *The Chinese Prime Minister* at The Globe Theatre in London. In 1966 she auditioned for BBC's schools radio and was cast as a boy by producer Richard Wortley. More radio work followed including parts in *The Dales* and *Waggoners' Walk* before *The Archers*. Judy's voice can be heard in numerous television cartoon and puppet shows and she presented the pre-school radio programme *Playtime* for nine years. She has also taken lead roles in many radio plays. Judy is married to Charles Collingwood (Brian Aldridge) and has three children, Toby, Barnaby and Jane.

Timothy Bentinck 🍂 *David Archer*

Tim joined *The Archers* in 1985 to play David Archer. He is one of the few members of the cast to have some direct experience of agriculture as he was born on a sheep station in Tasmania and after his family returned to England he worked on farms for pocket money throughout his childhood. After school in Berkhamstead, Tim was educated at Harrow before going to the University of East Anglia and the Bristol Old Vic Theatre School where he won the Carleton Hobbs Radio Drama competition. This resulted in his joining the BBC Radio Drama Company for six months which was to lead to the recording of many radio plays. As well as a busy career in the commercial and subsidised theatre, Tim's television credits include starring roles in *By the Sword Divided*, *Square Deal*, *Boon*, *Grange Hill*, *Sharple's Rifles* and *Three Up, Two Down*. His film appearances include *North Sea Hijack* and Trevor Nunn's *Twelfth Night*. He lives in London with his wife, Judy, and two sons, William and Jasper.

Charlotte Martin plays Susan Carter.

Mark Hebden (Richard Derrington), who acts as Susan's solicitor.

Susan is getting tired and depressed and is skiving off work. On September 29th, Clive phones her at home demanding that she gets his passport from their mother's house and some clothes. He will meet her at Digbeth coach station in Birmingham as he intends to leave the country. On October 4th a tense and distraught Susan meets Clive with the clothes, passport and some cash. Neil knows nothing of the meeting and is spending time with Mo, helping to fix the farm gate. On October 5th, Emma lets slip to her father that her mum has bought clothes for 'Uncle Clive'. Neil is horrified and the atmosphere is further strained as Susan and Neil argue about Susan's continued involvement. The fact that Clive has told Susan that he is going abroad is of little comfort to Neil who finds himself increasingly drawn to chats at Hill Farm where the lonely farmer's wife listens to him more than his own wife seems to do.

On 16th October, Neil, having been detained talking to Mo, gets home late. Susan is distressed because Clive has been arrested. Will he take her down with him as he has threatened? Sure enough, on October 21st, the police call early at the Carters' and arrest Susan on suspicion of harbouring her brother. The peroxide bottle is found during the search of the house

Brian Hewlett (Neil Carter) with Charlotte Martin (Susan Carter).

and Mark Hebden, called by Susan to be her solicitor, advises her to say nothing. But Susan wants to confess and on October 22nd she tells all in a recorded interview. She is bailed and the report is sent to the Crown Prosecution Services who will decide whether to prosecute.

Life is becoming very difficult for Susan and Neil as Susan worries about village gossip when the news of her situation gets out. Ironically it is Maureen Travis to whom she turns for help in looking after the children when the going gets tough. On October 25th, Mark sees Susan and tells her that if she is prosecuted he would expect a fine or community service. He also says that her best defence is that Clive threatened her, even made oblique threats against the children which forced her to help him. The police, he tells her, don't have much evidence apart from her own confession and Clive's unreliable testimony.

The peroxide bottle, he believes, is purely circumstantial evidence as Clive didn't touch it. By the end of October Neil is telling Mo all about Susan's arrest and she gives him a comforting kiss. He pulls away from her but she says that she will always be there if he needs her.

On November 1st, Neil tells Mo they can only be friends and, terrified of losing him, Mo readily agrees. He also somewhat guiltily asks her not to tell Susan how much she knows about Clive, but the friendship between Susan and Mo is getting stronger, as increasingly Susan looks on Mo as a support for the children in troubled times. On November 18th, Susan answers her bail but when she does so is charged with attempting to pervert the course of public justice. In an ironic scene later, she confides in Mo, and Mo has to pretend that she knows nothing.

Susan's solicitor, Mark, is aware that the prosecution has chosen a tougher law under which to prosecute her than it might have done and on November 22nd he mentions a prison sentence as a remote possibility. On December 3rd, Susan is committed to the Crown Court for trial at the same time as Clive. Mark tells her that he doesn't think the case will come to court before Christmas but by December 15th he hears that the court date will be December 23rd, a bitter blow to the Carter family. The trial takes

---

THE COURTROOM 2.45pm

JUDGE   And, Mr Horrobin, on the second count of escaping from prison custody, contrary to common law, I sentence you to twelve months' imprisonment, to run concurrently with the six years I have already imposed.

NEIL   Does that mean he's only got six years altogether?

GUY   Yes, it does.

JUDGE   (OFF) Mr Horrobin, you may go down.

CLIVE   (LEAVING DOCK) (OFF) Well, Susan, I hope you're satisfied.

JUDGE   Now, Mrs Fellows. I sit in these courts every day and have to listen to counsel, not all of whom are as eloquent as you, telling me that people commit crimes because they do not have any choice. But let me tell you Mrs Fellows, that they do have a choice – a choice between obeying the law or breaking the law. It's as simple as that. I recognise that Mrs Carter is of good character. I have listened to many good things that Mr Pemberton has said about her. But I cannot ignore what she did. The due administration of our system of justice is the core of a civilised and democratic people. It is becoming increasingly common for people to try and undermine this. I sadly hear from other courts about attempts at jury interference and witness intimidation. Any attempt to undermine the judicial system is a serious criminal act and I would be failing in my duty to the public and to the victims, if I did not impose a custodial sentence today. Therefore, Susan Carter, I have no alternative but to send you to prison for six months.

SUSAN   (SHARP INTAKE OF BREATH) What?

JUDGE   Take her down.

SUSAN   (OFF) You're sending me to prison!

JUDGE   (OFF) Mrs Carter, you may go down.

NEIL   They're not taking her straight to prison now?

GUY   I don't believe it! I'm sorry Neil...

NEIL   (RAISING VOICE) Susan –

SUSAN   (MOVING FURTHER OFF) Neil –

NEIL   (RAISING VOICE) Susan, don't worry! It'll be all right, we'll get you out. It'll be all right, I promise.

place on that day and in spite of her employer Guy Pemberton's appearance as a character witness, the verdict is seven years for armed robbery for Clive Horrobin and six months for Susan. The Court has viewed Susan's actions very severely. Because Clive had not yet stood trial when he escaped, Susan – in helping her brother – had hindered the police and undermined the judicial system. This the Judge regards as something that cannot be condoned. Susan's sentence will be an example to others.

Her solicitor Mark takes advice on mounting an appeal but reluctantly concludes that by the time it is heard Susan will be out anyway, especially if she gets time off for good behaviour. In fact, Susan is to find prison life very difficult. Neil visits regularly, sometimes with Emma, but Susan is quiet and withdrawn. She makes one friend in prison, a woman called Carol. They work in the laundry together. On the outside Mo is exceptionally friendly and supportive to Neil and the children and the more Susan withdraws, the more Mo's attentions threaten the status quo.

In March, the death of Mark leads Susan to go AWOL in order to attend the funeral. Neil is aghast when he sees her there and drives her back to prison. He wants to come in with her and explain but Susan refuses, saying she will face it out alone. When Neil visits a couple of days afterwards, she tells him that she has got five days suspended and loss of privileges. But that is not the only problem that Susan encounters while there. Later, she gets into a fight with another inmate who tears u a photo of her children. For this, ten days are added to her sentence. During this time Mo finds her moment to cook Neil a nice meal and suggest he stays the night. Though strongly tempted, Neil refuses and the listeners cheer.

On March 31st, Susan is finally released but hers is not the triumphal return of Tom Forrest. Instead, Susan is jumpy and afraid and, most of all, embarrassed to face her neighbours. And it takes considerable time and muc patience and kindness from her friends before Susan begins to be happy aga.

Susan is changed by the experience she went through and her crimina record sometimes haunts her. In 1996 she is worried that Simon Pemberton will find out she had been in prison, in case he refuses to continue to employ her. And when he does find out and rent money goes missing at the estate office, Susan is one of the first to be suspected. In 1997 her brother, Clive, is released from prison early and turns up in Ambridge, a further reminder of the turmoil of her recent past.

Susan Carter is a woman who is proud of the progress she has made in life and proud of her husband and family. For her, the loss of reputation involved in undergoing a prison sentence leaves a scar that will never go.

O ne of the extraordinary things about developing a long-running serial is the way in which story lines can be fashioned almost in real time, over a long period of time. A spin-off from a major event in one or more of our character's lives can go on and on and be charted with a complexity rarely matched in any other media. One of the biggest events in all our lives is, paradoxically, death and although the philosopher Wittgenstein comes up with the comforting notion that essentially 'death is not an event in life', for most people, at some time, the fallout from it most definitely is.

The Archers has never shied away from death, one of the most famous incidents being in 1955 when the programme killed off Grace in an audience-catching ploy on the evening that ITV started. The trick worked and the next morning much publicity was stolen from ITV. 'Listeners sob as Grace Archer dies' headlined the *Daily Sketch,* and the *Daily Express*

Grace Archer (Ysanne Churchman).

thundered, 'Why do this to Grace Archer?' The *Daily Mirror* reported people in villages standing at their doors openly weeping and quoted a Londoner as saying, 'I thought I was in for a lively party when I was invited next door for the first night of ITV; instead it was like a house of mourning.' Letters of sympathy poured into the BBC for Phil and the *Manchester Guardian* was moved to parody Wordsworth.

GRACE ARCHER'S 'DEATH' INEVITABLE

'TOO MANY CHARACTERS'

The "death" of Grace Archer, one of the leading characters in the radio series *The Archers*, was inevitable, as otherwise there would have been too many characters, which would have prevented the development of the plot, it was stated yesterday by Mr. D. Morris, head of B.B.C. Midland regional programmes, when he spoke at a news conference in Birm[...]

The decision w[...] eight months ago [...] of six men who run [...] The board consist[...] Programme, the [...] the producer, the [...] Morris.

"We knew sor[...] out to leave othe[...] Mr. Morris. "[...] informed some m[...] not be wanted in [...] She is a very acco[...] and we wanted t[...] to come back broadcasting."

Mr. Morris said that it was known, w[...] Grace Archer was "married" to P[...] Archer, that she was to be "killed off," the decision for the "wedding" was t[...] long before.

Death in the Family Ⓢ

The people who write the "Archers" serial for the B.B.C. have every right to feel proud at the lamentation that has followed the "death" of Grace. Respectable ladies felt dizzy and took to brandy after hearing the news; children telephoned the B.B.C. to ask about sending flowers; one angry housewife complained that she could not get the children to sleep and had missed the beginning of I.T.V. (Jerhaps this had been intended?) [...]tural concern should [...]s the symptom of the age. It is trifling in nation's grief during of little Paul Dombey. and writers soaked ith their tears as they tens not to let Paul the novel's tragedy and even those most if the child knew well he wild waves were mself, when he had [...]ecution.—in a passage so long and so elusive that it is hard to say when death occurred.—went out into the streets of Paris and walked the whole night through in mourning for this fictional on. The cast of the "Archers" were not, apparently, so moved. One of them is reported to have said "This is the third death. At this rate we shall all be out of work in no time.' The lady who actually played the part of Grace commented: I am very flattered by the reaction. But don't want to discuss my departure from the programme. I have other engagements with the B.B.C."

DEATH OF BBC SERIAL CHARACTER Ⓢ

Grace Archer, one of the main characters in the B.B.C.'s serial *The Archers*, "died" in last night's instalment while an ambulance was taking her to hospital. She had been trapped in a blazing stable.

A spokesman for the B.B.C. said last night: "We had considerable reaction to the death of Grace Archer. Some people rang up to make sure that it was the character in the serial who had died and not the actress. Most of the people who rang up said it was a pity she had died."

GRACE ARCHER

Dulce et decorum est pro BBC Mori

> She dwelt unseen amid the light
> Among the Archer clan
> And breathed her last the very night
> The ITV began.

> A maiden in a fantasy
> All hidden from the eye
> A spoken word: the BBC
> Decided she must die.
> She was well loved and millions know
> That Grace has ceased to be.
> Now she is in her grave but Oh,
> She scooped the ITV

The story itself is fairly simple. Grace is the only child of George Fairbrother who made a fortune in plastics and bought an estate farm in

Ambridge in 1951 to retire into the role of gentleman farmer. His daughter is fun and glamorous but pampered, with a volatile nature which is, at times, charming and at times, infuriating. She is the perfect charismatic and well-heeled match for the young Phil Archer, but her changeable and sometimes spoilt nature bodes stormy times in the years to come.

Phil proposes to her on September 8th 1954 and they marry soon after. Marriage seems to soften Grace a little and her unwillingness to have

Another farming day. Phil Archer (Norman Painting), Simon (Eddie Robinson), George Fairbrother (Leslie Bowmar) and Dan Archer (Harry Oakes) inspecting the stock in 1954.

children changes, much to Phil's
delight, after a holiday at her friend,
Isobel's, in 1955. When she and
Phil arrive they find Isobel in bed
with a scalded foot and Grace has to
take over running the house and
taking care of the baby. When they
return home the pleasure of
looking after the child has led to a change of mind.

*Phil with his wife-to-be
Grace Fairbrother.*

When George makes Phil a director of the estate, he arranges a
celebratory dinner party at Grey Gables with Grace, Carol Grey, John
Tregorran and Reggie and Valerie Trentham. During the course of the
pleasant evening Grace finds she has lost an earring. She goes back to her
car to look for it and sees, to her horror, that the stables are on fire.
Impulsively she dashes in to save Christine's horse, Midnight. But a burning

beam comes down on her head and, although she is rescued from the fire, she dies in Phil's arms on the way to the hospital.

The next day the village is in shock but farming life goes on and Dan Archer is in the dairy as usual seeing to the morning milking, as the continuity announcer tells us, 'glad to concentrate on hard work'. Simon a workman from the estate kindly arrives to help, knowing that Phil will not be there. The scene in which Simon expresses his sympathy reminds me of Bert Fry coming in early to help out with the morning milking after Mark's death in 1994.

Christine Archer (Lesley Saweard) on Midnight.

Simon (Eddie Robinson) and Dan Archer (Harry Oakes) mucking out the cowshed.

Later, when Dan sees young Christine in the farmyard, she is clearly very upset and his honest homilies are perhaps a little heavier than we would go in for nowadays. Peggy and her first husband Jack, on the other hand, have just the right mix of sympathy, desire to help and guilty relief

that they themselves are all right, which most of us, if we are honest, have felt at times when someone close to us suffers a bereavement.

Phil remains in shock for some time and his mother Doris arrives at Coombe Farm to stay with him. On September 26th the details of the will are read. Grace has left everything to Phil except her interest in the stables which she leaves to Christine. On that day too, listeners hear Dan, Doris and Christine back at Brookfield after the funeral. It was decided not to dramatise the funeral itself as the production office was worried that it would get too many wreaths.

Life must go on for Dan, even in the face of the death of his son's new wife, Grace.

DAN	...Me and Simon, there... in the milking shed... we've got the same feelings as you and everybody else but we've still had to carry on milking, just the same as you've had to carry on feeding and watering those horses you've got here...
CHRIS	I never said anything about not doing the milking or not feeding the horses, did I? Of course those jobs have got to be done.
DAN	And the same applies to breakfast and housework and ploughing and muck-spreading, and everything else, Chris. Life must go on, my love...it's heart-breaking and dreadful but it's not the end of the world. Life must go on, for you, for Phil, for all of us. So let's all get busy and do something to help it.
CHRIS	But... but Dad... why should a thing like this have to happen to us – why? Why to us?
DAN	Things like this are happening to people every day Chris...every day of the week somebody somewhere has a thing just like this to face up to and contend with. Why should we consider ourselves any different from other people just 'cos we're the Archer family. We're not any different, y'know. So this thing happens to us...now. And all we can do is the same as folks somehow manage to do in similar circumstances. Just carry on.

The prevailing tone in the programme is one of sadness and sympathy for Phil who is left so alone. The tone is also one of 'stiff upper lip'. Whether it be Dan to Doris, Walter Gabriel to Tom Forrest or boyfriend Paul to Christine, the emphasis is solidly on 'life must go on'. Preparations for the village concert, organised by John Tregorran, continue just as Phil and George Fairbrother have asked them to. On September 27th Dan comes upon Doris making a crazy paving path and they are interestingly tetchy with each other. Ostensibly the scene is about Doris's frustration with the path and Dan's irritation that the new farmhand he has just interviewed wants a house to live in as well as the job. This is a tricky one for Dan as Simon, the old farmworker, is still in the cottage and he cannot throw him out. The scene clearly shows the strain that all the Archer family are under. Even an event as big as the death of Grace, however, could not hold up normal life in Ambridge for long and in those early days there was less awareness in the scripts of the communal memory of major events as the months and years went by.

Dan Archer with his daughter, Christine.

Every so often though, Grace is remembered. On September 23rd 1957, Phil is having a meal in a restaurant with his new girlfriend Jill Patterson, later to become the second Mrs Phil Archer, when he suddenly and rather guiltily remembers that it is the second anniversary of Grace's death. Although it is, by then, quite late in the evening, Jill persuades him to pick some flowers and go with her to put them on Grace's grave. In 1959 Helen and George Fairbrother pay for a memorial window in the Church for Grace.

From the day she married Phil to the present, Jill Archer has that curious blend of affection, jealousy and irritation when Grace's name is mentioned. She knows Phil loved his first wife dearly and would never seek

Jill Archer (Patricia Greene) in 1962.

to ask him to forget her or take her place, but just sometimes she wonders if she is living with the ghost of a saint.

On March 2nd 1994, 37 years later when the Archer family are reeling from another family tragedy, Phil, sitting with his youngest daughter Elizabeth, remembers Grace. It is the morning of Mark Hebden's funeral.

On February 17th 1994, the death of Shula's husband Mark is as sudden and unexpected as that of Grace, but the powerful events surrounding the tragedy affected more characters directly and the resulting inter-connecting storylines were more complex.

Mark is driving home after a hard day at work using the car phone to do some last-minute

ELIZ	(THOUGHTFUL) Look at me. I haven't any right to cry.
PHIL	Of course you have.
ELIZ	I don't know how Shula's doing it. I couldn't.
PHIL	You don't know until it happens to you. (PAUSE)
ELIZ	Dad, what was Grace like?
PHIL	Oh, beautiful. Funny. Strong-minded – we used to have such rows. Still, we were both very young.
ELIZ	You must have been even younger than Shula.
PHIL	Yes. Yes, and I thought my life had ended. But it hadn't.
ELIZ	I suppose that's some sort of hope.
PHIL	There's always hope for the people left behind. Somewhere. Sometime. Eventually.
ELIZ	(CRYING) Oh Dad. I'm so sorry.

business. He is expected home as early as possible to help with the supper party hen night which Shula has organised for Caroline Bone. Caroline is to marry Robin Stokes, the local vicar. Shula and Mark had a small tiff about things only that morning when Mark said he might have to be late home, but thankfully they made up before he left for work. That evening, too, Debbie persuades Caroline to go out for a ride. The plan is that she will take Caroline and casually drop in on Shula when the surprise party will take place. Elizabeth and Nigel are already at Glebe Cottage helping with the preparations. Mark phones home to say he is on his way and he won't be late.

Caroline Bone (Sara Coward) with Robin Stokes, the local vicar (Tim Meats).

There follow four tightly inter-cut scenes between Debbie and Caroline on horseback on the road and Mark in the car. A speeding car overtakes Mark, scares Caroline's horse and throws her into the road. In a split second Mark rounds the bend and, trying to avoid the body of Caroline on the road, swerves and crashes into a tree. Listeners had to wait until the next day to learn that Mark was dead.

Caroline is in intensive care with a fractured skull, broken arm and abrasions, Shula is obviously numb with shock, and Caroline's wedding to Robin, which should have taken place the next day, is cancelled and Robin is at her bedside.

For me the death of Mark was a particularly poignant and powerful storyline because I was involved in a real-life car accident in which I almost died about a week before Mark's car crash. I will never forget lying in intensive care, tubes everywhere, just grateful to be alive, and tuning into the episode which I knew ended with the enormously realistic collage of

Vanessa 'on road to recovery'

Vanessa Whitburn at her desk in the BBC's Pebble Mill studios before the accident

Archers soap chief in crash

VANESSA Whitburn, of the The Archers, w serious but stable con in hospital last nigh being involved in a ca dent close to the BBC ble Mill studios.

A corporation spol said Miss Whitburn s a fractured pelvis a ken ribs in the colli tween her VW G another car at the of Bristol Road and Mill Road, Selly O mingham, shortly noon.

Firemen used equipment to free the wreckage.

She was taken to ham General Hospi

Three men in t car, also a Golf, we ken to hospital but badly hurt.

David Waine, BBC Broadcastin Midlands and Eas accident was a shock, not just fo of The Archers, b whole of the BBC

He said: "Van close personal fri wonderful lady a be a doughty figh

Miss Whitburn was appointed e Archers – dubbe day story of cou in 1991 and has duced several controversial storylines including sending one of the main characters to prison for helping her criminal brother after he escaped from custody.

The BBC said recordings of the programme were not affected.

Editor of Archers hurt in car crash

MISS Vanessa Whitburn, editor of The Archers, was last night very seriously ill and s undergoing an emergency operation after being involved in a car crash near the BBC's Pebble Mill studios.

A corporation spokesman said the condition of Miss Whitburn, 39, who is in Birmingham General Hospital, had deteriorated since she was admitted shortly after the lunchtime accident.

Firemen used cutting equipment to free her from the wreckage of her VW Golf after it was in collision with another vehicle at the junction of Bristol Road and Pebble Mill Road, Selly Oak, Birmingham.

Three men in the other car, also a Golf, were taken to hospital but were not badly hurt.

Mr David Waine, head of BBC Broadcasting in the Midlands and East said the accident was a terrible shock, not just for the cast of The Archers, but for the whole of the BBC and listeners to the Radio Four series

"Vanessa is a close personal friend and wonderful lady, and she a doughty figh e said.

Flowers flood in for Archers boss

By ROZ LAWS

road to recovery. We have been overwhelmed by the flowers, cards and messages of support from her colleagues and listeners,"

mingham.

Miss Whitburn was trapped 40 minutes before being cut free by fire crews.

She was conscious when taken to hospital, but her condition ed and minute ternal ed 39, atford ointed rs in

June 1991. A BBC spokesman said last night: "Our studios have been inundated with calls from listeners. Some fairly well-known people have been asked to be kept in touch with her condition.

The hospital has also had a large number of flowers and asked us to ask people not to send any more."

Deputy editor Joanna Toye will be taking over.

Archers editor cut from crash wreckage

THE editor of The Archers was seriously ill in hospital last night after a crash.

Fireman cut Vanessa Whitburn, 39, from her Volkswagen Golf after it collided with another car as she drove to the BBC's Pebble Mill studios Birmingham.

She was taken to mingham General 1 tal with rib and injuries. Three peop

the other car were injured.

Miss Whitburn has introduced several controversial storylines since taking charge of the BBC's longest-running radio programme in 1991.

A BBC Midlands

Archers editor in crash

THE editor of BBC radio's The Archers was "very seriously ill" last after emergency surgery for abdominal and chest injuries following a car crash near the BBC's Pebble Mill Birmingham.

said the condition of 39-year-old deteriorated since she was admitted eral Hospital shortly after the

Editor ill

BIRMINGHAM: Vanessa Whitburn (39), editor of radio soap The Archers, was seriously ill in hospital today after a car crash.

e being appointed of The Archers in Miss Whitburn has duced several controversial storylines, including sending one of the main characters to prison for helping her criminal brother after he escaped from custody.

Archers woman in crash

Vanessa Whitburn, aged 39, editor of the Radio 4 series The Archers, was in serious condition after emergency surgery last night for abdominal and chest injuries she suffered in a car accident near the BBC's Pebble Mill studios in Birmingham.

Graham Blockey ✿ *Robert Snell*

Graham was born in Manchester and brought up in Scotland.
His father was an orthopaedic surgeon and so, not surprisingly,
finding himself with similar interests, Graham went to Newcastle
University to study medicine. During his medical studies he spent
three months working in a mission hospital in Kenya and after he
qualified he worked at Shottley Bridge Hospital in Durham and in
casualty at St Marys, Paddington before becoming a G.P. But it
wasn't long before Graham realised that he had another ambition
he wanted to fulfil – that of becoming an actor. To this end he
spent a year at the Bristol Old Vic Theatre School, working as a
medical locum in the holidays to help support his studies.
Afterwards he spent three years in touring theatre in the
West Country and Lake District. Finding that medicine pays
better than theatre, Graham has now returned to being a
full-time G.P. but somehow he still manages to find time
to continue to create the long suffering but loveable rock
on which Lynda Snell's life stands. In real life, Graham is
married to writer and journalist,Chris Ingram and they have
two children, Olivia and Jamie.

Carole Boyd ✿ *Lynda Snell*

Carole was born and brought up in London, considering herself a
townie through and through until arriving in Ambridge to play
Lynda Snell in 1986. Coming to the BBC's Pebble Mill studios for
recordings was, however, something of a homecoming, since
Carole trained at the Birmingham School of Speech and Drama
before going on to win the Carleton Hobbs award for Radio
Drama in 1966. Since then, Carole has recorded many radio
dramas and features and she is also no stranger to radio soaps
having played Shirley Edwards in Radio 2's *Waggoners' Walk* for
four years before joining *The Archers*. In a theatre career
spanning over 25 years, Carole remembers a favourite year
working for Alan Ayckbourn in Scarborough where she created
the role of June in *Way Upstream* and her television appearances
include *The Specials, Virtual Murder* and *Frontiers*. Carole's voice
is well loved by thousands of children as she plays all the female
voices in *Postman Pat* on television, video and tape and she has
recently been involved in the first live recording of Radio 4's
Poetry Please which she found both challenging and enjoyable.

Margot Boyd ❧ *Marjorie Antrobus*

While studying at the Royal Academy of Dramatic Art, Margot had the unforgettable experience of taking part in George Bernard Shaw's *Heartbreak House* directed by the great man himself. And that was the beginning of a successful theatrical career which has included numerous West End productions, her favourite being Noel Coward's *Waiting in the Wings* at the Duke of York and *Harvey* with James Stewart at the Prince of Wales. It was in 1953 while at Stratford with The Royal Shakespeare Company, that Margot was invited to make her first radio broadcast from the BBC's Birmingham studios. It soon became clear that the microphone loved her voice and many radio plays followed. She was, however, busy elsewhere, and her television work includes *Dixon of Dock Green,* and film work, *The 39 Steps* with Kenneth Moore. It was in 1984 while Margot was doing a stint at the BBC Radio Drama Rep that she was given a small one-off part in *The Archers*. Her creation of the role of Mrs Antrobus was so memorable however, that once they had heard her the writers couldn't resist keeping her in as a regular. Luckily Margot agreed to the prolonging of the engagement and she is still enjoying her role twelve years later.

Kellie Bright ❧ *Kate Aldridge*

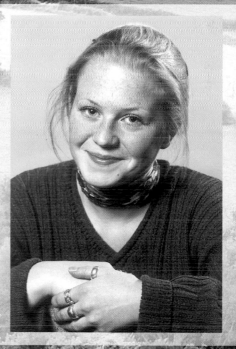

Twenty-year-old Kellie Bright plays Kate Aldridge, Jennifer's difficult daughter and one of the leading members of *The Archers* notorious brat pack. Born in Basildon, Essex, Kellie trained at the Sylvia Young Theatre School and made her first professional appearance in *Les Miserables* at the tender age of nine. Her theatre credits already include *The Wizard of Oz* at The Barbican for the Royal Shakespeare Company and *The Chalk Garden* at the King's Head Theatre in London. On television, Kellie has become well known for her role as Joanna in *The Upper Hand*. She is enjoying playing bad girl Kate and hopes to continue to expand her career in radio, theatre, television and film.

sound effects which made up the car crash. We had, after all, worked hard to perfect it for maximum effect. I thought I would be able to listen to it again. But I switched off just before the final scene. It made me think long and hard about the effect of powerful drama and how, with the best will in the world, we cannot control the circumstances of the listener and therefore the way in which it is received. If that crash had come upon me unexpectedly, how shocked would I have been? I do not know, but I do know that I couldn't listen to that sequence for several months. And yet, it seems to me, on reflection and even then, that drama has to dare from time to time to paint our lives in all its difficulty as well as its happiness. That after all, is what makes it relevant and powerful.

The shock of Mark's death with its almost graphic portrayal through sound effects, reverberated through the programme for many months, even years, in a way that a scene of reportage simply would not have done. So, we felt for Shula and travelled with her on her long journey into the light again. And as the ripples of the storyline extended out from the main event itself, so the programme looked, too, at how many other lives were affected and were beginning to put themselves back together.

On the day after what would have been Mark's 39th birthday, Shula blames herself for the accident, remembering that she had told Mark to hurry home and that was why he phoned from the car. It isn't until February 23rd that Caroline recovers consciousness, but it is clear that she is confused and unable to grasp what has happened. Debbie also takes it hard, remembering that she had talked Caroline into going for the fateful ride when Caroline had wanted to finish earlier, but she, Debbie, had insisted on staying out. Debbie's mother, Jennifer, tries to comfort her, reminding her that if it was anyone's fault, it was 'that criminal who overtook Mark on a blind bend'.

At first Shula cannot go to visit Caroline in hospital and Robin is relieved. He has not found the moment to tell Caroline about the accident. She does not even know that Mark is dead.

On February 25th, by one of those glorious twists of fate, Doctor Richard Locke is able to tell Shula that her IVF treatment has worked; she is pregnant. A light in the dark tunnel, but a light that demands a lot of courage from stoic Shula. On February 28th Shula tells her mother the good news. She also tells her father that she feels strong enough, at last, to visit Caroline.

It's not cricket

SOME cur has used the personal columns of *The Daily Telegraph* to play a practical joke on mourning fans of *The Archers*. The radio soap opera is still reeling from the fatal car crash of one of its main charac-

GRAY-NICOLLS CRICKET bat for sale. As new. Never used. Apply Mrs S Hebden, Glebe Cottage, Ambridge, Borcs.

ters, Mark Hebden. It was terrible. His wife Shula had just bought him a cricket bat for his 39th birthday.

Seizing on that pathetic detail, ... advertisement

advertising staff and, well, you can see the result for yourselves. My telephone barely stopped ringing yesterday after the ad's appearance. Typical was the response of Patrick Pool, an *Archers* fan from Flamsted, Herts. "Swine!" he opined. "I am appalled." The Friends of Hebden are in ugly mood. The mystery advertiser does well to remain anonymous.

Archers agony

Death shocks soap fans

Archers anguish

Fans protest at everyday tra...

New tragedy for Archers fans ...lk

More trauma for shaken Archers' fans

Accident puts Archers wedding in jeopardy

Robin warns Phil that he wants her to stay away a little longer. The truth is that Caroline still hasn't grasped the fact of Mark's death and any visit would be painful for them both. Between then and March 4th, when Shula finally does visit Caroline, Robin gently coaxes his fiancée into remembering what happened and encourages her not to be afraid to meet Shula and to stop blaming herself for Mark's death. But even as he does so there is a distance building up between him and Caroline. She will not talk of their wedding or confide in him. It is as if Robin's God has let her down.

Mark's funeral takes place on March 2nd, very much 'on air' in contrast to that of Grace all those years ago. The production office got many cards but no wreaths! It is a tough time for Shula and Elizabeth, who cries. And, in a different way, it is a tough time too, for Susan Carter who goes AWOL from prison to pay her last respects.

Two days later the time comes for Shula to visit Caroline at last, and there is a tearful reunion. She tells Caroline that she doesn't blame her for Mark's death and that Caroline needs to stop blaming herself. She shares the good news about her pregnancy.

All through this time, Shula's life-long friend, Nigel Pargetter, now going out with her sister Elizabeth, provides enormous support.

At first Elizabeth is, of course, understanding and sympathetic, but by May 9th the strain begins to show, as Elizabeth feels Nigel has begun to care

Alison Dowling plays Elizabeth Archer.

more for Shula than for her. Thankfully it is a temporary problem, however, because Elizabeth, deep down, can see Shula's great need for old friends at this difficult time, and it is not long before Nigel and Lizzie make up again and announce their engagement.

Meanwhile, strong Shula is finding it difficult to cope with the practicalities of sorting out Mark's business affairs with Usha, and in the end she leaves most of it in Usha's capable hands.

Nigel Pargetter (Graham Seed) and Lizzie announce their engagement.

Over the next year the programme charts carefully the pattern of Shula's grief. There are highs, like the single wicket competition in May, where she presents the new trophy in Mark's honour, and lows, like Elizabeth's hen night in September when she falls apart and has to go home early.

On September 29th, Elizabeth and Nigel get married and Shula is strong throughout the wedding. Shula's pregnancy goes well and she chooses her old friend Caroline to be with her when Daniel Mark Hebden is born on November 14th.

On December 2nd Shula breaks down in front of her sister-in-law, Ruth. She feels so alone; she wants Mark. Somehow she manages to get through the first anniversary of Mark's death but on his birthday on February 20th 1995, she takes a walk on Lakey Hill with Caroline and cries into the wind 'it's not fair, it's not fair'.

In 1997, much has changed. Realising his marriage to Caroline was not to be, Robin has left Ambridge. Guy Pemberton has successfully wooed and wed Caroline, but he has died of a heart attack six months into the marriage. Shula had tentatively begun to fall in love with Simon, Guy's complicated son, until she found out that he was having an affair and broke off the relationship. And Simon, after attempting to oust the Grundys from Grange Farm, has also left Ambridge. The second anniversary of Mark's death has been remembered quietly by Shula and all the family. No guilty forgetfulness while courting another for Shula – not yet.

The idea for this story, one of the biggest and most sustained the programme has ever done, came from a late-night discussion that I had with Louise Page, one of the writers. We wanted a big story that would touch the lives of many of the characters and into which other

SHULA	How long is it going to keep hurting?
CARO	I...
SHULA	Do you know, Caroline... (STRUGGLING) every morning when I wake up...every single morning... the first thing...the first thought I have every day is... Mark's dead.
CARO	I know.
SHULA	Even since this little chap was born. (PAUSE. SAD LAUGH) People think...at least she's got the baby. But...
CARO	That's not the point.
SHULA	It doesn't take away the pain. Oh, I love Daniel so much, of course I do. And his being here gives a real purpose to my life. But...it doesn't make Mark's not being here better.
CARO	No.
SHULA	Sometimes, when I look at Daniel, I miss Mark more. I look forward to...to his first words...his first steps...and then I think I shall never be able to share those moments with the only person who ever could share them...and I think...(PAUSE).
CARO	Go on.
SHULA	I know I shouldn't, and I know it's selfish...but I just think... (PAUSE)...it's not fair.
CARO	(LONG PAUSE. GENTLY) Go on, Shula. We're at the top. (PAUSE) As loud as you like.
SHULA	(YELLS) Oh Daniel, it's not fair! It's not fair! (SOUND OF THE WIND AT THE TOP OF THE HILL)

stories could weave and merge. We brought a rough line of the idea – that Mark should be killed in an accident which also involved Caroline and her horse, and which would injure Caroline to the extent that her wedding would be postponed and maybe even cancelled – to one of our long term storyline meetings. The team has at least two per year. There it was further crafted into an idea that would also involve Nigel, Lizzie, Susan, Neil, Jill and Phil.

Jo Toye, senior producer on *The Archers* at the time, then set to work on researching and establishing every detail from the coroners court and the British Horse Society for the crash, to the police for details of phantom speeding cars. She also went to our medical adviser, Dr. John Wynn-Jones, for the details of Mark's death itself.

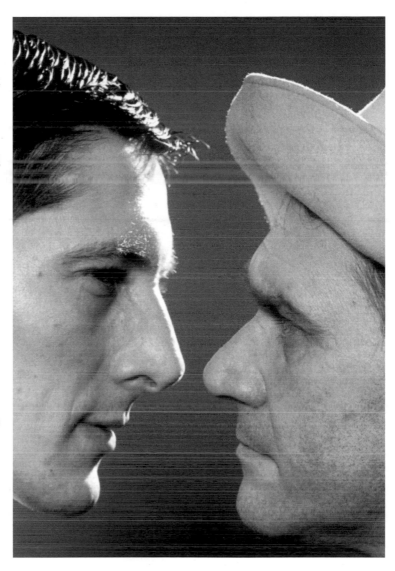

Eddie Grundy nose-to-nose with dastardly landlord Simon Pemberton.

A consultant in major injuries and neuro-surgery helped out with Caroline's head injury and slow recovery, which was again charted over the year, and our consultant obstetrician and gynaecologist, John Pogmore, continued his excellent advice on Shula's IVF treatment. There was crucial timing involved in the pacing of the storyline so that Mark died one week before Shula could find herself pregnant and much research went into the role that Richard Locke, both doctor and friend, would play in carrying forward Shula's IVF injections even while she was grieving for her husband.

Tabling a really big storyline at one of our script meetings is like throwing a large stone into water. The bigger the stone, the more ripples bounce out from the centre. The bigger and better the idea the more storylines flow from the centre of the main story and into the rest of the programme. It is a very exciting process but the right stone is the hardest one to find.

When I joined the programme as editor in 1991, I knew that I had to begin with a story which reached right into the heart of the Archer family itself. It had to be a big, bold story, true to the characters and one which would change, in some ways, those characters directly affected by it. Most of all, I focused on Elizabeth. This delightful, amusing, but selfish 24-year-old, needed, it seemed to me, to begin to grow up and have to take responsibility for her life and her actions. It wasn't the first time that such a storyline had been attempted, of course. In December 1966 the swinging sixties were upon us. The contraceptive pill had arrived and although Germaine Greer's book *The Female Eunuch* had not yet heralded the beginning of feminism in such striking terms, women were unshackling their chains and were out to have a good time.

In Ambridge on December 16th, an unhappy and, like Elizabeth, selfish 21-year-old, Jennifer Archer, tells the most worldly wise of her family, her aunt Laura that she is pregnant. She is worried. By December 23rd, feeling increasingly anxious and isolated from her family, she spends Christmas in Wolverhampton with Max, an old boyfriend. On January 6th 1967, the day before her 22nd birthday, she sees the vicar and tells him about the baby. She asks him to

Young Jennifer Archer (Angela Piper).

speak to her parents, Peggy and Jack, but he tells her gently that she cannot run away from telling them herself.

Jennifer expects a sermon on morality from this rather traditional vicar, but he is admirably restrained. She says that she regrets what she has done, because of the position in which it puts herself and her family, but that she is not ashamed. Mr Wreford tells

Jennifer's parents, Peggy (June Spencer) and Jack Archer (Denis Folwell) are hard at work cleaning the eggs.

her that after she has told her parents, he will come and see them and support her. He will 'hate the sin' but 'not the sinner'. He then goes on to talk about Twelfth Night which is the next day, and how the three wise men went in search of the baby Jesus, a baby that needed love just like her child would do and that she must be there to give that love. At the very end of the scene he offers Jennifer one or two practical tips, but sadly the scene fades out before we know what they are. In fact, Jennifer does not pluck up the courage to tell her parents until January 16th. The script writers, knowing they had a good hook, had her try several times, but someone always interrupts or she fails in courage!

Interestingly, however, she does manage to tell Jill, who after all has children of her own. She also tells her gran, Doris. Doris, in contrast to Jill, doesn't handle things at all well. She is shocked and horrified, eventually demanding that Jennifer tell her the identity of the father and that he should, regardless of the fact that he doesn't love Jennifer, be made to marry her for the sake of the child. Jennifer stands her ground and softly but firmly refuses to reveal the name of the father. What she needs, she says, is practical help. Making very little progress, Jennifer finally apologises for causing her gran, or anyone, any embarrassment and leaves.

The kettle boils but a stunned Doris no longer wants any tea. It is left to Jill, who comes round with a wallpaper pattern book that she has promised to drop in, to bring Doris out of her gloom. While agreeing with her mother-in-law that 'the thing itself is bad enough in all conscience', she gently points out that Doris seems most upset because she was not the first to be told the news.

There are, of course, a lot of the given moral values of the times in these scripts and a lot of unquestioned assumptions. For example, Jill says that Jennifer will obviously move to teach in a different school when she has had the baby. But there are also seeds of the more liberal pragmatic Jill that we would recognise today as she stands up for Jennifer's point of view. 'But surely, Mum, to marry someone just to get some sort of legal status for a child is a travesty of the whole idea of marriage?' And there is humour too as Doris leaps into a diatribe about what Mrs. P. will say '...especially when she finds that half the village knows and she doesn't.'

Dan Archer defends his granddaughter to her father.

When Jennifer does tell her mum and dad, Jack, at first, tries to throw her out of The Bull, but Peggy stops him. Again, Jennifer refuses to disclose the name of the father. It is, wonderfully, Jennifer's grandfather, Dan Archer, who defends his granddaughter to her father and to his own wife Doris. In a scene of considerable insight and power, Dan reminds the family that Jennifer is 'a human being in trouble', as well as his granddaughter. It is a courageous confrontation. In the end Dan accuses the family of a lack of charity and by implication he challenges them to let her have the baby in Ambridge and stand up to the critics. Interestingly, the most powerful lines in the original script, in which Dan talks about the birth of Christ, were cut on transmission, presumably for time.

Jennifer is determined to have the child and keep it, and slowly we see the rest of the family come round to the idea and the gossip in the village quietens down. In February Aunt Laura offers her a home, but Jennifer decides to brave it out at The Bull. All goes well with the pregnancy and by June 2nd a baby boy, Adam, is born.

DAN	...ay... and she's Jack's daughter and my granddaughter and a human being in trouble. The way Jack talks it sounds like he'd be very relieved if Jennifer did away with herself and saved a lot of embarrassment all round.
DORIS	(HORRIFIED) Dan Archer...what are you saying...
DAN	Well it's true... the pair of you are thinking more of the disgrace to the family than you are about the plight the girl's got herself into...
JACK	You sound as though you condone her behaviour...well I don't.
DAN	Oh get down off your pedestal Jack and take off your halo. It doesn't really suit you.

Aunt Laura (Betty McDowall).

Unlike today, and Shula with Caroline, Jennifer does not, in the absence of a father, invite a friend or member of the family to be her moral support during the birth. But all reservations and problems are forgotten, at least for a while, when the phone rings and Dan, Doris, Jack and Peggy receive news of the successful birth. Even Doris is delighted and desperate to know the weight of the little boy, and proud grandfather Jack takes no time in opening a bottle of champagne to wet the baby's head.

It isn't until July that listeners find out the identity of the mystery father and it is Jennifer's own father Jack and then her Aunt Laura who first compare the distinctive shock of red hair on the baby's head with that of farmhand, Paddy Redmond. Paddy was an attractive but unreliable young Ulsterman who worked at Brookfield in 1965. He captivated Jennifer but then arrived back from Belfast with a fiancée, Nora McAuley. The engagement didn't last long however because

Top: Paddy Redmond (John Bott) is the father of Jennifer's baby.

Above: Nora McAuley (Julia Mark) was briefly engaged to Paddy.

Paddy wanted to move down south and work for himself and Nora refused to go with him. On August 31st, Jennifer received a letter from Paddy, but she never replied.

The mystery of the father wasn't the most important thing about this storyline, however, even though it provided a wonderful hook for the listener. More important was the self-examination of values undertaken by many of the central characters involved in the story – the movement from blind prejudice when many first heard the news to sympathy, empathy and acceptance and in many cases, eventually, celebration. The growing-up process for Jennifer was important too. And who would have thought it of Dan, playing the real patriarchal role – the healer uniting the family. Looking back at his stout defence of Jennifer in January 1967, he even manages to broach what was, in those days, the unthinkable and unsayable. Of course, Jennifer keeps the baby and no-one ever comes up with that 'dangerous piece of foolishness', not then.

DORIS	Well I'm blessed if I know about you, Dan Archer... I'd have been willing to bet a hundred to one you'd have gone right up in the air and never come down again when you heard about this little lot.
DAN	That's a natural first reaction...the second one, as I see it, is to try and make the best of it. The baby's on its way and nothing's going to stop it short of a dangerous piece of foolishness which I don't imagine Jennifer would ever consider...
JACK	I should hope not...
DAN	Then I wouldn't continue with your present attitude, Jack, because if you can't talk to her about anything but the shame and disgrace she's bringing on the family...then there's no knowing what she might do out of desperation...

In 1992 the situation is very different for Elizabeth Archer. Again, this is a story which involves and intertwines several other storylines. It is not simply the story of Elizabeth Archer and her decision to have an abortion, big though that story is; it is also the story of Cameron Fraser. Who is this strange brooding Scotsman who has bought the estate in Ambridge? He appears to have plenty of money, but no-one knows quite how he got it or what he does for a living. It is also the story of Shula's childlessness – her desperate desire to have a baby, her ectopic pregnancy and resulting depression. How will she feel when her younger sister, who has been given a gift that she herself has longed for, decides to throw that gift away?

It is February 1992 and the listener begins to hear the stirrings of financial problems for Cameron Fraser. A Mr Cawood is on the phone saying that he hasn't been paid and threatening legal action.

Later, we hear that Cameron is selling the land connected to Red House Farm to Phil Archer for £85,000. Joe Grundy stirs the gossip. He is suspicious of Cameron's motives for selling. There had been talk of him merely renting the land out.

On February 28th, Elizabeth announces to Shula that she is going to propose to Cameron on Leap Year Day. She has, after all, been going out with him since October. Sadly, however, Cameron stands her up and she discovers that he is out of the country on business.

Elizabeth is now working for her old friend, Nigel Pargetter, at Lower Loxley Hall as his marketing manager. She is taking the job very seriously and doing some part-time training and examinations to develop her skills. Nigel is delighted but he still carries a torch for his Lizzie and wonders if she will ever really look his way.

On March 9th, Elizabeth has to be brought home from work early by Nigel because she feels ill. However, Elizabeth is quick to get rid of Nigel when Cameron turns up and Nigel continues to be bitterly jealous of Cameron. On March 13th, in conversation with Debbie, Elizabeth says that she feels torn between her feelings for Cameron and Nigel's devotion to her and this is why she is feeling ill. But Debbie, hearing a list of her symptoms, tells her she thinks she is pregnant.

Cameron Fraser (Delaval Astley).

Elizabeth is shocked and frightened. She has been sleeping with Cameron for some time and she knows that if she is pregnant, the child is his. On March 16th, Elizabeth and Debbie do a pregnancy test with a home kit. The result is positive.

By March 18th, instinctive Jill guesses that her daughter is pregnant and Elizabeth, upset, confesses that she doesn't want anyone else to know until she has had a chance to tell Cameron, who, she says, will be delighted. Cameron is still abroad, and she must wait for his return because she doesn't want to tell him by phone.

Meanwhile, she won't let her mother tell her father. On March 23rd, Jill can stand the deception no longer. It is obvious to Phil that something is worrying Elizabeth and Jill eventually tells him the truth. At first he is angry, especially as the man in question is Cameron Fraser, whom he does not like. But Jill talks to Phil and in contrast to Jack Archer's tough response to Jennifer all those years ago, Phil is calm and reflective when eventually Elizabeth comes into the living room to face him.

He makes it clear that whatever she decides, she will get his support but, unlike Jack or Doris to Jennifer, he also makes it clear that just because Cameron is the father of her child, it does not mean she has to marry the man. But Elizabeth is infatuated with Cameron and wants to marry him. Both Phil and Jill are worried.

On March 26th, Cameron returns to the village and Elizabeth tells him the 'good news'. She is shocked and distressed by his response.

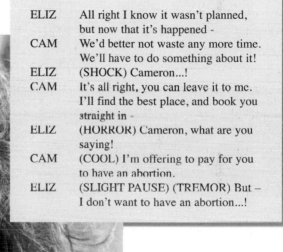

ELIZ	All right I know it wasn't planned, but now that it's happened -
CAM	We'd better not waste any more time. We'll have to do something about it!
ELIZ	(SHOCK) Cameron...!
CAM	It's all right, you can leave it to me. I'll find the best place, and book you straight in -
ELIZ	(HORROR) Cameron, what are you saying!
CAM	(COOL) I'm offering to pay for you to have an abortion.
ELIZ	(SLIGHT PAUSE) (TREMOR) But – I don't want to have an abortion...!

*Elizabeth Archer
(Alison Dowling).*

Charles Collingwood ✹ *Brian Aldridge*

Charles was born in Canada in 1943 but his family moved back to England the following year. He went to Sherborne School and later trained at the Royal Academy of Dramatic Art. After a lot of work in rep, by 1973 he was in *How the Other Half Loves* with Penelope Keith at Greenwich. Shortly after that he met actress Judy Bennett who was playing Shula in *The Archers* and they recorded three children's puppet series together for ATV, *Mumphie, Clopper Castle* and *The Munch Bunch*. This proved to be the start of more than a successful working relationship and they got married in 1976. Charles's career is a varied and busy one. As well as playing Brian in *The Archers*, his radio work has ranged from performing with Richard Stilgoe to reading the news on the BBC World Service. His television credits include *The Bretts, Hannay, London's Burning, Inspector Morse*, Noel Edmonds's sidekick scorekeeper in the recent series of *Telly Addicts* and the part of God in *The Alexei Sayle Show*. Recently Charles has put pen to paper and become one of the three co-authors of *The Book of the Archers* – the dictionary of every character in Ambridge.

Sara Coward ✹ *Caroline Pemberton*

Sara joined *The Archers* as Caroline in 1979. A grammar school girl from South East London, she went to Bristol University where she gained an Honours Degree in English and Drama. She completed her training at the Guildhall School back in London, where she won the prestigious Carleton Hobbs award for Radio Drama in her year. The award ensured an Equity Card and a six-month contract with the BBC Drama Repertory Company. Sara has enjoyed work in radio drama ever since but is also very busy working in rep up and down the country and on the London fringe as well as in television. She has co-written plays for the London fringe and has a chapter to herself in Clive Swift's book *The Performing World of the Actor*. Somehow in this busy lifestyle she also manages to maintain her two homes in the Warwickshire countryside and in France.

Pamela Craig ❧ *Betty Tucker*

Pamela's first appearance on the professional stage was as Peter Pan at the Theatre Royal, Leicester, when she was fifteen. She caught the theatre bug and soon afterwards trained at the Birmingham Theatre School where a fellow student was Alan Devereux who now plays Sid Perks. Pamela has worked extensively in rep, including a season with the Traverse Theatre in Edinburgh, and in the West End she was directed by John Osborne in Charles Wood's *Meals on Wheels*. Her television appearances include *Z Cars, Coronation Street, Pickerskill's Primitive* by Mike Stott and a drama documentary about William Blake for the BBC. On radio, as well as playing Betty, Pamela has been heard in many plays recorded in Leeds and Manchester. She now lives in Warwickshire.

Helen Cutler ❧ *Brenda Tucker*

Fifteen-year-old Helen auditioned successfully for the part of Brenda in 1991. Helen is a member of the Central TV Workshop and has recently worked on Mike Leigh's film *Secrets and Lies*. In spite of this early experience, Helen is not dazzled by the glamour of the world of acting and is keeping her options open, saying she may well work in another part of the media. When she is not acting or at school, Helen can often be found on the football terraces supporting her local team, Aston Villa.

At no point does he ask Elizabeth what she wants. He professes to care for her but regards the baby as an 'inconvenience'. He clearly doesn't want it.

She backs tearfully away when he tries to touch her. 'I don't want your money, I don't want anything else from you, ever.'

The next day a shaken and lonely Elizabeth confides in Debbie and tells her she will keep the baby whatever happens. Jill once again knows that all is not well, simply by watching her daughter. By March 30th, Elizabeth knows that she has to tell faithful Nigel the truth. When he hears, he conceals his own pain and is supportive. In a later scene with her father, we sense Lizzie's confusion between Cameron and Nigel and their very different responses.

By April 1st, Cameron is admitting to a bruised Elizabeth that he has a cashflow problem with his investment business in Crieff. He offers this up as one of the many reasons why he is not settled enough to consider fathering a child at the present time. Elizabeth is not impressed, but Cameron insists that he still cares for her. She is clearly still in love with him, hoping that he will change his mind.

On April 1st, Elizabeth tells her mother that Cameron wants her to have an abortion. Jill is horrified and angry. The next day, Ruth and David are told about the baby but Elizabeth cannot pluck up the courage to tell Shula, sensitive to what her sister has been through, wanting to have a child herself. But she insists she will tell her. She will find her time.

By April 13th, things are hotting up at work for Cameron and a Mr Ainsworth calls early one morning chasing him for money. Cameron promises to datapost the cheque. In yet another meeting with Elizabeth, he opens up a little about his financial problems. It seems that his business is largely concerned with investing money for other people, but now that their shares are doing well and many want their money out, he does not have the funds to repay them. He has clearly been 'playing the stock market' with some of their earnings and embezzling the profits, but Elizabeth only partly follows his explanations and he further muddies the picture by telling her that friends gave him bad investment advice. Elizabeth gives him the support he seems unable or unwilling to give her.

Pressured by creditors, Cameron reduces Elizabeth to tears in the estate office on April 16th, and then talks to Shula about the pregnancy, assuming that she already knows about it. The next day, Shula seeks Elizabeth out, hurt that the family thought she needed protection. Struggling through her own pain, she assures her that the baby will be loved by all the family.

How you can avoid an Ambridge conman

Delaval Astley, who plays Cameron Fraser. The *Archers* character is suspected of fraud

The Independent on Sunday, *10 May 1992, ran a piece in the 'Your Money' section on Cameron Fraser.*

65

On Elizabeth's birthday, Cameron sends her a card. It says simply, 'I love you'. When she visits the Dower House, she notices that watercolours are missing from the wall. Cameron says his business problems are improving. While she is in there, though, another investor rings demanding money. Cameron assures the woman that her cheque is in the post. On April 24th, the same woman, a Mrs Carpenter, is getting angry with Susan in the estate office because she cannot speak to Cameron. The cheque, she says, has bounced. An embarrassed Susan mentions it to Cameron, but he says that the cheque was post-dated and that the silly woman has tried to cash it too early.

When Cameron opens a letter from his Scottish bank, he angrily asks Susan to book him on the Edinburgh shuttle first thing next morning. But before he goes he finds time to wine and dine Elizabeth, giving her an extravagant diamond bracelet and professing his love. Although Cameron never mentions the abortion or the child, Elizabeth thinks his attitude is changing. She is winning him over with time and trust and patience. Her confidence is further boosted when, after a week of declarations of love and romantic attentions, Cameron finally asks Elizabeth to go on a last-minute holiday with him. Elizabeth seizes the opportunity with both hands. A holiday and rest 'away from it all' is what they both need; time to concentrate on the future, the baby and perhaps even, dare she hope, a proposal of marriage? It is clear that Cameron seems to be coming round to the idea.

On May 1st, Cameron drives Elizabeth to Heathrow to board a plane for his 'secret destination'. Elizabeth hasn't had the courage to tell her family where she is going so suddenly, although she has taken time off work. Perhaps it is because she knows, deep down, that they would disapprove of her going away with Cameron. She intends to phone them from the airport just before she flies off. She is excited and talks nervously all the way down the motorway about her hopes for the future, the baby and their life together. As she talks, Cameron grows more and more silent but Elizabeth doesn't seem to notice. When they stop for food at the service station, he eats with her, tells her he is going to the gents and exits with the words, 'I'll be back in a minute',

Ten minutes later, Elizabeth goes into the car park to see that her cases are dumped on the ground. He has abandoned her.

She has to hitch-hike back to Ambridge, bereft and miserable. Later, humiliated and unable to sleep, her heart desperately tries to cling to some hope. Perhaps Cameron was under such great strain that he is having a breakdown? He will surely contact her soon, when he realises the extent of what he has done. She tries to go into work as usual but it isn't long before she has to ask Nigel for time off.

Looking back at the time when Elizabeth first told Debbie of Cameron's invitation, Debbie's response may have rung some warning bells, if only she could have heard them. But slowly, as the time goes on and Cameron doesn't phone, she feels she only has herself to rely on.

ELIZ	Cameron rang me this afternoon.
DEB	Oh yes?
ELIZ	I was just about to leave the office. Two minutes later and he'd have missed me.
DEB	And?
ELIZ	He's asked me to go away with him.
DEB	What? For a holiday?
ELIZ	Of course for a holiday.
DEB	Oh. The way you said it, I thought you were going to, you know, run away together.
ELIZ	Isn't that great?
DEB	Yes. When? I mean when are you going?
ELIZ	On Friday.
DEB	What!
ELIZ	The thing is, you know he's got a few problems with his business at the moment.
DEB	Has he?
ELIZ	It's nothing serious, but he's been up to his eyeballs these last few weeks, and he's completely wrecked. I mean, like total exhaustion.

Cameron Fraser with former girlfriend Caroline Bone, whom he also treated poorly.

All a-quiver over the A...

Radio

Val Arnold-Forster

MY POLITICAL friend is worried about **The Archers**. If Shula, or worse still Linda Snell, get to be church warden, there will be, he predicts, blood on the streets. What about Clarrie Grundy as the people's candidate?

Some of it is a sidelong reflection on present electoral trends. But mostly it's just part of that cod-serious Archers analysis that aficionados affect. In recent weeks the aficionados have gone into overdrive over Lizzie's pregnancy.

Bets have been placed. Debates conducted in pubs and stately drawing rooms. We know some of the answers already. And I know someone ...

assumption that no Archer would have an abortion.

But what next? Will she, won't she marry? If so, who? And what about Shula? Can she forgive? Or is she by any chance going a bit too far for a modern young estate agent? Place your bets.

Nothing is too far-fetched for ...

The Archers (7.05pm R4) They are probably enlisting the aid of moral philosophers in the script-room to sort out the ramifications of Elizabeth's abortion. Today's billing — "An unexpected visit to Borchester General" — may turn out to be a red herring ...

● The end of a dilemma for Elizabeth Archer? (Monday, R4, 7.05pm)

Radio 2 Young Musician Competition (Sunday, R2, 4pm) Music to soothe the troubled breast in this new series of ...

RADIO

Archers hit the target

A DISTINGUISHED opera critic said to me ... "Please ... ents to ... or. The ... cting's ... es, and ... plots ... om the ... y."

... t Sun- ... apers, ... on at ... ecture ... possi- ... the ... Am- ... Yet ... aper ... mma ... nant ... fore- ...

and Jill. She can be nice to decent but chinless Nigel Pargetter, hoping he will lead her to the altar and at least make the child legitimate. She can accept the adoption offer from her elder sister Shula, who seems to have infertility problems with her husband Mark. Or she can have an abortion.

In tonight's episode, after an emotional week which culminated in a raid by the Fraud Squad on Cameron's offices, Elizabeth makes known her decision. This is not an episode which any follower of The Archers should miss. Capricious, irresponsible but fundamentally good, Elizabeth has been dragged through a wheel of fire. It is an indelible portrait of a frivolous 25-year-old forced to grow up, all the more powerful for the conviction which Alison Dowling brings to the part.

He is promiscuous, selfish provocative, defiant and, by curious coincidence, has als... got a girlfriend pregnant Like Cameron Fraser, hi... first reaction is to advise abortion. Unlike Cameron, he then shows signs of con... science and remorse. But wil... this be enough to stop the station being taken over by evangelical Christians?

Shaun Prendergast, the author of *Open Mike*, clearly believes in stuffing his plot with issues, seasoning it highly with bold demotic and linking it with regularly reversed dramatic expectations. So much is going on you want to have a little lie down afterwards. But those of us who have encountered rebels in serials before can, I think, rely on Mike to carry on the tradition of spouting first, thinking second and finally rallying round.

IN EAST Texas there is an eminently practical tradition of eating things that have been run over in the road. We heard about it on Sunday's **Table Talk**, a regular Radio 3 lunchtime delight. Ed Swift, a chap from the Big Thicket, that corner of east Texas where they habitually dine on rattlesnake, possum, armadillo and squirrel, talked nostagically of his native patch to Alan Brown. Mr Brown sounded sceptical. "Isn't it rather crushed?" he inquired of the motorway menu, and "These were relatives of yours?" to some of Mr Swift's more lyrical descriptions of various finger-pickling, fiddle-making, hallucinating oddballs from the backwoods.

Of Texas caviare, a concoction of black-eyed peas, chilli powder, peppers and spices, I will say no more except to mention that Mr Swift makes up pots of it and sends it to perfect strangers such as Darcey Bussell, the ballerina. Mr Brown bet she wouldn't eat it. Mr Swift thought she would.

Everyday stories of crooks

REGULAR listeners to *The Archers* may have wondered if the saga of Cameron Fraser, who lied about investing money in gilts, reflects the real-life activities of convicted fraudster Robert Miller. The answer is abortion. Miller's wife had a miscarriage after he did a runner. To get verisimilitude, *Archers'* senior producer Jo Toye consulted not just the BBC's own *Financial World Tonight*, but insolvency experts Cork Gulley and regulators Fimbra. ...

PEOPLE

Kiss if you must, but please don't tell

S occasionally crossed my ... of late, that perhaps I ... write my memoirs. Go ... hog. Kiss and tell all. ... mes. Breach every con... hat has ever been made to ... eal everything I know ... eryone. As Mrs Annie ... the former mistress of ... p of Galway could testify, ... much to be had from such ... rise. Hollywood wants to ... movie of her story, and is ... to be offering $300,000 ... ry rewarding indeed.

... used to be a generally ... agreement between dec... le that whatever mis... urs you got up to in your ... fe, the one thing you did ... is kiss and tell. Whatever ... s you made, however ... u behaved, or however ... eone behaved towards ... took it on the chin, kept ... ind got on with your life. ... t accolade paid to a mis... lover in past times was ... y were exquisitely dis... tey took their pleasures ... ot embarrass anyone, did ... anyone, did not cause ... o be pained or pilloried.

That was the unwritten deal in any illicit love affair, whether it involved a priest, a married man or a homosexual. Adults knew the rules of the game when they were embarking on an affair, and to kiss and tell afterwards was ratting.

All such agreements are now called "brushing things under the carpet", "covering up" and "hypocrisy". But such "hypocrisy" prevented a great deal of gratuitous cruelty and was the glue that kept society on the rails. As my wise mother used to say: "There are things that people do not mind suspecting, but they still do not want to *know*." She adored a gorgeous Irish actor called Michael MacLiammoir: she didn't mind suspecting that he preferred chaps — she called it "artistic" — but she still didn't want to *know*. Poor old Mickey Mac wouldn't stand a chance in Dublin today: his face would be all over the front pages, with full details of his riot-ous living, after some vicious rentboy had kissed and told.

For it is in Dublin, in particular, that Bishop Casey has been crucified by the media, for his "hypocrisy", "humbug" and "arrogance". A Woman Abandoned And A Child Denied is a typical headline. "If he were anything other than a bishop he would be called a cad and a scoundrel," wrote Dublin's *Sunday Independent*. "But precisely because he is a bishop and an arbiter of moral standards, he is a cad and a scoundrel. And now a coward for running away."

Tut, tut. Gloat, gloat. Press, radio and television are united in this common theme. And why shouldn't they? A bishop has been caught out, not just in an affair, but for the more grievious modern sin of "hypocrisy". How dare anyone in a position of authority "cover up" his private life?

Yet it seldom seems to occur to

MARY KENNY

journalists that most of them have something to hide too. The media today is a much more powerful agency than the church. The arbiters of the media are far more influential than churchmen; they are, moreover, much richer and greatly protected by their own conspiracies of silence. Why do they not preface their personal condemnations of people in high places by "honest" confessions about *their* affairs, their visits to venereal disease clinics (journalists having the second highest VD ratings, after commercial salesmen), their sometimes less-than-honourable financial dealings, their drink problems, their disastrous marriages, their drug-addicted children and all the rest of it? Surely those who condemn "hypocrisy" should first take the beam out of their own eye and stop being so "hypocritical" themselves? Surely we in the media should ask ourselves: which of us, precisely, is in a position morally to condemn *anyone*?

Yet the eminent columnist who has been thundering against the "unchaste" behaviour of Bishop Casey would emerge, under any "honesty" regulation, as a thoroughly dirty old man himself. A writer railing against the bishop in a highly compromising professional position, which goes unmentioned. An investigative journalist does not even know the full truth about his own wife. A political columnist who advertises himself as a "male feminist" is personally an appalling male chauvinist. A famous face on Irish television is an unmarried father, without ever publicly confessing it. How would they like it if the honesty-at-all-costs spotlight were turned on them? Not one but Yet they are more powerful and much richer than any churchman.

The media has a duty to report, and commentators have a privileged public platform on which to air their views. Public figures are kept up to snap by critical comment. But it is just as much "hypocrisy" and "humbug" for media folk to represent themselves as impeccable — by carefully omitting their own failings when they go for the attack — as it is for bishops not to declare a secret child.

Luckily, I will not be writing my memoirs. Kissing and telling is shabby and cruel. And people in glass houses who throw stones eventually find that the effect on themselves, and their families, can be shattering.

ISN'T *The Archers*, on Radio 4, absolutely stunning at the moment? My daily schedule just *has* to allow for listening in at 1.40pm or 7.05pm. The acting is better than anything at the National Theatre — it is impressive how much an actress like Patricia Greene as Jill can communicate just using tone of voice — and the writing (currently by Mary Cutler and Louise Page) is up to the very best drama today.

The recent storyline has involved an anguishing abortion, and although there is a perceptible tincture of feminist political correctness about the script, it has still been superbly handled. Bravissimo!

Shula Hebden (Judy Bennett) would like to adopt Elizabeth's baby.

On May 8th after much discussion with Mark, Shula tentatively asks Elizabeth if she would consider her and Mark adopting the baby. Elizabeth is shocked. This tender and difficult moment is jarringly interrupted by a call from Mr Rodway for Shula. Cameron is wanted by the Fraud Squad for fraudulent share dealing; his assets have been called in. Elizabeth, when told, is deeply humiliated. It seems Cameron must have thought she was just a child and in some ways maybe that is what she was. He fooled her, along with everyone else.

Elizabeth leaves home early on May 11th, the family assumes for work. But later, she returns, with devastating news. She tells her mother she has had an abortion.

The next day the fallout in the family, among those few who know, begins. Debbie

ELIZ	I went to – I decided to – I've had an abortion.
PHIL	What!
JILL	Oh, Elizabeth, no!
ELIZ	I'm sorry, Mum. I thought about it so much – so much. You don't know how hard it was. But I just couldn't have the baby. I just couldn't.

consoles her and supports her. 'It's your decision, Elizabeth, it's your body, you had every right to do what you did.' Phil is shocked and Jill, dealing with her own strong views against abortion, is both angry and upset that Elizabeth didn't talk to her before making the decision. Others in this large extended family know nothing and possibly will never do so. To this day, for example, Peggy and Jack, Pat and Tony and Chris and George know nothing of Elizabeth's pregnancy or abortion. The immediate family, almost subliminally, by common unspoken consent, dealt with the problem between them and shut the doors on it. Ambridge at large, so busy gossiping about Cameron's misdemeanours, missed the domestic tragedy that was unravelling just a few miles away from their own doorsteps, at Brookfield. Interestingly, in those early scenes after the event, when Jill struggles to come to an understanding with her daughter, it is Phil who provides the most immediate solid support. He has little to say about what his daughter has done but, like Dan for his granddaughter in the sixties, Phil comes up trumps for his daughter Elizabeth in the nineties. His anger is reserved for Cameron Fraser.

On May 15th, Elizabeth is interviewed by the Fraud Squad as she was the last person to have seen Cameron. She can tell them so little that she feels very foolish. On the same day she faces Shula, telling her of the abortion. Shula takes it very hard, most particularly because she had offered to adopt the baby.

A rift develops between the two sisters, exacerbated by the news of Ruth's pregnancy in June. This does not change until Christmas when time begins to heal and Elizabeth and Shula tentatively talk together in the garden at Brookfield. Eventually it is the birth of Pip which provides the catalyst that is needed. Shula is instrumental in getting Elizabeth to visit Ruth and her baby in hospital and when Pip is christened in July 1993, both women can, once again, talk through their feelings about having children.

And so the cycle of life goes on. Cameron is still not found – maybe a backpacking traveller is talking to him today in some remote country without even knowing it. Elizabeth's misery is compounded by a deep loathing of Cameron in the village. Caroline Bone and Mrs Antrobus, to name but two, had money invested with him which they lose. The Red House Farm land deal with Brookfield falls through and the house and land are sold off by the liquidators as a single lot, separate from the rest of the estate. In February 1993, Guy Pemberton buys the estate and moves to Ambridge.

Again, the research for this important storyline was significant. Senior producer Jo Toye went into the differences between liquidation and bankruptcy with a specialist firm of accountants. We then had to research Cameron's situation in Scotland, Scottish law being different to English law, and FIMBRA were extremely helpful with the details of compensation which Caroline and Mrs Antrobus might hope to receive. The abortion storyline got us involved with advisory clinics and the pro and anti lobby and the crucial thing was timing the build to the announcing of Cameron's business collapse and Elizabeth's decision that she could not go it alone. An abortion still had to be physically possible.

Difficult stories and sad stories then, and the big ones often are. Such stories, like the protracted and distressing 'racist' attacks on Asian solicitor, Usha Gupta, or the hitting of Shula and Debbie by Simon Pemberton, galvanise press and media interest and encourage a surge in listening figures. They are certainly exciting and challenging to create. *The Archers*, however, is a rich mix, and in searching for the added ingredient of charm to sit alongside such thought-provoking stories, one need not look much further than its comedy.

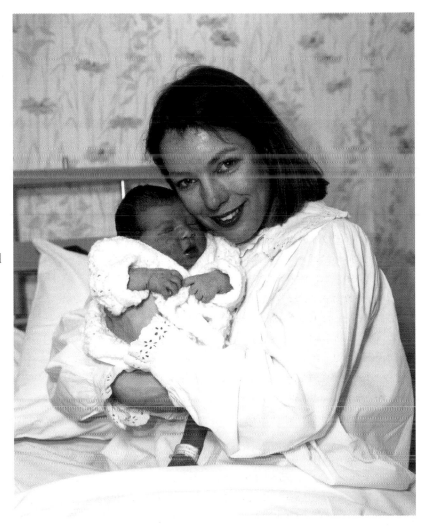

Ruth Archer (Felicity Finch) with Pip. The birth of Pip brought Shula and Elizabeth back together, after Elizabeth's decision to have an abortion.

Comic Creations
chapter three

Comedy characters and plots have always been an essential part of *The Archers*. Through the years, comedy has been treated in different ways from farce through sitcom to the gentle social comedy implicit in dialogue, refreshingly present in the most serious of storylines. And it is of course, the great comic characters of the programme who carry much of this comedy. From good old Walter Gabriel, that lovable rogue of the fifties and sixties, created by Godfrey Baseley and his team, to William Smethurst's splendid Grundy family in the late seventies and early eighties; from the archetypal busybody and incomer Lynda Snell, created by Liz Rigbey and team in the mid-eighties, to the nineties and our Julia, Nigel's monstrous mother with her social pretensions, fears of inadequacy and 'common as muck' past.

The best comic characters have always had a serious underbelly. They are rogues rather than villains, social snobs with community concerns, larger-than-life folk whose

*Walter Gabriel
(Chris Gittins).*

*Lynda Snell
(Carole Boyd).*

confidence covers vulnerability and sometimes even despair. Comedy in the programme has always been at its strongest when the situations grow from the characters and at its weakest when the situations seem grafted on.

Walter Gabriel bought a minibus and became the village carrier.

*W*alter Gabriel worked because he was always sympathetic, even at his most wicked. He had other uses, too, in the programme. It was Walter from whom listeners heard all about old remedies and Borsetshire customs and with whom they took trips, yes even in the fifties, down memory lane. His catchphrase 'me old pal, me old beauty' has gone down in broadcasting history. In some ways he was similar to Eddie or Joe Grundy today. Like Eddie, he was musical but instead of the guitar he played the euphonium. This was usually successful at the annual carol-singing party at The Manor, but the coach-horn he blew at vital moments in the local cricket matches went down far less well. Like Joe and Eddie he had a heart. For years he carried a torch for Mrs Perkins. He showered her with gifts, some more acceptable than others, even though they argued a lot.

At Christmas in 1976, he plucks up the courage to steal a kiss. Mrs P. is furious with him and refuses to go to the Woodfords for New Year's Eve if he is to be there. Determined to get back in her good books however, Walter turns up with champagne to welcome her, but all hopes for forgiveness are dashed when he pulls the champagne cork and it hits her in the back of the neck.

Walter Gabriel offers Mrs Perkins (Pauline Seville) a cauliflower.

Like Joe, Walter had a son who was capable of causing him considerable worry. Nelson was the apple of his father's eye, although a far from perfect fruit in many other people's eyes. Up until 1980 when Nelson comes back to Borchester to open a wine bar and look after his ageing dad, Walter spends many an hour of anxiety over his son's whereabouts and shady business deals. Since Nelson's return, things have quietened a little and Nelson restricts his 'dubious activities' to his other business, the antiques trade. But until the day he died on November 3rd 1988, Walter could never be quite sure of what his son was really up to.

Like the Grundy's farm today, Walter's farm in the fifties was a bit of a disgrace. He is shocked when his landlord, Squire Lawson-Hope, puts it under supervision. It is only a loan of £400 from Mrs Perkins which enables Walter to do the necessary repairs and get the landlord off his back. And Mrs P., though she had two husbands and never married Walter, is a true and loyal friend throughout his life.

In 1957, Walter gave up the farm and moved into Honeysuckle Cottage, where his son now lives. He bought a minibus and became the village carrier. He was keen on village activities and ever helpful with ideas and hard work to back them up. Like Joe and Eddie today,

Nelson Gabriel (Jack May), Walter's errant son.

he was always trying new scams to bring in money. He was part owner of the pet shop with Mrs Turvey for a while, he opened a junk shop in Hollerton and when that shut, opened another one in Ambridge with a stuffed gorilla called George as a signpost. He bought a field with Ned Larkin and they tried several money-making schemes with it. Nothing came of the schemes but they incurred the wrath of Mrs Turvey, whose garden backs onto the field.

In fact, Walter's altruistic ventures did better than his business ones. He organised many trips for the over-60s in his younger days and formed the White Elephant Society to raise funds for the Youth Club. In 1965, somehow, he managed to buy an Elephant called Rosie with her baby Tiny Tim and brought them to the Ambridge Summer Fete; something of a scene stealer from Miss Anne Sidney, the Miss World of the time, who was amazingly, to open the fete. It was Walter too who was the proud owner of the giant exploding marrow at the annual flower and

Joe (Edward Kelsey) and Eddie Grundy (Trevor Harrison).

Nelson Gabriel at his father's grave.

produce show; Walter who fitted new door handles the wrong way round to all of Doris's doors and Walter who invited Pat Archer and her children to see *Snow White and the Seven Dwarfs*, not realising that he had rented the adult version. But it was also Walter who was the wood carver, who carved a beautiful rocking horse for Christine's adopted son Peter and ended up making them for most of the kids in the village; who organised the home-coming celebrations for Tom Forrest after his trial for manslaughter; and who wrote his own epitaph which shows his true love of country life, 'All the beasts of the forest are mine; and so are the cattle upon a thousand hills'.

By the late 1970s editor William Smethurst was beginning to focus on Jethro Larkin, son of Ned Larkin, as the vehicle for his 'social comedy'. But it could be a cruel comedy at times, resting heavily on Jethro's slow Cotswold dialect and plodding pace. In March 1977 we hear about his dentures and how he was always taking them out and leaving them all over the place. In September 1980 he drops a bale of hay on Phil Archer's head by accident. Phil is mildly concussed and when the Grundys, on the way to The Bull, dump a piano at Hollowtree to shelter it from the rain, Jethro comes across Phil playing it in the pig unit and blames himself for causing Phil to go soft in the head.

In March 1984, Nigel, who is selling swimming pools for a living, persuades Jethro that, while drunk the night before, he signed a contract to buy a Jacuzzi for £950. Jethro doesn't even know what a Jacuzzi is and his daughter, Clarrie, is worried when she hears about it, thinking the next step will be her dad frequenting massage parlours in Borchester. Jethro finally confides in Phil, who tells him it must all have been a joke and gets Nigel to apologise.

William Smethurst, editor of The Archers *1978-1986.*

The most enduring of the comic creations of that time has to be the Grundys. Joe Grundy is first heard from in 1970, receiving a letter about his tenancy from the estate owner Ralph Bellamy in which he is told to quit. How little life changes! Of course, as usual, Joe doesn't do as he is told and so thankfully he is still here to entertain us today. Although Joe hardly

Haydn Jones as Joe Grundy. Haydn played Joe until the actor died in 1984

Buffy Davis 🍂 *Jolene Rogers*

Buffy joined the cast of *The Archers* in 1996 to play Eddie's country and western singing partner the Lily of Layton Cross Jolene Rogers. Buffy has a great singing voice and ever since her first professional job with the Mikron Theatre Company in which she performed on narrowboats up and down the country, Buffy has often used both singing and acting talents in her career. She was born in Vancouver in 1955 where her father had a rope-making company. The family returned to England when Buffy was in her early teens and after school in Cheshire, Buffy went on to study acting at the Guildhall School in London. Her theatre credits include Ruth in *The Norman Conquests* at Scarborough, Sugar in *Some Like It Hot* at the West Yorkshire Playhouse, Peter Pan in *Peter Pan* at the Drill Hall in London and Gloria in *Sunday in the Park with George* at the National Theatre. On television Buffy's work includes *Casualty, Harnessing Peacocks, My Sister Wife, The Bill* and *Wycliffe* and she has appeared in the film *Orphan Annie*. Radio experiences include *Little Women, The Handmaid's Tale* and *Spiderman* and she has also read *G is for Gumshoe* and *Second Nature* for *Woman's Hour*. Buffy enjoys most sports and is a keen skier. She lives in London with her partner who is a sculptor and musician.

Lucy Davis 🍂 *Hayley Jordan*

It was Lucy's splendid comedy timing which got her the part of John Archer's bossy girlfriend Hayley, when she auditioned in 1995. The daughter of Birmingham comedian Jasper Carrott, Lucy trained as a member of the Central TV Workshop in Birmingham before doing a two-year course at the Italia Conti. She has appeared in *The Widow Maker* for Central Films and her television credits include *The Bill, Casualty, Woof, Blue Heaven* and the BBC's recent adaptation of *Pride and Prejudice*. Lucy has worked extensively in theatre in the UK and abroad, most recently in *The Threepenny Opera, Henry IV, Part One* and *Hedda Gabler* in which she played the title role.

Alan Devereux 🍃 *Sid Perks*

Born in 1941, Alan went to school in Sutton Coldfield. At the age
of fourteen, he started going to evening classes to study speech
and drama and a year later he went to the Birmingham Theatre
School. BBC radio plays and walk-on parts in television soon
followed and he made his first professional stage appearance at
the Birmingham Repertory Theatre in 1956. Alan went on to
spend five years working as an assistant stage manager and
playing small parts at the Alexandra Theatre in Birmingham and
The Grand in Wolverhampton. He remembers this time as a very
thorough way to learn about the theatre. He has played the part
of Sid Perks since 1962. He has also performed in over 100
radio plays, supplied voice overs for countless audio visual films,
voiced thousands of radio commercials and appeared in many
television ads. Alan's daughter Tracy-Jane is also an actress and
plays his daughter in the programme, Lucy Perks. He also has
one son, Ross, who is a veterinary nurse.

Alison Dowling 🍃 *Elizabeth Archer*

Born in Malta in 1961, Alison really wanted to be a ballerina but
says that she outgrew it, literally, at the age of eleven. Instead
she developed a passion for acting and a successful pantomime
audition in Shepherd's Bush in London led to the offer of a place
at the Barbara Speake Stage School in 1972. While there for five
years, Alison appeared in many television plays and serials
including *Grange Hill*, *Bless Me Father* and *Quatermass*. More
recently she has toured Scotland, Canada, Thailand, the Middle
East and Egypt with the London Shakespeare Group and has
worked in theatre in London, Horsham, Newbury, Ary and
Latchmere. Her television credits include *Crossroads*,
Emmerdale Farm and *The Camomile Lawn* and she has
appeared in the films *Mahler, Tommy, Bugsy Malone, Silver
Bears* and *Little Dorrit*. In the early 90s she presented
Granada's Saturday morning children's TV show *TX*.

Clarrie (Heather Bell) and Eddie Grundy (Trevor Harrison) on their wedding day, 21st November, 1981.

features in the programme until the late seventies and eighties, he has, in fact, been around Ambridge albeit silently for some time. He inherited the tenancy of Grange Farm from generations of Grundys.

When Joe's much-beloved wife Susan dies in 1969, he is left with two unruly boys to bring up, Eddie and Alf. Eddie, in spite of Joe's constant moans, grows up to be a reliable son of sorts, helping to manage the farm, marrying the capable Clarrie Larkin and producing two sons, William and Edward. Alf, on the other hand, is a bad lot. He hates farming and leaves home as soon as he can.

Clarrie and Eddie's wedding reception at The Bull. Clockwise: Sid Perks (Alan Devereux), Pat Archer (Patricia Gallimore), Phil Archer (Norman Painting), Joe Grundy (Haydn Jones), Martha Woodford (Mollie Harris), Nelson Gabriel (Jack May), Caroline Bone (Sara Coward), Jethro Larkin (George Hart) Walter Gabriel (Chris Gittins).

He goes into the scrap metal business at Gloucester but is soon hauled up before the magistrates and charged with receiving stolen copper wire. His luck is in and he is acquitted but shortly afterwards is caught breaking and entering, and sent to jail. He has been in jail on and off ever since and was last seen in Ambridge in 1986, when he stole from William's money box and left with Eddie's car radio.

Having got such rich comic characters, much of the comedy in the late seventies and eighties was based around incident rather than major plotting. The Grundys were particularly useful in this way and Eddie frequently got banned 'for life' from The Bull. In 1980, for example, he has a grudge against P.C. Jim Coverdale

The Grundys in the 1990s, William Grundy (Philip Molloy), Joe Grundy (Edward Kelsey), Clarrie Grundy (Rosalind Adams) and Eddie Grundy (Trevor Harrison).

and he phones the Borchester police to tell them that Jim has girls staying over at the Police House. In fact, it is only Jim's current girlfriend, Eva, the German au pair. But the sergeant ticks him off all the same and he has to tell Eva she cannot stay again. Eva is so furious that she tips beer all over Eddie and, coming in on the row, Sid issues the ban. The only thing that Sid has forgotten is that Eddie is a key member of the darts team due to play an

Eddie often annoys Sid Perks by supporting the Cat and Fiddle agains The Bull.

important match against The Cat and Fiddle the following week. On the night of the match, Eddie gets his revenge by turning up at The Bull as the captain of the Cat and Fiddle team. The Cat and Fiddle win the trophy and to cap it all, Eddie arranges for the Yibberton Yobboes to hold a motorbike scramble in The Bull car park.

Also in 1980, Eddie gets involved in a pyramid-selling scheme of Nelson Gabriel's when Nelson pays for 100 gallons of soap solution to be stored at Grange Farm. Both Joe and Clarrie are involved in turning it into shampoo by adding colours and herbs. They then bottle, label and sell it. Inevitably, sales do not go well and Nelson is left with 700 bottles to get rid of before Christmas. Offered a good deal, Eddie races around in a hopeless attempt to offload them, but even Martha won't buy for the village shop. Eventually Eddie has to flog them for a nominal price at Borchester Market. Nelson leaves Eddie the last crate (70 bottles) as payment for his trouble.

THE BULL DARTS MATCH
29 December 1989

Teams:

	The Bull	The Cat and Fiddle
Captain	Neil Carter	Eddie Grundy
	David Archer	Herbie Sykes
	Mike Tucker	Snatch Foster
	~~Shula Hebden~~ *Kathy Perks*	Jolene Rogers
	Tom Forrest	Baggy Bagshore
	Keith Horrobin	Fatty Partridge

Shula's car breaks down and she doesn't make it to the darts match, so Kathy takes her place.

Eddie's on and off relationship with local country and western singer, Jolene Rogers, has always provided an opportunity for comedy but also reveals a poignant side to Eddie's character. In 1981 he is invited to make a record with Jolene. Clarrie Larkin, who is courting Eddie at the time, is never pleased when Jolene, 'the Lily of Layton Cross', turns up on the scene, and she is even less pleased this time as the phone call with the offer comes just as Eddie is about to propose. In the end he doesn't get around to the proposal but he does ask Clarrie for £15 to cover the cost of making the record. She is soft enough to promise it to him because she loves him dearly and by May he is off to London with Jolene and her husband, Wayne

In 1981 Eddie was all set to make a record with Jolene Rogers.

Tucson, to make the demo tape. By now Nelson is on board as Eddie's manager, though 'managing' him doesn't extend to giving him expenses for the London trip. It does, however, extend to sorting out a recording contract for the release of the record.

By July, Clarrie is tired of waiting for Eddie to propose and pops the question herself. Eddie is about to accept when news that his record is to be released changes his mind.

Poor Clarrie. She feels even more put upon when Eddie announces he is about to embark on a three-month tour to coincide with the release! By late August, however, Eddie is back in Ambridge and broke. The recording company has gone bust and the record is never released, so the tour dates go down.

Clarrie is always having to bail Eddie out.

Jolene and Wayne decide to try again, this time without Eddie and his dubious contacts, and worst of all, Eddie has to admit to Clarrie that her £15 wasn't the half of it. He's borrowed £250 from Baggy, who is now knocking on his door to be paid back. Magnanimous Clarrie agrees to give Eddie the money to repay the loan from £500 left to her by her mum's insurance, but in return she tells him he must marry her. Needless to say, gallant Eddie proposes there and then and on November 21st, the happy couple are wed. From that day to this, Clarrie has been bailing Eddie out whenever required.

'Get rich quick' schemes and abortive business ventures continue to abound in the Grundy household and as the eighties go on, among other scams, Eddie borrows Neil's water tank and fills it with caustic soda to strip chairs for Nelson. The venture is a failure as the chairs fall apart. Next, he tries to sell 700 hamburgers which he buys cheap from Baggy. Finding nowhere to store them at Grange Farm, Joe persuades Laura Archer to put them in her freezer in return for 'keeping mum' about a deer

she knocked down while taking driving lessons. Jill comes to the rescue, however, by telling Laura that if anyone has committed an offence it is Joe, who dragged the deer away after the accident. So Laura tells Joe and Eddie to take the burgers away. They wrap them in blankets then store them in the village shop freezer, then at The Bull. They eventually try to fob them off on Mary Pound and Nelson. In the end I don't know who had the pleasure of eating them.

No matter how many scrapes Eddie gets involved in, he always returns home to Clarrie, and it is from their enduring relationship that the best comedy comes. In 1992, Clarrie's energy for life and naturally outgoing personality leads her to develop an interest in all things French. Eventually she suggests an Ambridge Town twinning project and she even goes to France with Eddie to look at French farmhouses on a pipe-dream that they might one day move out there. Eddie, however, is less taken with the place, particularly when he is served red wine instead of English beer and has to watch the estate agent, Bernard Valmer, using his gallic charm on Clarrie. He isn't at all sure about all this French romanticism. Clarrie, on the other hand, seems to thrive on it. When she gets home, she begins to cook French food and play her Roch Voisine tape, asking Jean-Paul to translate the lyrics. This means that Clarrie is spending quite a lot of time in Jean-Paul's company, and so when Jack Woolley asks him to

BRIDGE FARM: 5.15 P.M.
(CLARRIE IS PLAYING PAT HER ROCH VOISINE TAPE, 'JAMIE'S GIRL'.)

CLARRIE Do you like it?
PAT   Yes, very much.
CLARRIE The French side is more romantic, but I can't understand all the words.
PAT   Maybe that helps.
CLARRIE Roch Voisine's French Canadian, you see. He sings in both languages. I like the words to this one. Eddie hasn't written me a song for years.
PAT   You should ask him to.
CLARRIE I have. He says I don't inspire him. That's nice, isn't it?
PAT   Considering the last thing that inspired him to write a song was a pig, Clarrie, I should take it as a compliment.
CLARRIE You're probably right. So it's a swap? I lend you my Roch Voisine and you lend me A Year in Provence.

French chef Jean-Paul (Yves Aubert) inadvertently causes a problem for Eddie and Clarrie.

name a new pudding after Clarrie as a thank you to the Grundys for recovering Peggy's stolen garden statue of Aphrodite, Eddie becomes suspicious. And later, when he finds the translated lyrics of 'Pour Toi' addressed to Clarrie in Jean-Paul's handwriting, it is enough, in his mind, to prove an affair.

Getting a few drinks inside him, Eddie goes up to Grey Gables determined to punch the Frenchman on the nose. Whether it is the drink or simply that Eddie is beside himself with rage, we'll never know, but suffice it to say that Jean-Paul's nose comes off better than Eddie's hand and the wall in the garden where Jean-Paul had gone for a quiet smoke gets the worst of it all.

Poor Clarrie is appalled. What will Jean-Paul think of the Grundy family now? They will never be refined enough for the French way of life and culture. Eddie will always, somehow, let her down. It is no wonder that her friends and acquaintances in Ambridge do find themselves feeling sorry for her every now and again.

A few days later, still suffering from a smarting hand and struggling with the milking, Eddie is obviously beginning to feel guilty and decides to make it up to Clarrie by taking her on a balloon flight. But Clarrie will have none of it, telling him that at least she is looking forward to

CLARRIE	What's the matter with you?
EDDIE	This. (PRODUCES PAPER) A filthy bloomin' poem from your fancy man.
CLARRIE	Where d'you get that? You been goin' through my things?
EDDIE	Lucky I did, innit.
CLARRIE	You've got no right...
EDDIE	No right? No right to know what my wife's gettin' up to behind my back?
CLARRIE	Oh, you need your head examined.
EDDIE	I'm gonna have that Frenchman's guts for garters.
SHULA	Frenchman?
CLARRIE	He means Jean-Paul.
ROBIN	Oh come on, Eddie, don't be ridiculous!
EDDIE	Ridiculous? You listen to this. (READING) 'Your fingers running over my naked flesh.'
CLARRIE	It's a song.
EDDIE	'Your voice is dying in a sigh.'
CLARRIE	Off my Roch Voisine tape.
EDDIE	'And me, tremblin' with pleasure.'
CLARRIE	Jean-Paul translated it for me.
EDDIE	You think I was born yesterday?
CLARRIE	You ask Debbie. She knows the song. It's called 'Pour Toi'.
EDDIE	It's lewd. Lewd and filthy.
CLARRIE	No it's not. It's dead romantic.

her trip to the Norfolk lavender fields with the W.I., a real chance to get away from it all.

On July 31st, Clarrie sets off with Mrs Antrobus and the others on her big day out. Imagine her surprise when only an hour or so into the journey, Eddie, on his motorbike and in his best clothes, flies past the coach at great speed. What is he up to? No sooner has she turned her back and her husband is off on some unauthorised jaunt, probably 'making music' with Jolene. A momentary jealousy threatens to blight her day but she puts it to the back of her mind; she is out to have a good time and a well-earned rest. And she certainly does. So much so, in fact, that just before they are due to leave, Clarrie refuses Mrs Antrobus's invitation to join the other ladies in the herb garden in order to sit quietly for a few moments on her own among the lavenders and take in the smell and the colour. It is a gorgeous summer's day and she is alone for a moment with just the breeze and the sounds of the bees. It is so relaxing.

Suddenly and gently, in the distance, she hears music and a beautiful French voice seems to be singing to her through the bushes. It is Sacha Distel. All her love of France wafted on the breeze, coming nearer and nearer to her in the sunshine. But then, another voice joins in ...

In 1995, we decided to capitalise on Joe Grundy's 'farmer's lung' with a little black comedy. It all starts when one afternoon, before milking, Neil calls Eddie over to help him. Neither Mike nor John are around and Neil wants to move an old boar called Monty nearer to some gilts, ready for serving in the morning. Eddie begins joking about the old boar being on its last legs and how it won't be seeing much more action. Neil, however, disagrees. He reckons Monty's got plenty of life left in him yet. Eddie argues that Monty's legs are going and he's got a bad cough, but Neil says it's only a bit of worm.

(SUMMER SOUNDS OF BEES AND WHAT HAVE YOU)	
(CLARRIE SIGHS HAPPILY)	
(SACHA DISTEL SONG IS HEARD OFF A BIT)	
CLARRIE	Who's that? Who's there?
EDDIE	(SINGING A FEW LINES OF THE SONG OVER THE TAPE)
CLARRIE	Eddie!?
EDDIE	Hello darling!
CLARRIE	Eddie Grundy, what on earth are you doing here?
EDDIE	Impersonating a lavender bush?
CLARRIE	Eddie, what are you playing at?
EDDIE	Love-sick man courting the most wonderful woman in his life?

Finally a bet is struck. Eddie bets Neil that Monty won't make it past Easter and they both get on with the job of moving him. Eddie waves his board about and drives Monty towards Neil. Suddenly, as if to get his own back, Monty turns round, runs through Eddie's legs, picks him up and, rodeo style, rides him around the field. Neil can't help but laugh as Eddie is pitched unceremoniously to the ground, twisting his ankle as he tries to get up. And he still can't stop laughing as he drives his friend back to Grange Farm and Eddie has to contend not only with his hurt pride but with Clarrie's disbelief. She just thinks he is trying to get out of the milking again.

Later in the day however, when the pain just won't go away, Clarrie hands Eddie the phone to speak to the doctor. To Eddie's embarrassment, Richard finds it as amusing as Neil, but he does offer some good advice and they go on to talk about Monty and the bet. Just as Eddie is recounting his belief that Monty's dodgy lung will not allow him to go on much past

Easter, Joe comes in and, overhearing the conversation, thinks they are talking about him. From that moment onward Joe harbours the belief that he is going to die and that Clarrie and Eddie know but won't tell him.

Joe starts to behave in a very generous manner, even offering – to Eddie's amazement – to do the evening milking and help Clarrie with some of the household chores. Both Eddie and Clarrie think he must be up to something or 'going soft in the head'. Undeterred, he takes Eddie and Clarrie out to lunch, spends more time with William and Edward and even more time quoting *The Bible*. He takes to quoting gloomy poetry and, most unusually, paying secret visits to The Laurels to see Pru Forrest.

Tom (Bob Arnold) courts Pru Forrest (Mary Dalley)

Eventually, Tom Forrest catches Joe arriving with flowers for Pru. At first, Joe claims he's visiting Jimmy Dawson, the blacksmith, but when it is clear he can't get away with that, he scarpers. But Tom won't let sleeping dogs lie and the following week he finds Joe in The Bull and gets the truth from him.

Way back in 1957, it seems, just before the time when Tom was up for manslaughter for shooting Bob Larkin, Joe had set his eyes on Pru and they had had a brief romance. Tom is aghast; Pru has never said anything about it, and Joe was, after all, married to Susan at the time. But Joe is quick to assure Tom that it only led to a quick kiss and cuddle after closing time at The Bull, nothing more. 'But it might have been. Powerful feelings were unleashed' he cannot resist continuing. Then he reveals how he sent Pru a Valentine's card. Tom says that he thought it was from Bob Larkin. Joe then divulges that he and Pru saw each other from time to time while Tom was in prison, and cannot resist speculating on what might have happened if Tom hadn't been cleared of manslaughter. As it was though, Joe and Pru went for a long walk by the Am, tears were shed and they parted. After all these years, says Joe, he now wants to set his house in order before he dies.

The confession may have made Joe feel nearer to God, but it doesn't do much for Tom Forrest or his relationship with Pru over the next few weeks. Eventually, of course, Tom and Pru are reconciled and Joe decides to take to his bed.

By now Clarrie is beginning to get really worried about Joe's odd behaviour; his over-concern for others, his cheerfulness one minute and deep depression the next.

Seeing him looking ill and tired all the time, she decides to call the doctor. Richard Locke arrives, diagnoses a touch of the flu and, when pressed by Joe to tell him the truth, reveals that not only is Joe not about to

Is Joe swinging the lead? Clarrie has to find out.

die but that he should, with care, have many active years still ahead of him. Joe recounts the overheard phone conversation which led him to believe that he had six months to live and Richard bursts out laughing, telling him the story of Monty the boar and the bet. Joe is mortified. When he thinks of all the pints he has bought people, all the folks to whom he has been nice and all the secrets he has revealed, he feels like killing Eddie.

In fact, he decides on a better plan. When Dr Locke departs, he calls Clarrie and tells her that his lung has got a lot worse and that he will need plenty of bed rest and nursing. Poor Clarrie believes him and tells Eddie that he will have to do the work of two on the farm while Joe rests. Time goes on, with Clarrie running around to do all she can for Joe, but Eddie is by no means as convinced of his father's condition. Clarrie, however, is adamant. Joe is not 'crying wolf' this time. And so for a month, Joe pretends to be bedridden, though able to creep out of bed for the food and drink supplies he has hidden when Clarrie isn't looking. As Joe gets happier and happier being waited on hand and foot, Clarrie gets more and more worried.

Eventually, suspecting that Joe is swinging the lead, Eddie decides to confront Richard. Richard, amazed Joe is still in bed, tells Eddie the truth and Eddie storms back to Grange Farm to have it out with Joe. Seeing that the game is up, Joe argues that he has almost been frightened to death, to say nothing of being publicly humiliated by Eddie's bet which led him to believe he was going to die. In the end, Eddie sees the funny side and they agree to call a truce. Clarrie returns to find both men promising to work even harder on the farm. In spite of everything, soft-hearted Clarrie cannot really bring herself to blame Joe. How terrible, she thinks, to believe you are going to die.

Ambridge's greatest comic heroine, Lynda Snell, makes her first appearance in Ambridge in September 1986. Immediately she seems to be a self-styled expert on the countryside and much of the comedy is found in exploiting the gap between her opinion of herself in this respect and the reality. Meeting Eddie for the first time, she thinks his ferret is a rat and encountering Brian Aldridge while out walking, she berates him on the state of the footpaths, only to be invited a few days later to Home Farm by Jennifer for 'embarrassed' drinks.

As soon as Lynda arrives from Sunningdale, it is obvious that she is a great organiser of people, a woman whose sense of self worth comes from being needed by others in her community. She is determined to make Ambridge 'her' community. Immediately she launches into many do-gooding and environmental concerns, eventually opposing Phil Archer's barn conversions in 1987 and standing for the parish council on the platform of 'a

VOTE FOR A GREENER AMBRIDGE

VOTE

LYNDA SNELL

ON THE PARISH COUNCIL

Lynda Snell (Carole Boyd) with Persephone.

greener Ambridge'. She is not elected. In 1988 both she and Mrs Antrobus, each unaware of the other, carry out a footpath survey, and in the next few years her campaigns involve everything from cleaning up ponds to rescuing hedgehogs and preserving rare birds. She also becomes interested in animals, purchasing two Anglo-Nubian goats which she names Persephone and Demeter.

Lynda with Dame Edna

Lynda's heart, of course, is always in the right place. Her need for her fellow human beings is so blindingly obvious, even when she herself will profess to have little time for any of them. And she can be tactless and excruciatingly irritating to all around her as she drives fearlessly on in her pursuit of the truth and better standards for all. In this respect she resembles another huge comedy heroine; or perhaps to be fair, that woman could be seen as an Australian parody of her good self, a larger than life version, if such a thing is possible, of Lynda Snell. How wonderful then, when on October 7th 1988, Lynda and her husband Robert go to see Dame Edna Everage at the theatre and find themselves sitting so close to the stage that Lynda, inevitably, is called upon to participate. The scene was recorded as live, in front of the real audience for the show and most of it was ad-libbed. However, Lynda's gloriously competitive reaction afterwards was not.

In 1989 we begin to learn a little more about Lynda's domestic life. She tells Shula that her marriage to Robert is complete, in spite of the fact that she couldn't have children, and she is thankful that Robert already has two daughters, Leonie and Coriander, from his first marriage. In 1990 she sends the progeny of her beloved billy goats to Africa under the Farm Africa scheme in an altruistic gesture so typical of Lynda. She goes to Heathrow herself to wave them off.

LYNDA	(GLOATS) She made a big mistake when she picked on me! I could tell she was regretting it, right from the start.
ROBERT	Yes.
LYNDA	The poor creature, I almost felt sorry for her. I mean, she'd obviously never heard of eau de nil.
ROBERT	No.
LYNDA	And I don't suppose she's ever set eyes on a watered-silk bedspread.
ROBERT	No, I'm sure you're right.
LYNDA	And then she tries to cover up her embarrassment by making cheap jibes about ensuite bathrooms! Well I ask you.
ROBERT	Yes, it was – (FROM THE HEART) – terrible.
LYNDA	I can't wait to get home and tell everyone in Ambridge.
ROBERT	(QUALMS) Right.
LYNDA	I mean, I've just upstaged a megastar! And it was more than a mere victory, it was a complete humiliation! (MUSIC)

Souad Faress 🍃 *Usha Gupta*

Souad joined *The Archers* in 1994 to play Asian solicitor Usha Gupta. Her father is Syrian, her mother is Irish and Souad was born and brought up in Ghana. Her family travelled extensively when she was young eventually settling in Southport where Souad spent most of her early teens. Trained at the Guildhall School of Music and Drama, Souad's extensive career in television includes roles in *EastEnders, Prime Suspect 2, Inspector Morse* and *Shalom Salaam*. Her filmwork includes *My Beautiful Launderette* and *Bhaji on the Beach* and in the theatre she has played a variety of roles from Sita in *The Great Celestial Cow* at the Royal Court Theatre to Vittoria in *The White Devil* at The National Theatre. In 1995, she won Best Actress Award from the Asian Film Academy for her role as Usha, facing up to a campaign of racial harassment in *The Archers*.

Felicity Finch 🍃 *Ruth Archer*

Felicity's first professional job was a real baptism of fire working backstage on a national tour of *The King and I*. She remembers many long nights altering twenty costumes to fit each new group of Siamese children and being so tired that the chorus dresses were sewn back to front. After eight months as an assistant stage manager, she spent three years training at the Drama Centre in London and then went on to work in rep in Leeds, Leicester, Nottingham, Northampton, Newcastle and Cardiff, and further afield in Hong Kong, Australia and Europe with the Old Vic Company. Felicity still loves doing theatre work and she has played a great variety of parts from Laura in Tennessee Williams's *The Glass Menagerie* and Hazel in John Godber's *Up and Under* to Violet Beauregarde in *Charlie and the Chocolate Factory*. Her TV appearances include Rosa in *Bleak House,* Lady Lucan in the drama documentary, *Murder in Belgravia* and Sally in *The Sculptress*. Felicity comes from Teeside where her family still live and she has played the part of Ruth from Northumberland since 1987. When Flick is not acting, she spends time perfecting her circus skills for, amongst her other talents, she is a great trapeze artist.

Patricia Gallimore 🍂 *Pat Archer*

Patricia won the Carleton Hobbs Radio Drama Award while still at drama school in Birmingham and was offered a six month contract with the BBC Radio Drama Company. A wide variety of radio work followed including leading roles in classic serials such as *Wuthering Heights*, *The Forsythe Saga*, *War and Peace*, *Cold Comfort Farm* and *Persuasion*. In addition to reading a large number of *Morning Story* scripts and serialised books on radio, Pat was for some years a presenter of *Listen with Mother*. Pat also records a number of audio books, does television and radio commercials, film and TV commentaries and dubbs foreign TV serials and films into English. Recently she has been involved in devising and presenting a number of poetry recitals on stage. Pat joined *The Archers* in 1974 as Pat Lewis and married Tony Archer later the same year. In fact *The Archers* is Pat's third radio soap. She has previously played in both *The Dales* and *Waggoners' Walk* where for a time she shared a flat with a character played by Rosalind Adams (Clarrie Grundy). Today Pat lives in Warwickshire with her husband.

William Gaminara 🍂 *Dr Richard Locke*

William joined *The Archers* in 1992 to play the Mancunian Dr Richard Locke. He started his acting career at Worcester and York Reps, and with the Chung Ying Theatre, a half Chinese, half-British company based in Hong Kong. His theatre work since then includes seasons at the Leicester Haymarket, the Liverpool Playhouse, the Old Vic Studio and the National Theatre in London. On television, William's TV credits include *The Bill*, *Casualty*, *Soldier Soldier*, *The House of Elliott* and *The South Bank Show* and in film he has been seen in films *Paradise Postponed*, *Comrades* and *Leave to Remain*. William works a great deal in radio for both BBC Radio 4 and The World Service.

A few days later, missing them terribly and comforted by the ever-faithful Robert, she declines his idea that she should join the health club to occupy her time because, she says, there would be children running around everywhere.

In August she collects the runt of a litter of Afghan pups from Mrs Antrobus. She calls the pup Hermes.

In the last few years we have built on the idea of Lynda's vulnerability and childlessness. But she still continues to play a key role in Ambridge's many community activities. And who could forget the village fête of 1991 when, having put her back out practising for the 'Tug-a-truck', she is carried around the site on a litter so she can still take full control of the proceedings. Or the video she makes about an altogether different kind of litter. It shows secret footage of villagers carelessly dropping paper on the village green and upstanding members of the community like Peggy Archer accidentally dropping eggs which smashed outside the village shop. Jill Archer is so offended by Lynda's approach when the video is shown in the village hall that she wipes the floor with her in a speech so heartfelt and strong that Lynda, for once, feels guilty. And radio critic Gillian Reynolds admitted to throwing her tea towel in the air with delight as she cheered Jill on from her own kitchen.

After all this, it is no wonder that Lynda genuinely feels isolated from the villagers. So isolated, in fact, that, to get back on good terms with them, she offers to put on a Christmas panto in the village hall. She even offers to donate the script, her own version of *Aladdin*, which had been so successful in Sunningdale a few years before. But when she submits the script for approval to the village hall committee they find that it was written in 1984 and is full of outdated references to the miners' strike so they turn it down in favour of Bert's script.

Lynda cannot understand their short-sightedness. Isn't it obvious that a woman of her talent and experience would update all the topical references? Apparently not to the village hall committee. She therefore resolves to put on her version of *Aladdin* herself. She will stage it in the conservatory at Ambridge Hall.

Thus began the saga of the two *Aladdins* and Eddie's unenviable task of playing in both productions at once – quite literally as it turns out, because a last-minute muddle over dates means that both pantomimes are playing on the same night and Eddie has to be frantically driven backwards

Aladdin

The Conservatory, Ambridge Hall

Directed by Lynda Snell

Aladdin	Debbie Aldridge
Abanazar	Joe Grundy
Wishee Washee	Eddie Grundy
Princess Balroubador	Caroline Bone
Widow Twanky	Nelson Gabriel
Music	Marjorie Antrobus

The Christmas pantomimes of 1991.

ALADDIN

The Village Hall, Ambridge

Directed by Bert Fry

Aladdin * Ruth Archer

Abanazar * Bert Fry

Wishee Washee * Eddie Grundy

Princess Balroubador * Kathy Perks

Widow Twanky * George Barford

97

and forwards between venues, changing costumes in the car as he goes. Thank goodness Clarrie has Velcroed everything in sight for quick removal and replacement! So Eddie gets through both shows with the audience believing that the confusion is part of the scripted fun. He is a star, and with the collusion of both casts, the directors Lynda Snell and Bert Fry, who would never have permitted cross-casting, are none the wiser.

Lynda's popularity in the village does not last long however, and during the collection for a promises auction planned in aid of Church funds in July 1992, Brian Aldridge jokes that Lynda should promise to mind her own business for a week. The joke is so popular that it spreads like wildfire and a good time is had by all until Joe tells Lynda what has been said. Hurt and humiliated, she vows to do no more for the village and retires to replan her garden borders, modelling herself on Vita Sackville-West.

Jack Woolley (Arnold Peters) is a shoulder for Lynda to cry on.

Eventually villagers notice that Lynda is no longer 'out and about' and Shula volunteers to try to tease her out. In fact, it doesn't take long to rekindle Lynda's enthusiasm, as Shula flatters her into offering to design someone's garden for the auction. But at the auction in August there are no bids for Lynda's garden design and Robert has to leap in and save the day by making a bid himself. It doesn't fool Lynda though and, for once, she wonders if she really is the right person for Ambridge.

All through the end of 1992 and the beginning of 1993 Lynda is quite low. In September, Robert goes away on a camping holiday with Leonie and Coriander and, although busy with her town-twinning video, Lynda misses him. While editing the video with Jack Woolley, Lynda pours her heart out about how isolated she feels from Robert's past life and how jealous she is of it. And no sooner has Robert returned from the holiday than he has to be off again on a business trip to Switzerland, leaving Lynda alone and with time on her hands once more. Time which she fills by taking an interest in 'off the rails' young Kate Aldridge.

Kate has taken quite a shine to Lynda, who seems to Kate so much more exciting, worldly wise and less censorious than her own mother. Or is it just that she can wind her round her little finger? Whatever the truth,

Lynda shines under Kate's spotlight and she really seems to be getting through to the girl. She draws Kate out about drugs and boyfriends and gently offers her opinions and advice. She is always careful not to overstep the mark but it is obvious, even to Jennifer, that some of the advice is getting through. By February, Lynda is inviting Kate to tea for half-term to meet Leonie and Coriander, and offering to print some of Kate's poems in the parish magazine.

Things seem to be looking up and it isn't long before surrogate motherhood is joined by the usual raft of community events once more: the videoing of 'the Battle of Hassett Bridge'; the HOOF – 'hands off our fingerposts' campaign, and more organisation of the town-twinning with Meyruelle. Eventually, Lynda is even able to lend a sympathetic ear to Shula and her plans for IVF. Little does she know what enormous upheavals lie ahead.

1994 is a busy year for Robert with, it seems to Lynda, even longer spells away from home on business or seeing his daughters. And as Leonie and Coriander are growing up they seem less and less inclined to stay at Ambridge Hall. Lynda puts on a brave face about this latest turn of events, remembering that, in any case, she used to find the children's visits very taxing.

Christmas 1994 arrives and Robert and Lynda spend the day alone before Robert visits his daughters and ex-wife Bobo on Boxing Day. On December 27th a woman keeps ringing Ambridge Hall and leaving

Difficult teenager Kate Aldridge (Kellie Bright) with her parents Brian (Charles Collingwood) and Jennifer Aldridge (Angela Piper).

Richard Locke (William Gaminara) re-enacting the Battle of Hassett Bridge.

urgent messages for him. So Lynda decides to phone Robert to find out who this woman is and why she seems so anxious to speak to him. But when she phones Bobo she finds that Robert isn't there. He had left, as arranged, the night before.

All Lynda's insecurities leap to the fore. Who is this stranger on the phone? Is Robert having an affair? When he returns home on December 29th she confronts him. Poor Robert denies everything – he had simply fitted in a quick business trip.

On January 18th, unable to rest, Lynda meets a private detective in a down-market café in Borchester. Dave Walker hands her a report on his first day's work following Robert. In spite of the dark glasses and scarf Lynda is wearing and the unusual nature of the rendezvous, she is spotted by Jennifer Aldridge who has popped in from the rain. Jennifer later jokes with Robert about seeing his wife with a mysterious stranger in a sleazy café. Now Robert thinks Lynda is having an affair. By January 24th, Lynda has been spotted with Dave Walker by Shula and the rumours in the village are beginning to grow.

Meanwhile, Dave is adamant that from what he has observed, Robert's problems are more concerned with financial matters than matters of the heart. Lynda, in total disbelief, simply sacks Mr Walker. On February 9th though, she is puzzled when her director's salary is not paid into her account. As Robert is away she rings the bank and is told that the business account has been frozen as it is heavily overdrawn.

LYNDA	Where the hell have you been?
JILL	I think I'd better go.
LYNDA	I have been insane with worry. Where were you last night? I know you came back to Ambridge.
ROBERT	Who told you that?
LYNDA	Sid.
ROBERT	Oh.
LYDNA	Well?
ROBERT	I slept in the car.
JILL	(GOING) I'll see myself out.
LYNDA	In the car?
ROBERT	I parked down by the river.
LYNDA	You expect me to believe that?
JILL	(OFF) Bye.
ROBERT	Well look at the state of me...Oh, goodbye Jill.
LYNDA	You think I was born yesterday, don't you.
ROBERT	Lynda, I sat in the car all night because I just didn't know what to do. And there's nothing I can do. I've just got to tell you the truth. (FRONT DOOR OFF)
LYNDA	There's no need.
ROBERT	What?
LYNDA	I already know.
ROBERT	You can't.
LYNDA	The bank manager told me.
ROBERT	What? What did he tell you?
LYNDA	My salary wasn't paid last month. And when I queried it with the bank, they told me there were no funds to cover it.
ROBERT	No, well, that doesn't surprise me.
LYNDA	So I put two and two together.
ROBERT	But it's not just the money, you see.
LYNDA	I know. There's another woman.
ROBERT	Oh no.
LYNDA	I know all about her.
ROBERT	Lynda I've told you -
LYNDA	That's where all the money's gone, isn't it. Setting her up in a love nest somewhere.
ROBERT	What?! (HE STARTS TO LAUGH) A love nest? Oh Lynda...
LYNDA	This is no laughing matter, Robert.
ROBERT	You're going to tell me next that we had sex romps.
LYNDA	I don't wish to know the sordid details.

From this evidence Lynda cannot help but face the truth. Robert has been having a torrid and expensive affair and has frittered away the profits from the business on a floozy. Her suspicions are further fuelled by the fact that the first she knows of her husband being back in Ambridge from Swindon, where yet again he has apparently been on business, is when Sid phones her from The Bull to say that Robert had left his coat in the pub the night before. Not only did Lynda not know that Robert was back but he, most certainly, had not returned to Ambridge Hall that night. She is therefore in considerable distress and anxiety when he does eventually walk through the door. When confronted, Robert shows himself in an altogether unexpected mood. He tells Lynda that he has been sleeping in the car because he hasn't known what to do or which way to turn. As he tries to explain, Lynda keeps interrupting with her accusations about another woman. When she comes up with the idea that he has been funding 'a love nest' however, Robert cannot help but laugh. If only it was that simple. He patiently explains the much bigger problem. He tells her that their company has gone bust. For two years, he says, things have been tricky with a combination of bad debts and business being hard to find. This, he reminds Lynda, is why he has been away so often and working so hard. Also, the outgoings on their business have been high recently; the new computer system, the cars and the travelling expenses.

'Is that why you got rid of your mobile phone?' asks Lynda.

'They cut me off,' he replies, and then with a rueful smile, 'The bill wasn't paid.' He then admits that there are other bills. For example he owes Grey Gables over £1,000, for putting up prospective clients who then didn't come through with any orders. And it's not as if he hasn't tried to get himself back on his feet.

He did, after all, have one brilliant idea. He tells Lynda about the computer system he designed for the canning factory in Borchester which has worked so well. So well, in fact, that he decided to adapt it and advertise it in the trade press in the hope of selling it to several other companies. And his gamble seemed to be paying off. There was a fantastic amount of interest and he really thought he'd cracked the problem. Until one day, through the post, a letter arrived from solicitors acting for the canning factory. They threatened an injunction if he continued to offer the program for sale. They pointed out to him that they now owned the copyright in the program and that such fine tuning of detail did not alter that fact. The program was no longer Robert's to sell. Sweeping all thoughts of an affair aside, Lynda is outraged on Robert's behalf. She is all for fighting the canning factory but Robert calms her down. Sadly, he thinks the factory is legally watertight. From that moment onwards Lynda gives Robert her full support. On February 22nd Robert formally winds up his company. Together they face village gossip and an embarrassing and stormy creditors' meeting and Lynda shows great dignity in the face of adversity.

By mid-April, Robert thankfully gets a systems analyst's job in Birmingham but it is badly paid and the Snells prepare to tighten their belts. Throughout 1995 and 1996 much gentle comedy arises from the various schemes that Lynda puts into place to do just that. Not too proud to get a job, she applies for several secretarial posts when she sees them advertised. She even visits the Job Centre but it isn't long before she realises that her age and lack of training are against her and she retreats to fight another day.

Imagine her delight, then, when she hears that Kathy Perks is pregnant and will be taking maternity leave from Grey Gables. Airily she offers to cover for Kathy, creating an embarrassing situation for Jack Woolley and Caroline, who don't think she is right for the job. Lynda's assumption that she can have the job if she wants it puts Jack, particularly, in an awkward corner as he hasn't the heart to refuse her outright. Thankfully Caroline comes up with a solution. Trudy will stand in for Kathy running the health centre and Lynda will take Trudy's role as receptionist. Lynda, desperate for any job, accepts gratefully and launches in with her customary Snell panache. This, inevitably, is not to everyone's liking and it isn't long before she has offended Jean-Paul by ticking him off for smoking and irritated Caroline by using the Grey Gables computer system for her own outside activities: the design of the Ambridge floral carpet.

Jean-Paul (Yves Aubert) in the kitchen at Grey Gables – happy to be left to his own devices.

In general, though, Caroline has to admit that Lynda is very capable and efficient, even if, just occasionally, she still goes too far. As, for example, when she seems to be running a parallel business in her spare time, taking Grey Gables visitors on guided tours of places of interest in the vicinity. But before Caroline can step in to stop this wayward piece of entrepreneurialism, Lynda finds herself frightened off the venture by an over- zealous client who gets the wrong end of the stick and assumes she is a high-class call girl. Even Caroline finds it difficult to stifle a laugh when she hears about that one.

When Caroline goes on her honeymoon and Peggy Woolley stands in for her, Lynda finds life at Grey Gables a little more taxing. Faced with a sudden staff shortage in the chambermaid department, and finding it easier to get the agency to send her a temporary receptionist than a chambermaid, Peggy hurriedly insists that Lynda takes over as a temporary stopgap. Poor Lynda hasn't really cleaned anything thoroughly for years. Every day she wears a headscarf and scuttles across the lobby for fear that someone will recognise her. Her nails are breaking and she has to endure the ignominy of being pulled up by Peggy in front of hotel guests for not putting the proper bleach in the lavatories. How grateful she is when Caroline comes back from her honeymoon and, taking pity on her parlous state, returns her forthwith to the reception desk.

These days Lynda has a permanent job on reception and her social life is as busy as ever. She is directing Ambridge's first amateur Shakespeare production, *A Midsummer Night's Dream*, with Joe Grundy as Bottom and Nigel and Elizabeth as Oberon and Titania. All, of course, does not run smoothly but Lynda remains determined to be in artistic control.

Very few people can get the better of Lynda Snell, but one woman who can make a

Caroline Bone's introduction of Nouvelle Cuisine put the restaurant at Grey Gables on the culinary map.

good stab at it is Julia Pargetter. When Lynda is shooting the town-twinning video to give the people of Meyruelle a glimpse of Ambridge life, Julia manages to change considerable chunks of the script by the sheer force of her personality, even though as 'director' Lynda stands before her.

Nigel's formidable mother speaks for the first time in the programme on June 29th 1989 when she, Nigel, Kenton and Elizabeth have lunch together to discuss how to get Lower Loxley back on its feet. Nigel's father died in April 1988 and it has slowly become clear that there is a crisis. The family estate, Lower Loxley Hall, was steadily run down towards the end of his life and something will have to be done if it is not simply to crumble around them. Nigel suggests, in a tactful way, that his mother might make the estate over to him to avoid death duties and enable him to sort things out. The idea, unfortunately, is not well received and Julia leaves before the end of the meal, prophetically, with a bottle in her hand.

Debbie Aldridge (Tamsin Greig), with her natural father Roger Travers-Macy (Peter Harlow). Julia Pargetter has her sights set on Debbie as a suitable partner for her son.

After this outburst she does, however, make some attempt at working with Nigel but she soon finds the necessary economies tedious and decides to leave everything to her son after all, and spend her time abroad. And so Nigel takes it on, but 'Mummy' has never signed over total control and he walks a tightrope whenever she looks like taking an interest.

And take an interest she does, once again, when after two years jetsetting around the world with her wealthy Iranian friends, she finally runs out of money and announces that she is to return home in August 1992. During the interim it has become obvious to Nigel that opening Lower Loxley to the public on high days and holidays is not going to be enough. The Jacobean building is desperately in need of repairs to the roof and interior decoration, too, is a priority. So he has set out a business plan and appointed and trained Elizabeth Archer as his marketing manager.

The day of the launch of Lower Loxley as a conference venue is now fast approaching and when mother announces her plans to return on that very day, Nigel is apoplectic. Mummy will surely hate much of the necessary new-found commercialism of her home and on that day of all days, she

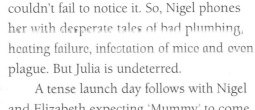

couldn't fail to notice it. So, Nigel phones her with desperate tales of bad plumbing, heating failure, infestation of mice and even plague. But Julia is undeterred.

A tense launch day follows with Nigel and Elizabeth expecting 'Mummy' to come through the door at any moment. But thankfully, and in typical Julia style, she simply doesn't turn up. Instead she arrives one week later, without comment on her lateness, and with Asty, an interior designer she met in Minnesota, on her arm.

Nigel's relief is not, however, to last long. She is astounded at some of the changes Nigel has made and even more horrified at the clear influence exercised by 'the yeoman farmer's daughter' Elizabeth Archer. Finally, she orders Elizabeth out, reclaims her role as chatelaine and instructs Asty to redecorate her bedroom to her own taste. Nigel flies to Elizabeth's defence and insists that his mother accepts her as a key member of the Lower Loxley organisation. Reluctantly and tentatively, in the end, she does so but it will never be a comfortable relationship.

Meanwhile, Julia spends her time getting in the way at Lower Loxley, mopping up Titcombe's day by cultivating an interest in horticulture and setting her sights on Debbie Aldridge as a richer and, therefore more suitable, partner for her son. To Debbie's acute embarrassment, she is invited regularly to tea at Lower Loxley and Julia loses no opportunity in suggesting that she and Nigel go off on business trips together. If Nigel is to marry 'new' money, at least Julia is determined to see that it is considerable.

As time goes on, Elizabeth grits her teeth and waits in vain for the moment 'Mummy' decides to take off again. But somehow the invitations from her friends never come. The Peacock Throne crowd are looking elsewhere for their entertainment and impecunious freeloaders are not on the guest list. Elizabeth manages to offload Julia on Nelson from time to time and a friendship seems to be growing between them as he takes Julia off for a concert or tea on several occasions. But he is a busy man with the wine bar and antique shop to run and Elizabeth knows that she cannot rely on him for ever. So 'Mummy' continues to get in the way at Lower Loxley, and her primadonna tantrums place more and more strain on her son. Meanwhile Nigel's relationship with Elizabeth grows warmer as the business at Lower Loxley gets steadily stronger and as it grows, Julia, feeling more excluded than ever, becomes an even bigger 'thorn in the flesh'.

By December 1993 the writers decided to turn the tables on comedy and give Julia a drink problem. On December 14th she slithers down the stairs and crawls into a table and by December 16th she is complaining of dizzy spells. Nigel is worried enough to insist that she sees her private doctor in Harley Street. On the way back from London in the car, Julia is strangely quiet, which confirms Nigel's suspicions that something is wrong. By December 21st, Nigel announces to Lizzie that he has decided to spend Christmas with his mother and not at Brookfield because Julia is obviously not well. Elizabeth, hearing maternal manipulation in every word, is frosty.

Three days before Christmas, Julia tells her son that the doctor has told her that this could be her last one. A worried Nigel goes to Mrs Antrobus for help. She advises him to ask the doctor for more details. On December 23rd, Nigel phones the doctor. The doctor tells him that he has indeed told his mother this could be her last Christmas but only if she doesn't stop drinking. On Christmas Eve, Nigel confronts his devious mother who finally, when pressed, admits to having a 'little problem' and that she could do with his help. But, when she returns later in the day from a shopping expedition, she is laden down with alcohol for the festivities and Nigel, disgusted, goes off to Brookfield leaving 'Mummy' to a lonely Christmas.

Christmas cheer for Nelson in the wine bar.

He should have known that lonely Christmases were not resilient Julia's style and Nelson is soon able to report details of a house party of London friends on Christmas Day and that Julia intends to leave to spend New Year's Eve with the same friends on the day after Boxing Day. Nigel sighs with relief but on December 29th, Julia mysteriously returns announcing that she hasn't touched a drop since she's been away and insisting that she wants to spend New Year's Eve with her son. By January 4th, Nigel is telling Lizzie that he is sure that Julia is secretly drinking early in the morning and later that day they find her swigging gin in the summer house. Caught in the act, she cannot deny it so she turns defensively on Nigel, accusing him of cutting her off from all her friends.

By January 7th, Julia has taken to regular visits to The Bull and is becoming a subject of gossip in the village. When she returns home drunk that evening, Nigel is furious with her. By January 14th another drunken session leads to Elizabeth refusing to give Julia her car keys back. A dreadful row ensues and Nigel, coming in upon it, orders his mother to her room and comforts a distressed Elizabeth. Something must be done.

Once again Julia is ahead of them all and the next day, unpredictable as ever, she takes off for a holiday with friends in Bath. When she returns in February, she pronounces herself on the mend again and asks Nigel to

Conflicting plans for Elizabeth and Nigel's wedding reception as Phil and Jill decide on a marquee at Brookfield, while Julia favours the great drawing room at Lower Loxley.

lock the drinks cupboard and keep the key. She is even polite to Elizabeth. But she is obviously tired and, Elizabeth thinks, 'a shadow of her former self'. On February 11th, she is due to spend another weekend with her friends and both Nigel and Elizabeth find her slow to pack. When they press her, the truth comes out. The friends have cancelled. She was drunk when she was with them last time and they do not want her to go again. She has to face the truth but even as she looks her son in the eye, she distances the problem by putting it in the third person: 'Your mother is an alcoholic' It is a breakthrough nevertheless and, finally, she agrees to go into a clinic for help.

The regime at the clinic seems to suit Julia and, apart from one minor blip when she walks out for a few days, life seems to be getting brighter for her. Finally, in May, having tentatively controlled her drink problem, she checks out and returns to Lower Loxley. The writers can, once again, turn their attention to things comic for a while.

Never one to do anything by halves, Julia now decides to plough some of the spare energy and time previously absorbed by her alcoholic haze into renewed interest in the business of Lower Loxley. She promptly sets about 'helping' Elizabeth: messing up the fax machine; muddling bookings and confusing clients on the end of the phone. If Elizabeth had less of a heart, or less of a memory, she may well have wished that Julia had never taken the pledge. But relief is at hand when Julia decides to move out of the office and turn her attention to developing a herb garden with Titcombe. This new venture lasts until August Bank Holiday when a day trying to sell plants to the public convinces her that she is not cut out for the job!

Julia's new, more reasonable, attitude even extends to gracious acceptance of Nigel and Elizabeth's wedding. A wedding is always a project for any prospective mother or mother-in-law and Julia loses no time in assuming that the reception will be at Lower Loxley as it usually is when a Pargetter gets married. It is just a pity as she gets preparations under way, that she does not consult Jill, who is, of course, going ahead with her own preparations for a Brookfield reception. Parallel plans unfold: a marquee on the Brookfield lawn versus a sit down dinner in grand style in the Great Drawing Room at Lower Loxley. Julia even wants to control the music at the Church. Finally, on June 29th, at the florists in Felpersham, the two mothers and their ambitions collide. Julia complains that for some reason which baffles her, Jill has instructed Nelson to provide sparkling wine for

Patricia Greene 🍃 *Jill Archer*

Paddy studied at the Central School of Speech and Drama and was one of the first actresses to go to Eastern Europe after the War. After that she had a series of jobs from bus conductress and waitress, to model and cook, but she always worked in the theatre whenever a job came up. At one point she was invited to join the Rank Organisation as one of their starlets, but she decided against signing the contract, concentrating instead on the theatre in England, working in many repertory theatres, on the fringe in London with George Devine and touring Europe with the Oxford Rep. When she joined *The Archers* in 1956 she was given a six-week contract and has now been with the programme for forty years. Recently she took on a different but related role when she became one of the three co-authors of *The Book of the Archers* with fellow cast members, Hedli Niklaus and Charles Collingwood. Paddy has one son, Charles, who is studying accountancy.

Tamsin Greig 🍃 *Debbie Aldridge*

Tamsin joined *The Archers* in 1991 as Debbie Aldridge and is considered to have one of the sexiest voices in the programme. She grew up in Camden in London and studied at the University of Birmingham, gaining a first class Honours Degree in Drama and Theatre Arts. Her television credits include *Blue Heaven*, *The Upper Hand*, *Kinsey* and *Neverwhere* and on film she has appeared in *Glasses Break*. Tamsin enjoys working in the fringe theatre. She is also a dancer and a founder member with Flip Side Dance Company. One of her favourite jobs was working with Theatre of Play, a theatre arts project, with young Ukrainian performers in Vinnitsa, Ukraine. She currently lives, a little nearer to Ambridge, in London.

Trevor Harrison ❧ *Eddie Grundy*

Trevor Harrison, like Chris Gittins, who played Walter Gabriel, is a Stourbridge lad. He trained at the Birmingham Theatre School and went on to work in rep in Birmingham and Coventry. TV appearances followed in *Get Some In Hazel*, *Stig of the Dump*, *Richard II* and *State of Emergency*, as well as several programmes for children, including *Jackanory* and *The Basil Brush Show*. On radio, Trevor could be heard reading countless stories on *Listening Corner* for Radio 4. It is, however, for the loveable rascal Eddie Grundy that he is best known. He has been playing the part since 1979 and in that time has released several country and western records including his latest album, 'The World of Eddie Grundy'. He particularly enjoyed working with Chris Difford from Squeeze who produced the album. Trevor is on the board of directors of The Archers Addicts fan club and he lives in the Malvern area where he is a keen bird watcher. Eddie would like to assure readers that Trev means of the feathered variety.

Brian Hewlett ❧ *Neil Carter*

Brian has played the part of Neil Carter since the character's first appearance in Ambridge in 1973. Although not directly connected with the world of farming, Brian is an amateur naturalist and photographer who cares deeply about the environment and the need to conserve wildlife. He spends his holidays, when time and money allow, exploring in the remoter parts of the world and remembers several wonderful visits to the game parks of Kenya, and observing rare mountain gorillas in Rwanda. Brian trained at the Rose Bruford College in Kent and first trod the boards at London's Mermaid Theatre in *Lock Up Your Daughters*. Since then he has balanced a busy schedule of theatre, film, television and radio. Brian loves doing musicals and favourite roles have included Amos Heart in *Chicago* in London's West End, Herr Schultz in *Cabaret* at Coventry and Salisbury, and Tevye in *Fiddler on the Roof* at Ipswich. He has also played the dame in panto on numerous occasions. Radio has played a big part in Brian's career and he has been with the BBC Radio Drama Company on four long-term contracts and recorded hundreds of plays for Radio 3 and 4. Today, Brian lives in a 17th century cottage in Norfolk where his overgrown orchard and pond serve as his own wildlife garden.

the reception when it was clear that she, Julia, would only consider champagne. Poor Jill defends her decision by explaining that champagne will be served for the toast, but that it is perfectly acceptable to serve a good sparkling wine up until that time. The energy with which Julia over-rules the decision and announces that she has already cancelled the wine and substituted champagne, leads faint-hearted Jill to realise that Julia is not talking about the same reception!

In the end, Nigel and Lizzie have to tell Julia, as kindly as possible, that the Lower Loxley reception is off. But once again, Julia, expecting the blow, beats them to it and, going for maximum effect, disappears once more. This time Nigel is worried that she will 'go on a bender', undoing all the progress she has made in previous months. In fact, it turns out that Julia has gone to Eastbourne to 'lie low' with her AA sponsor and presumably recover. The trip is a success and she returns unabashed to Lower Loxley on July 4th.

The wedding day arrives on September 29th and provides one of the biggest comic turning points in Julia's life in Ambridge to date. Nigel and Elizabeth have organised a surprise guest for Julia; it is her sister Ellen whom they have flown over from Spain. The two sisters

ROBIN	Morning Mrs Pargetter. (CAR BOOT LID SLAMMED) Lovely day.
JULIA	Marvellous. Off on your rounds?
ROBIN	Yes, I've rather a lot of calls to make this morning.
JULIA	Then I shan't hold you up. I just wanted a quick word about the wedding.
ROBIN	Oh yes?
JULIA	Well the music actually. What you thought would be suitable.
ROBIN	That's something I usually leave to the bride and groom.
JULIA	But you have some guidelines? I must say I prefer the more traditional approach myself.
ROBIN	And what do you call the traditional approach?
JULIA	None of these wretched choruses we get thrust at us these days.
ROBIN	You don't like them?
JULIA	No I do not. There's ample variety in *Ancient and Modern.*
ROBIN	Well if Nigel and Elizabeth want traditional hymns that's fine.
JULIA	But you're not going to insist?
ROBIN	Of course not. Why should I?
JULIA	And what if Elizabeth wants some sort of pop song?
ROBIN	It depends on the words. But I can't imagine Elizabeth asking for anything too profane.
JULIA	Mr Stokes, may I explain something to you?
ROBIN	I am a bit pushed for time.
JULIA	You may or may not know that the Pargetter family have been associated with the church in this county for nearly three centuries.
ROBIN	So I understand.
JULIA	I won't say they've all been devout. But they can certainly claim to have been staunch defenders of the faith.
ROBIN	I'm sorry, I don't quite see...
JULIA	A tradition like that places certain obligations on each succeeding generation. I'm sure you can appreciate?
ROBIN	Up to a point, yes...
JULIA	Well I'm far from certain Elizabeth does.
ROBIN	Oh I expect she does.
JULIA	All the same I'd feel happier if you and I saw eye-to-eye on the sort of service that would be appropriate.
ROBIN	I really think we should wait and see what they have in mind for themselves. Now if you'll excuse me?

haven't seen each other for several years. But during the ceremony, to the happy couple's surprise, the sisters sit on opposite sides of the church. It is only at the reception the reason for their distance becomes apparent. Julia does not like her sister. As the reception goes on there is still no sign of 'glasnost on the long-lost sister front', as Nigel puts it, and Elizabeth is anxiously watching Nelson, who is supposed to be making sure that Julia doesn't drink. In fact, Aunt Ellen is charming and is the hit of the afternoon. Debbie, Richard Locke, Phil Archer, and even Shula all crowd round as she proudly chatters away about her sister, whose real name is Joan, not Julia, and whom she remembers fondly as saving her pocket money for dancing lessons so she could become a dancer at the tail end of variety in the early forties. And that was where she met Gerald Pargetter.

Wedding bells for Nigel and Elizabeth.

'She was playing Bridlington,' Ellen recalls. 'He was stationed near there with his regiment. Went to see the show and fell madly in love with her.' More and more details of Joan's ordinary early life come out as good-hearted, garrulous Ellen continues to the increasing delight of the enthralled company. 'Finishing school? Good Lord no. Our father was a greengrocer in Lewisham,' Ellen tells Elizabeth. But as for her sister's dancing, Ellen is proud. 'I mean she really was very very good. And she had a string of admirers. You never saw the like. Gerald wasn't the first offer she had, not by a long chalk.'

Julia, overhearing snippets of the conversation and only too well aware what is going on, eventually makes a vain attempt to stop her sister. 'Nobody wants to hear about it.' But it seems they do and Julia retreats for the bottle.

When the time comes for Elizabeth and Nigel to leave for their honeymoon, all of Julia's pretentious bubbles have been burst and this greengrocer's daughter from Lewisham, who refused to train as a secretary but went on the stage instead, and who has been kept sober by much deft swapping of glasses by Nelson Gabriel and Richard Locke, does manage to compliment Jill on a reception 'very pleasantly done'.

After the wedding, good-hearted Ellen decides to stay on for a few weeks and keep 'Joan' company, and it isn't long before her beguiling ability to ignore Julia's little insults reveals a hidden strength. Ellen actually knows what makes her sister tick and can, perhaps better than anyone, control her sister's excesses. When Nigel and Elizabeth return from their honeymoon, Ellen takes one look at the situation and decides that what this young couple need more than anything else is time to themselves. She therefore,

with Nelson's help, contrives to make Julia take up her invitation to stay with her in Spain.

Ellen's ploy is a great success and Julia, to Elizabeth's immense relief, stays away for over a year. But good things never last for ever and in early 1996, Julia returns with yet another new obsession. This time it is the Hay diet. She drives Elizabeth mad by throwing out various ingredients from Elizabeth's kitchen, by donating all her Lower Loxley frying pans to the playground jumble sale and by insisting on never being served starch and protein on the same plate. And then almost as suddenly as she came, she is gone again, back to Spain. But Elizabeth's relief does not last long for in the summer, she reappears – this time to take part in the feature film at Lower Loxley. This is one commercial venture of which Julia certainly approves. The filming of *Isabella, An Orphan Jilted*, lets her down, however. Her roles turn out to be 'walk-ons', and her co-star is a pig!

The happy couple on the steps of St Stephen's with (left to right) Jill (Patricia Greene) and Phil Archer (Norman Painting), bridesmaid Debbie Aldridge (Tamsin Greig), best man Richard Locke (William Gaminara), Nigel's mother Julia Pargetter (Mary Wimbush) and bridesmaids Alice and Rosie.

Farming Matters

chapter four

"There's not as much farming in the programme as there used to be', so runs a common complaint familiar to the ears of successive *Archers'* editors as well as the broad-shouldered Tony Parkin, who, as agricultural story editor looked after the farming matters on the programme from 1972 to 1996.

In fact, nothing could be further from the truth. If anything, there is more and more farming in the programme as the ever escalating phone bill of Tony's successor Graham Harvey and his increasing research notes for script meetings testify. It is simply that these days the farming is more integrated into the drama as a whole. We do not stop, as they sometimes did in the fifties, to read a Ministry handout while sitting on a log; our writers do not write scenes based solely around how to control warble-fly in cattle or scab in sheep and our remit is no longer, and has not been since the early seventies, to educate farmers on new farming practices and townsfolk on countryside matters.

The nature of farming, over 46 years, has changed too. These days

Agricultural editor
Graham Harvey.

Tony Parkin, who retired as agricultural editor in 1996, proudly displays his unique award from the Royal Agricultural Society of England for his outstanding contribution to communication in agriculture.

farming can be as much about IACS forms, debates on set-aside and plugging in your computer to monitor the cattle feed as about harvesting, drilling the sugar beet or tidying the silage clamp. It is the constant backdrop to our drama and like all constant backdrops, it is often just gently there, unobtrusive and ongoing. Sometimes, and usually when there is trouble, it takes centre stage. Then, as when Brookfield suffered an outbreak of foot and mouth in 1956 and a TB outbreak in 1994, or when, as recently, the Grundys are threatened with eviction by Simon Pemberton, it is central to the drama and there is no mistaking it.

Over the years, villages too have changed and although Ambridge, off the B3980 from Borchester, is still a relatively small village of less than 600 inhabitants, incomers have moved in. Some, like Robert Snell and many of the residents of Glebelands, commute to the nearby towns to work. With less need now for manual labour on the farms, local work is hard to find. These days, *The Archers* follows 'country life' as well as 'farming life'.

In 1951, however, the remit was very clear. *The Archers* was part of the 'putting the country back together' effort immediately after the War, a popular way to disseminate information to farms and townsmen alike, through entertainment. Godfrey Baseley was even able to quantify, in percentage terms, the mix he required in the programme. It was '60% entertainment, 30% information, 10% education'. In July 1950, following the Whit week trial, he outlined for the benefit of T.W. Chalmers, then controller of the Light Programme, the purpose and general tenets of *The Archers:*

The most important thing here is accuracy. To keep a good tolerance between the purely factual and the more entertaining aspects of country life and to keep in mind always that the programme is directed to the general listener i.e. the townsman and through the entertainment develop an appreciation of the inexhaustible diversions to be found in the countryside.

And it must not be forgotten that *The Archers* was one of the few sources of farming information around after the War. The world of specialist farming advice, the publicity machines of government, the environmental lobbies; the big food companies and pressure groups, did not exist in the vast numbers that they do today.

By January 1952, one year into the national transmission of the programme and the year in which the Omnibus edition started, every farmer and farmworker in the country seemed to be listening. The

production office received a huge postbag, including many suggestions for storylines, praise and, inevitably, complaints. The complaints were often from farmers in other areas of the country, picking up on the regional differences in farming practices, which in the fifties were much more marked than they are today. Topical inserts were also considered a very important part of the programme and Godfrey wrote that 'should any important matter be discussed in the House of Commons, we should include the natural reaction of our characters to this subject.' This was considerably easier to do in those early years, as the programme was broadcast live or on the same day of recording. These days we record one month ahead of transmission and have a topical insert procedure which involves much last-minute calling of actors and rewriting of scenes well after the original recording. An altogether more cumbersome process. Major farming events like the recent furore over BSE involves Graham and myself in much second-guessing of the future and we closely monitor the

Godfrey Baseley (left) discusses the finer points of large white pigs with John Ryman, another broadcaster on For Midland Farmers.

farming news so that we can respond on the day if necessary. A tricky and exhausting business for a drama production team producing, in any case, a daily serial. Progress doesn't always make everything easier.

The quest for authenticity in the farming detail has been central to the programme since the beginning and it isn't only the scripts that come in for strong scrutiny. Sound effects, both recorded and invented on the spot with the actors in the studio, are scrupulously chosen and there is a story from the fifties which illustrates this concern. Producer Tony Shryane wanted the sound of a cow having warble-fly removed from its hide. The studio manager, who was providing the sound effects at the time, dutifully brought out a scrubbing brush and rubbed it across a doormat. Tony didn't believe the effect for one moment and sent sound recordist John Pierce off to the farm to record the real sound of a cow's hide being brushed. When John proudly returned to the studio with the effect safely recorded, Tony listened, smiled and, turning to John, said, 'Yes, sounds all right, but did the cow really have warble-fly?'

George Barford (Graham Roberts), Neil Carter (Brian Hewlett) and Tom Forrest (Bob Arnold) on location. The microphone is covered with an enormous wind-shield!

Looks like someone's knocking at the door at Brookfield. Dan (Edgar Harrison) turns towards the sound.

Nowadays, Louise Gifford, our programme assistant, frequently finds herself out on the farm recording new effects and we also have a full-time archivist, Camilla Fisher, who documents the daily goings-on in Ambridge on our computer database. Today, it is Camilla to whom we turn if we want an up to the minute list of what each farmer has on his farm. In 1951 Godfrey Baseley and writers Edward J. Mason and Geoffrey Webb each had a toy farmyard which was a model of Brookfield. Each cow and pig represented a portion of Dan's stock and animals were literally placed in the farm and taken out again as Dan bought and sold.

In those early days, many country organisations, perceiving *The Archers*' propaganda role, wanted to get in on the act and the production office had over two hundred letters a year from organisations asking for airtime. Godfrey was strict about the BBC's editorial independence and retained the final say over what went into the programme.

Today we have many similar requests and there is an even tighter control of, for example, the representation of charities across the BBC. Our storylines, which spring from our characters and their perceptions, tend to determine what information we need from outside bodies and we usually approach them for help rather than the other way round. Requests for inclusion in the programme for its own sake would rarely be agreed.

John Tregorran (Philip Morant, second from left) comes home to share a pot of tea with his wife Carol (Anne Cullen, far right). The studio managers create the sound effects for the scene.

We also have far less contact with Government than in the fifties and, now unshackled from our educational remit, tend to take our agricultural advice from farmers 'on the ground' or local representatives of organisations who have anecdotal information and evidence rather than dry facts or propaganda to disseminate. This is in sharp contrast to the minutes of *The Archers* liaison meeting in 1953, which showed that it was attended by the editors, writers and no less than sixteen heads of department from the Ministry of Agriculture. Today we really do go our own way.

At the height of the BSE problem, we had John Archer saying he wouldn't be eating beefburgers. While also representing the many farmers who believed that British beef was safe, we nevertheless mirrored the frustration that farmers felt when Government advice seemed to be muddled, as well as the confusion over what to do when the slaughtering of cows began. This is in sharp contrast to 1955 when, astutely, Godfrey and the writers wanted Dan Archer to change his herd from dairy Shorthorn to Friesians. It was becoming common knowledge that Friesians had a better milk yield and Godfrey could see that this was the way many in the farming community seemed to be moving. However, when he mentioned the idea to the secretary of the Dairy Shorthorn Society, the man was aghast. Eventually the Society made representation to the BBC and the debate reached the Director General, Sir Ian Jacob, as the Society expressed strong fears that Dan's changeover to Friesians could have 'serious

Walter with Boxer.

implications' for the British Shorthorns. In the end the BBC conceded the point and the plan was shelved. However, Godfrey and team, seeing the way the wind was blowing outside in the farming world, merely regrouped and when Dan's herd got foot and mouth the following year and had to be slaughtered, they then replaced the lot with Friesians.

Reading through the early continuity cards for the programme in the fifties, one can see clearly how the agricultural mirrored the progress of the times. In 1951 when the programme started, Dan buys his first tractor, selling his horse, Boxer, to Walter Gabriel and putting the other one, Blossom, out to grass. On 16th June 1952, a new egg-washing machine arrives and in 1953 lucerne is grown and silage made for the first time at Brookfield. In 1954 Dan and Doris are able to buy Brookfield when the squire sells the Estate. Many listeners forget that the Archers were only tenants when the programme began. In 1954 too, Dan bought a diesel tractor on H.P. and Phil, who was then living at Coombe Farm and working for George Fairbrother, started to build up a herd of Herefords and some pigs. In 1955 Dan finally sold Blossom but haymaking at Brookfield was still unmechanised. This was the year in which Phil was offered a directorship by George Fairbrother and Ambridge, like much of the country, had to cope with an outbreak of myxomatosis.

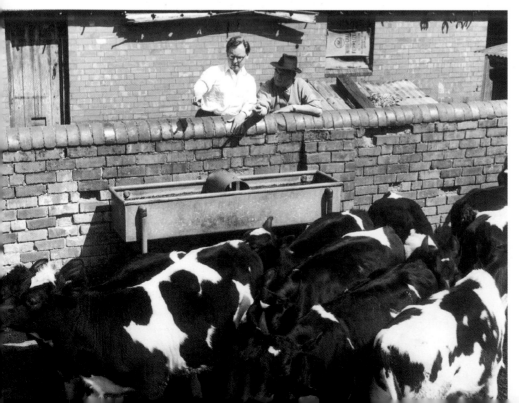

Phil and Dan inspecting the Brookfield herd in 1958.

*I*n 1956, the agricultural storylining of *The Archers* really did take centre-stage as Brookfield was hit by a devastating outbreak of foot and mouth. The storyline ran for ten months, certainly a long-runner in those early days. In 1994, a similarly devastating outbreak of TB in Phil's herd provided a storyline which went on for eighteen months and Brookfield has regular TB checks, even today, as a result of the outbreak. There are similarities, of course. Both stories involved big changes at Brookfield and both put Dan and Phil respectively under considerable stress as their livelihoods were threatened. But, as usual, the story in the 90s was less conclusive and more densely interwoven with other stories.

In 1956 the trouble started for Dan on 13th January when two pigs were reported sick by farmhand Simon. Immediately the vet was called and foot and mouth was suspected. By 20th February, much to Dan's distress, the outbreak was confirmed. Brookfield was put into isolation and P.C. Bryden had to stand guard on the gate to prevent anyone from entering or leaving. Scenes, in the spirit of the times, conveyed the educational information so valuable to farmers.

Young Phil and Christine are away for the night when the outbreak is confirmed and are first told the news, dramatically, by a hotel receptionist, who, noticing that they are from Ambridge, tells them the village was mentioned on the news headlines. But she does not know which farm is affected. So brother and sister have to drive back to Ambridge in suspense.

In 1997 we may well have chosen to place the listener in the same position as Phil and Chris, but in the fifties, the choice was different. We are already party to the dreadful news, having heard the earlier scenes with Dan and the vet when the trouble was confirmed. Whilst driving home, Phil mentions quite casually to Christine that his father is not insured against the disease but that his employer, George

DORIS	But how could we pick up foot and mouth at Brookfield?
VET	Any number of ways...
DORIS	But look, Mr Robertson... it's the pigs that seem to have it... not the cows or sheep. I mean... they're locked up in sties, they don't run wild.
VET	Swill?
DORIS	Boiled, naturally.
VET	You're absolutely certain of that?
DORIS	We know better than to give pigs swill that's not been boiled, Mr Robertson.
VET	H'm... in that case – I can only suggest that... either I'm wrong or else your other animals are infected and have passed on the infection.
DORIS	The dairy cows are all right... that I'll swear. And the sheep must be – otherwise Len would have reported it. Haven't even had a touch of foot rot. You might be mistaken, mightn't you?
VET	I might be, yes. But I'm taking the precaution of phoning my wife and asking her to prepare a change of clothing for me – and I think you'll find that P.C. Bryden will be outside your gate very shortly... keeping folks from going out and coming in... better to be too careful than the other way.

Fairbrother, is. Eventually though, the worry is just too much and they stop to phone home. Using a public phone box is a lengthy procedure, but they, eventually, get through.

Christine, movingly, offers her father an inheritance of £2,500 which she has just received to help out in the crisis. Dan is grateful but, with tears in his eyes, says he cannot touch her money.

It is a particularly harrowing time for Dan and Doris who must stay on the farm whilst their animals are slaughtered. The outbreak started in the sheep but as Dan patiently explains to Doris, even if the cattle show no signs of infection, the Ministry cannot take the

OPERATOR (DISTORT BUT CLEARER)	Go ahead caller... you're through now.
PHIL	Thank you. Hello... Dad... that you?
DAN	(DISTORT) Ay... hello Phil, lad.
PHIL	Dad... just heard on the radio... foot and mouth at Ambridge.
DAN	Ay.
PHIL	Where is it... who's got it?
DAN	Haven't you heard, then?
PHIL	No?
DAN	We've got it lad... here at Brookfield.
PHIL	Oh Dad... not really.
DAN	True enough.
CHRIS	(OFF) Oh no.
PHIL	But...but how... I mean...
DAN	Lord knows. Anyway we've got it... the Ministry vet's here on the spot living with us as y'might say. Specimens have been sent away to Pirbright and they've confirmed it.
PHIL	Your dairy herd?
DAN	Pigs. But it makes no difference... they'll all have to go. (BRISKLY) But look, Phil... we're isolated. You and Chris are darned lucky not to be here. Don't come back... go to Fairbrother's... they'll put you up. We'll keep in touch by phone.

Christine (Lesley Saweard) offers her father (Harry Oakes) £2,500 to help out in the foot and mouth crisis.

risk of sparing them; all cloven-footed beasts must be slaughtered. Amongst all this emotion, the scripts are careful to set out clearly the Ministry compensation and there is a warning to farmers to insure against the loss of income incurred whilst they are without stock.

As the days go on, Dan and Doris are devastated. Doris even thinks about giving up farming, asking Dan to get a job in a factory and move to the town. And amongst it all, there is the mystery of where the disease came from in the first place. Some villagers say it can be brought in by birds flying in from France. For the man from the Ministry, the problem is tracing the eight sheep which Dan sent to market the previous Thursday. These may have the disease. All stock within two miles of the affected area cannot be moved and all dogs within a five mile radius must be controlled. Walter Gabriel, who farms nearby, is one of the farmers who is stuck.

Farm workers, Len and Simon, worry about their jobs. Will Dan be able to keep them on? And if he can't, will they find it difficult to get another job because they come from an infected farm?

A couple of days later, Dan, shattered, goes away for a while to rethink the future of his farm. Part of him wants to retire, so shocked has he been, but his son, Phil, is not willing to take over yet and so, by March, Dan buys six sheep at market for £7 10 shillings and begins to look to the future once more.

On 10th April, he visits the bank manager to outline new plans for the farm. The country is suffering from a credit-squeeze and so he knows he will not be able to get a loan. But he is concerned that the bank manager will not back him if he falls behind with the mortgage repayments. Meanwhile, his plans are to use his compensation to bring in some sheep and pigs, increase his poultry, particularly the turkeys, and continue to grow cash crops. His big idea is reserved for the cattle. Dan explains that he doesn't want to buy a second-rate herd and has decided instead to build up a top-notch herd slowly. First he will buy some nurse cows and a few first-class dairy female calves to suckle off them. He will then sell the calves on, keeping the odd really top-class animal when he finds it. In this way he will build up his herd slowly but surely. Without milking immediately, he won't need so much labour so he will save costs by letting his oldest worker go and possibly replacing him later with a younger, cheaper lad.

By 20th July, Dan has rebuilt his flock of sheep to 20 ewes and 27 lambs. He plans to buy 68 Radnor-type ewes in August and put a couple of

Edward Kelsey ♦ *Joe Grundy*

Ted has been playing the role of Joe Grundy since 1984 when he took over the part after the death of actor, Haydn Jones. Trained as a teacher of Speech and Drama at The Royal Academy of Music, Ted graduated with the Howard De Walden Gold Medal as well as winning the Carleton Hobbs Radio Award which was then in its second year. As well as hundreds of radio plays, Ted has done a lot of work in film dubbing and voice overs. He created the voices of Greenback and Col. K. in the cartoon series *Dangermouse*. His theatre work began with the tour of *Reluctant Heroes* and was followed by many years in rep, notably at Guildford. His television credits include *Z Cars, Dr Who, Campion* and *Anna of the Five Towns*. For nearly thirty years, Ted was an examiner in speech and drama for the Associated Board of the Royal Schools of Music and in 1992 he was elected an Associate of the Royal Academy of Music. Ted is also a writer. He has written several musical plays and in 1991 he wrote *The Ambridge Pageant* which went on a national tour with members of *The Archers* cast. He is married with three children and two grandchildren.

Graeme Kirk ♦ *Kenton Archer*

Graeme was born in Crowborough in Sussex, educated at Sunbury on Thames and trained at the Drama Centre, London. As a youngster he was a member of the National Youth Theatre and was in their London productions of *Zigger Zagger* and *Macbeth*. After drama school he toured with Brian Way's Theatre Centre and then spent two very enjoyable years with Peter Cheeseman's Victoria Theatre in Stoke on Trent where he appeared in over a dozen productions. He has worked extensively in rep including the Liverpool Playhouse, where he appeared as David in the successful production of *Love on the Dole* which transferred to the Tricycle Theatre, London. His TV appearances include Jack in *Brookside*, Ralph Ward in *Coronation Street* and Dave in the BBC series *Sea View*. When not working he likes to play golf and cricket and spend time at home with his wife, actress Roberta Kerr, and their son Jack. Roberta has also been in *The Archers*, playing Mo Travis, the woman with whom Neil Carter nearly had an affair.

Rosemary Leach 🍃 *Ellen Rogers*

Rosemary joined *The Archers* in 1994 to play Julia Pargetter's down to earth sister, Ellen. Rosemary was born near Ludlow and trained at RADA in the early fifties. Her first job was as an acting assistant stage manager, followed by a summer season at a Butlins Holiday Camp in North Wales. In the late fifties however, her theatre work really took off and she joined Caryl Jenner's Theatre Group which toured the UK. Rosemary began her hugely successful TV career in 1960 with *Z Cars* and has appeared in many TV dramas since, including *The Roads to Freedom*, *Othello* with Anthony Hopkins, *The Jewel in the Crown*, *Cider with Rosie*, *Blood and Peaches* and *The Buccaneers*. Her film work includes *A Room with a View*, and *That'll be the Day*. In the theatre she has worked in both the West End and the provinces playing leading roles in plays ranging from Terence Rattigan's *Separate Tables* to Alan Ayckbourn's *Just Between Ourselves* and from *The Beggar's Opera* to *Hedda Gabler*. An extensive radio career includes *Tender Loving Care* and *No Commitments*. She enjoys coming to Ambridge whenever possible.

Moir Leslie 🍃 *Janet Fisher*

Moir joined *The Archers* in 1996 to play Janet, the new woman vicar of Ambridge. It is a far cry from the part she played in 1985, that of David's dizzy and dumb girlfriend, Sophie Barlow. Moir was born in London and trained at The Guildhall School of Music and Drama and her first professional role was in *Babes in the Wood* at the Porthcawl Pavilion. Since then she has worked extensively on stage, radio and in television, particularly enjoying a long stint with the Compass Theatre Company under the directorship of the late Sir Anthony Quayle. Moir played Ariel alongside his Prospero in *The Tempest*. She has played numerous leading roles in plays and serials on Radio 4, including the classic serial *Cousin Basilio*, Charlotte Bronte's *Shirley* and Katherine Mansfield's *The Voyage*. She made her directorial debut last year, directing touring productions of *Educating Rita* and *Private Lives*. Moir lives in London with her partner and their daughter.

Downland rams with them. But by 17th September, his bank manager is worried. When Dan goes to see him this time, he is advised to get back into milk as soon as possible. He tells Dan that he thinks his plan to build up a first-class herd, although admirable, will be too slow. And that his dairy, milking sheds and equipment lying idle, represent depreciating assets. It's not a sound business proposition. He persuades Dan to buy some dairy cows which he can afford, just to keep him going in milk until he can build up the splendid herd he really wants. Thinly disguised advice to farmers in real life comes thick and fast now as he also warns Dan that he must remember he will have to pay tax on his compensation money, or at least on that part which represents the growth value of the animals since the beginning of his financial year.

Dan takes his bank manager's advice and buys seven Friesian cows and six heifers at a farm sale and shows them off to Walter Gabriel with great pride. The road to recovery is set. There are several hills to climb, of course, but Dan will get there in the end.

What went into the behind-the-scenes decision to go with the foot and mouth outbreak in 1956 is, unfortunately, long since lost in history, although we do know that *The Archers* was faithfully mirroring what was happening to a lot of farmers at the time. There were several opportunities too, to make useful educational points. It also provided a splendid chance for the writers to change Dan's herd from Shorthorn to Friesians in one swoop.

The decision to cover the TB outbreak in 1994, was, however,

DAN	Why yes... calves had grown into cows – pigs had multiplied...
B.M.	So the difference between the two figures must count as income... and as such is taxable. Less the expenses and so on of course...
DAN	My golly I'd not allowed for that. Looked upon it as me own... tax free – like a football pool win or summat.
B.M.	I know. So many people do... but they still have to fork out to the Inland Revenue just the same...
DAN	Even if they've spent it?
B.M.	That's nothing to do with it.

The road to recovery is set for Dan Archer (Harry Oakes).

a fairly protracted and angst-ridden one. We spent a lot of time in a long-term script meeting which was solely devoted to the agricultural stories in the programme, wondering whether Brookfield could take such a difficult story after we had only recently left the inhabitants reeling from the death of Mark. And then there was the challenge of doing a story spread over such a long time and keeping up the momentum of the problem it presented to Phil, to say nothing of finding different ways of dramatising the seemingly endless Ministry tests required. The big difference between this story and the foot and mouth outbreak was that the latter was sudden in its impact and dramatic in the force with which it hit Dan, whereas the TB started slowly and almost imperceptibly, gathering momentum like a ticking clock on a time-bomb.

Phil (Norman Painting) looks to the future after the disastrous foot and mouth outbreak at Brookfield in 1956.

Phil in the milking parlour at Brookfield in the eighties.

Having decided to ignite the fuse, we began gently on 25th March 1994 with a possible reaction to a routine TB test by one of the cows in Phil's herd. As the vet, Robin Stokes, takes the first results, he is in a relaxed mood and he talks with Phil about other things. Once the reaction is suspected he has to issue a movement order on Brookfield which, thankfully, is revoked by the MAFF divisional vet after the weekend, on the grounds that the history and status of the herd makes it unlikely that it really is a case of TB. Phil is relieved but to be on the safe side the cow is milked last and her milk kept out of the tanker.

From March to May, Phil has to go about his daily business trying to forget that he may have TB in his herd. The nature of the test means that the cow cannot be re-tested for seven to eight weeks and there is nothing he can do but wait.

In mid-May, the MAFF vet returns and injects the tuberculin, once again, into the suspect cow. Two days later he comes back to look for any slight swellings which could indicate that the test

is positive. It is bad news. The cow has reacted and will have to be slaughtered. All movement of bovine stock is forbidden. The Ministry agrees compensation at 75% of the cow's value and arranges for her to be picked up for slaughter and post-mortem early the following week.

Phil and David try hard to convince themselves that it could be an isolated case. The post-mortem on the slaughtered cow reveals suspicious lesions in some of her lymph glands. It is looking more and more like TB and the divisional veterinary officer rings Phil to arrange to re-test the whole herd the following week. They will also test any cattle which may have had contact with Brookfield's. This means Tony Archer and Brian Aldridge's herds will both be tested and so will the estate cattle. Jill has to serve pasteurised milk to her bed and breakfast guests.

The results of the tests the following week show one reactor and two doubtfuls. The reactor is slaughtered and the doubtfuls kept apart and milked separately. By mid-July, Home Farm and Bridge Farm are clear but both Phil's slaughtered cattle are finally confirmed as having had TB.

Ruth (Felicity Finch) with the cows at Brookfield in happier times.

When the whole herd is re-tested in August, there are eleven reactors and Phil has to face the prospect of having to slaughter the entire herd. No-one knows from where the infection may have come.

In August Phil gets further news from the Ministry labs. The eleven cows did not have TB in their lungs which meant that they were not passing it to each other, but all must have caught it from the same source. In some ways this is good news, because it means that if the test has picked up all the TB cases and there are no new ones developing, the end is in sight, providing the source of the infection has gone.

Meanwhile, Jill notices that her bed and breakfast guests have fallen off and wonders if it is as a result of village gossip. Ruth, to be on the safe side, is getting pasteurised milk from the shop for Pip, and Peggy talks to Jack about the terrible foot and mouth outbreak in 1956 and how it all brings back such dreadful memories.

So far all lines of enquiry on the possible sources of the infection have proved negative and it isn't until mid-August that, controversially, the possibility of badgers is brought up. This leads to much speculation as villagers take up strong pro and anti views on the vexed question of whether badgers are responsible for spreading TB.

Phil clings to the hope that the infection may now be over. In September, however, his hopes are dashed as tests find one more reactor. But MAFF reassures him that this is probably the last. In October Phil has to cope with the knock-on effects of not being able to sell his calves. Every available space on the farm is commandeered to over-winter the large number of calves and, as if that isn't problem enough, Bert makes some of the temporary accommodation too snug and the calves catch pneumonia as a result.

Things look brighter for David Archer (Timothy Bentinck) as the herd is pronounced clear for the first time

On 31st January 1995, MAFF conducts more tests. By 2nd February the herd is pronounced clear for the first time. There is much relief as Phil is, at last, able to sell his stock. The final test will be in six months' time but things are looking good. The source of the infection is still not known, however, and some have even suggested that it could have come from deer. The possibility that it is badgers from Lakey Hill has meant that the case has gone to the Badger Panel of the Ministry of Agriculture. David, for one, is convinced that the badgers are to blame. Pro-badger animal rights activists cause £450's worth of damage to Phil's car when it is parked in Borchester in early February but by late February, the Ministry of Agriculture, acting on advice of the Badger Panel, decides the evidence is not strong enough to destroy the badgers. William Grundy, who is looking after a sick badger called Stripey, is highly relieved.

On 6th March, David, tired from busy nights in the lambing shed, frustrated by the apparent lack of information on the cause of the outbreak and still worried about the test in the summer, comes upon a badger foraging in a feed trough in one of the cattle sheds. He shoots the badger and buries it, in secret, in rough ground at the back of the bungalow.

But Phil's sheepdog, Jet, digs it up and Phil is furious. It is a frustrating time for them all but he warns David that he cannot take the law into his own hands. What David has done is against the 1981 Wildlife and Countryside Act, and the last thing Phil needs, as a magistrate, is to be obliged to cover up an unlawful act. However, this is, of course, precisely the position David has put him in and together they re-bury the animal. Phil has very few words for David as they do so. But David is adamant. He blames the badgers for all their problems.

To further complicate the situation, on 30th March Jill gets a letter from the wife of a Mr Clark, one of their bed and breakfast guests. Mr Clark always took a particular interest in watching the milking while on holiday with them. But they didn't come last year and now, sadly, they won't be able to come this year, she says, because her husband has TB. Phil contacts the Ministry of Agriculture who can only say that it is possible, but unlikely, that the cows at Brookfield could have been infected from a human source. Phil, David and the family must resign themselves to the fact that, in the complex world in which we now live, it is impossible to identify one simple source. On 7th September 1995, 18 months after the outbreak began, the Brookfield herd finally tests clear and life goes on once more for Phil, just as it did for Dan in 1956.

In the early sixties Geoffrey Webb, the man Godfrey Baseley described as 'a countryman through and through' and a key member of the writing team, died, and it took a while before Godfrey really found a settled team to work alongside Ted Mason. Eventually the actor, Norman Painting, who played Phil and who had considerable experience in feature writing for the BBC, was chosen. Norman obviously knew the characters well and with Ted and Birmingham-born writer Brian Hayles he wrote as well as starred in the programme for many years.

During this unsettled time, however, Godfrey backed a hunch that many farmers would react to the increasing pace of change in the countryside and the apparent need for ever larger farms and increased modernisation by forming co-operatives. Such things were being talked about and even tried out. But the formation of Ambridge Dairy Farmers in 1961, which in 1962 became Ambridge Farmers Ltd, when Dan, Phil and neighbouring farmers Jeff Allard and Fred Barratt decided to amalgamate, was in retrospect a rather precipitate idea.

Dan Archer (Monte Crick) attends the official opening of Britain's Sixth June Dairy Festival National Inauguration at the Royal Exchange, London. Here he is seen with Harold Macmillan.

In some ways Godfrey was way ahead of his time. Nowadays we do see increasingly large farms - many run by commercial companies rather than individual farmers - but in the 1960s the idea of large co-operatives never really took off and by 1966 the programme was winding the storyline down. In 1962 Phil and Jill had already bought out Jeff Allard and moved into his farm, Hollowtree. In 1966 Fred Barratt retired, allowing Phil and Dan to pay off his interest in the company in instalments. Eventually, Fred's land was bought by Laura Archer who rented 100 acres of it back to Phil and Dan.

The last two years of the sixties involved Dan in much soul searching about whether he should retire. This obviously fuelled gossip in the village as folk wondered what changes young 'Master Phil' would make and whether Dan would ever really be able to let him take control. Not so very different to the concerns expressed by David to Phil in 1997. Although Phil, in spite of the setback over his dodgy hip a few years ago, has not yet set the date.

The 70s opened with Dan having decided to semi-retire and move with Doris to Glebe Cottage, allowing Phil and Jill to move into Brookfield. On the other side of the family, Jack and Peggy's 18-year-old son Tony, is about to start work for Ralph Bellamy on the estate.

In a document disseminated by the production team called '*The Archers* as Radio Entertainment in 1970', Godfrey Baseley wrote:

It must be appreciated that over the years, very great changes have taken place in the whole pattern of rural life and that this is likely to accelerate over the next few years ... The whole status of village life has changed, particularly in those villages within an hour's journey by motorway from a big urban area.

Phil and Jill at the gate of their new home, Brookfield.

And Ambridge, within 25 miles of Birmingham, was certainly in that category. The village was likely to grow and it seemed clear that the way forward was to concentrate on a widening group of villagers with the ever growing Archer family at its centre. Phil was slowly to take on the role of father figure while Dan and Doris played an important but subsidiary role. The team restated their support for the old mix of 60% entertainment, 30% information and 10% education, but expressed a wish to add a slight documentary flavour by exploring more social, political and economic issues through the characters; i.e. sharpen up the realism of the programme.

When Godfrey retired and Malcolm Lynch was appointed as editor it was felt that his largely urban background necessitated some help on the

farming side and Tony Parkin, then the BBC's foremost editor of farming
programmes, was brought in to advise on the agricultural storylines from
that time. And from that time too, there seemed to be a marked shift in the
way the farming detail was integrated into the programme.

A review meeting in London was quick to praise the new team. The
feeling was that there had been 'a great all round improvement ... more
action, better dialogue and, in particular, a rather better way of using
farming material'. By 1973 Charles Lefeaux, who had succeeded Malcolm
Lynch as editor, was describing the programme as one that 'should reflect
rural events and new developments in farming, but is no longer intended to
be an information programme'.

The emphasis was clearly now on drama and entertainment with
farming providing the unique setting which gave the programme its
originality. Rural events and new developments were still to be reflected
accurately and fully but 'always subservient to the dramatic intention'.

*There's always some
problem for the Grundys
at Grange Farm.*

In fact, Tony's influence was quickly apparent
as the ironic counterbalance to those rather
dry internal memos became obvious; the
more skilfully the farming background was
built into the ongoing dramatic storylines,
the more farming detail sat easily in the
programme. The simple truth, as I am
increasingly aware as editor in the nineties, is
that the more sophisticated the mix, the more
farming one needs and wants to get in.

*I*n 1972 the goings on of the Grundys
began to be mentioned as a
replacement, at last, for Walter Gabriel's
farming exploits which ceased when Walter
retired from farming on Lady Day in 1957.

In some ways the Grundys have always
been examples of the slightly incompetent
farmer – 'the townsman's idea of the character
farmer' as Godfrey Baseley put it. But when all
is said and done, Joe and Eddie keep that
farm going year by year with very little money

and a lot of hard work. And in recent years the caricature elements which Godfrey Baseley created and William Smethurst refined into splendid situation comedy, have been balanced too by a more realistic approach to the family. There will forever be Grundy scams and nothing quite succeeds in the way that they plan. But we are also interested now in the way the Grundys build up their farm again after the fire and their recent eviction order; in the more human side of Eddie's marriage to Clarrie and in Joe's aspirations for his grandsons' inheritance. And as Graham Harvey, our agricultural story editor reminds us, Eddie is the power behind the rebuilding of Grange Farm – he can't be stupid.

No rest for Eddie!

In 1973, Tony Parkin reflected the growing number of apprentice schemes in the countryside by introducing Neil Carter, a young man from Oxfordshire, who had to learn all about farming from scratch. Neil was apprenticed at Brookfield and the situation provided considerable opportunity for comedy. Neil, particularly in his working relationship with his older mentor and friend, Jethro Larkin, became and continues to be one of the most popular characters in the programme.

In 1974, Tony decided to take the bull by the horns and do a story about swine vesicular disease (SVD) which had been causing considerable

trouble in the country since December 1972. By then the programme was
being run, much as it is now, on a three-month lead time and the team had
resisted doing a story on the disease for fear that it could have subsided
by the time the episodes were transmitted. Their fears were further
supported by the fact that the Ministry kept insisting that they had the
disease under control.

Eventually it was agreed that Ambridge would have an outbreak, but
not before Tony Parkin had extracted a promise from the Ministry that they
would not announce eradication of SVD, if it happened, until after the
Ambridge outbreak. In fact, there were still cases around when the
episodes were transmitted but Tony remembers the
time as nail-biting

By the mid-seventies Tony had decided that
farming mainly on the estate and Brookfield's 400
acres meant that Ambridge didn't have enough
different-size farms to represent what was going on
in the countryside at the time. He therefore proposed
that the owner of the estate, Ralph Bellamy, should
sell off some of his land. This successfully carved out
a central large holding of 1500 acres bought by Brian
Aldridge and 100 acres known as Willow Farm
which was bought by Haydn Evans for his son
Gwyn. Willow Farm was especially useful as it
reflected the average holding in Britain at the time
which was quite small. Home Farm, Brian Aldridge's
1500 acres, however, gave *The Archers* the
springboard it needed into the world of the large
business farmer in the expansionist eighties,
interested in high-yield intensive farming.

*It's just another day at
Hollowtree for Neil
Carter (Brian Hewlett).*

The size of farms can be planned in advance, of course, but elemental
forces are more difficult to control and one of Ambridge's more precarious
ingredients, the weather, caught us napping again, and not for the first or
the last time, in 1976. It was the year of the extraordinary summer drought
and the year also in which much trouble was caused by the corn-drier
breaking down at Brookfield. Red faces all around as farmers rushed to put
pen to paper to tell us that Ambridge must have been the only place in the
country that needed to use one.

When William Smethurst became editor in 1978, he immediately brought in a larger and more flexible writing team, many of whom had no direct countryside background. This meant that Tony's job became even more crucial and the agricultural notes he provided at script meetings more detailed. He created an agricultural calendar which showed who was doing what and when, and organised frequent forays into the country for the writers to meet farmers and farmworkers at first hand.

As the seventies came and went, Tony made sure that *The Archers* reflected the major changes of the decade. Increased mechanisation led to fewer men working in the fields; the countryside opened up as farmers, particularly in arable farming, took out hedges to accommodate the bigger machinery and create bigger fields; hedges were trimmed rather than laid and black and white Friesian cattle almost entirely replaced the red-coloured Shorthorns. Hayricks and milk churns tended to disappear as the hay was carted into the barns and the milk was taken away by the tanker. Increased specialisation led to larger flocks or herds and farms did not tend to dabble with a bit of everything as they had done in the fifties, sixties and early seventies.

Tony (Colin Skipp) and Pat Archer (Patricia Gallimore).

1980 for Phil meant reorganisation at Brookfield. Phil had just bought an additional 30- acres of land, which had belonged to Meadow Farm, and his son David had just returned from a two-year course at Cirencester's agricultural college brim-full with ideas for Brookfield. One of the first things he did on his return was to persuade his father to get in the ADAS man. ADAS suggested increasing their sheep flock to 300, expanding their potato acreage and selling their beef cattle which they did later to Brian Aldridge.

Throughout the early eighties the listener heard David Archer flexing his muscles at Brookfield and ironically

encountering some of the same sort of friction which Phil had done in the fifties and sixties with Dan.

Lambing is a busy time for Ruth and David. They must ensure that all the newborns are thriving and healthy.

In 1984, milk quotas were introduced in Ambridge as in the rest of the country. As a result, Brookfield had to reduce its herd from 110 to 95. At Bridge Farm it was the final push that Tony and Pat needed to make them go organic. They commit to converting over five years at thirty acres per year.

The eighties was a disastrous time for Mike Tucker - his troubles beginning in 1982 with TB in his herd and ending in 1986 with bankruptcy. When Dan Archer died in the same year, the rules of inheritance tax were different from today and Phil faced a huge bill. He had to sell fifty-five acres of Willow Farm and three acres of Meadow Farm for barn conversions to pay it. There was further friction too, at Brookfield, when Phil, worried about David's latest girlfriend Sophie, refused to make him a partner in the farm. In fact, although Phil didn't know it then, help was soon at hand when, in 1987, Ruth Pritchard, a 19-year-old agricultural student from Northumberland, arrived for a pre-college year's work experience. Her combination of strong opinions about farming but lack of practical experience made for several early mistakes which did not endear her to David but the animosity didn't last long. Mutual respect grew and they were married in December of the following year.

In 1987 too, Brian Aldridge began to diversify. In April he went into deer and in the summer ran shooting weekends in partnership with Grey

Gables. By 1988, he was jumping on the conservation bandwagon and, much to Lynda Snell's delight, constructing a farm pond. In 1989 there was a setback for Brian when he was kicked by a cow suffering from BSE and as a result he suffered post traumatic epilepsy for several years afterwards. Meanwhile Pat and Tony declared themselves fully organic and were able to apply for Soil Association status, by bringing in their last two years' acreage in one go.

Brian Aldridge (Charles Collingwood) takes an interest in the Brookfield herd in 1983. He has other things on his mind, though: he is having a very discreet affair with Caroline Bone.

In the nineties, diversification, particularly for Brian, continues. He now runs a fishing lake and an off-the-road riding course and, as part of a consortium, has bought the estate. Jill Archer at Brookfield has inevitably gone into bed and breakfast and increased attractions at Lower Loxley Hall and Grey Gables show how the countryside is playing an ever increasing role in the leisure industry.

Set-aside has been a major bone of contention amongst farmers and non-farmers alike, and many a heated debate about the morality of it all has taken place across the table at Brookfield and at The Bull. Arguments regularly rage between those who favour subsidising farmers and those who do not.

Tony and Pat look with a mixture of envy and disdain on the latest IACS cheque to drop on Brian Aldridge's doorstop as they bemoan the paltry subsidies given to the organic farmer. Brian, on the other hand, protests that he would be happy in a free market with no subsidies at all but isn't about to look 'a gift horse in the mouth'. The Grundys are too busy just keeping afloat to qualify for much and Mike Tucker, who went bankrupt just one year too soon to get his share of the milk quota which could have given him a leg up in troubled times, cannot resist an ironic smile.

The nineties have been good to some farmers with the average income up in 1996 by as much as 30%. But times are tougher for the farmworker. Today there are fewer workers employed regularly on farms and labour is often provided by men like Steve Oakley, freelance contract worker, with his own tractor and willing to travel. Some of the old farmhands like Neil Carter have gone into white-collar jobs, but even Neil, working for Borchester Mills as a seed rep, is now working freelance, on a commission only basis. Mike Tucker, who started his own market garden with the compensation money he received when he lost an eye while working on the estate, is in one sense one of the lucky ones. But even he juggles several jobs at once, still keeping on his milk and egg round because of the precarious nature of his new business.

The estate has been sold again, first to Cameron Fraser and then to Guy Pemberton. And in 1996, as a result of Guy's death, is split once more between his wife Caroline and his son Simon. Caroline inherited the Dower House and the immediate surrounding land whilst Simon kept the rest of the estate. After Simon's abortive attempt to evict the Grundys and his shocking beating of Debbie Aldridge, he has sold the estate. It has now been bought by a consortium from Felpersham which includes Brian Aldridge.

The nineties have, so far, been good to Tony and Pat at Bridge Farm. In 1991, Pat expanded her yoghurt business into ice cream and secured a lucrative contract to supply both to Underwoods food store in Borchester. In 1992, she and Tony opened a farm shop at Bridge Farm and in 1993 their 10-year-old son John decided to supplement his college allowance by rearing conservation-grade pork. Pat and Tony were not very impressed, regarding his choice as a green gimmick and not a patch on real organics. But by 1996, he is making enough of a success of it to venture into Gloucester Old Spots and finally to rear them organically at Bridge Farm. Not bad for a boy only just out of college.

At Home Farm, Brian Aldridge, having bought into the estate, is looking to the future with the help not only of his wife Jennifer, but also his step-daughter Debbie. At 26, Debbie seems at last to have found a career she wishes to follow, after finally poting for agriculture over antiques in 1994. Since then she has been playing an increasingly important role alongside Brian.

Phil and Jill are still at the helm at Brookfield but these days David plays the key role. And his wife Ruth, juggling farming and motherhood, is vital to their dairy business. Phil increasingly looks to David to make the major decisions which will take Brookfield into the next century.

Charlotte Martin 🍃 *Susan Carter*

Charlotte was born in Fontainebleau near Paris where her father was working at NATO Headquarters and she grew up at the family home in Solihull near Birmingham. At the age of three she went to dancing school and when she was nine she took the lead in *Babooshka* a Christmas play and was in just about every school production thereafter. She trained at the Birmingham Theatre School and her first professional role was at The Birmingham Rep in *The Importance of Being Earnest*. It was shortly afterwards that she successfully auditioned for her role in *The Archers*. As well as enjoying playing Susan, Charlotte has appeared in numerous other radio plays including *Lark Rise to Candleford*, *The Golden Ass* and *The Brothers Karamazov*. TV credits include *Crossroads*, *Boon*, *Howards Way*, *The History Man* and *A Very Peculiar Practice*. She has also made a pop video for the group UB40 and had a part in the film *I Bought a Vampire Motorcycle*. She now lives in Birmingham with her school teacher husband and one daughter.

Jack May 🍃 *Nelson Gabriel*

Jack was born in Henley on Thames, educated at the Forest School, Essex and spent the War in India. When he came back to England he taught for a year before going on to Merton College, Oxford. After that he got a job at the Birmingham Repertory Theatre and stayed there for four years. Jack has probably got one of the best-known faces in the programme since his extensive career has involved him in numerous film and TV roles, including both versions of *Goodbye Mr. Chips*, *The Verdict is Yours* for Granada TV and *Spread of the Eagle*, *The Age of Kings* and *All Creatures Great and Small* for the BBC. His voice is well known as Igor the Butler in *Count Duckula* and he has been heard in hundreds of radio plays and serials over the years. In the theatre, Jack has played many leading roles in the West End and was the first actor to play Henry, consecutively, in the three parts of Henry VI at the Old Vic.

Philip Molloy 🍃 *William Grundy*

Philip joined the cast of *The Archers* as Eddie and Clarrie's son, William, in 1988 at the age of seven. Like Helen Cutler the drama business has always been part of his family life as his father is actor Terry Molloy, who plays Mike Tucker, and his mum is actress Heather Barrett, who played Dorothy Adamson, the vicar's wife, in the seventies and eighties. Philip's professional ambition is to be a lighting cameraman in films and his hobbies include playing the saxophone and sports, particularly tennis, scuba diving and snow boarding.

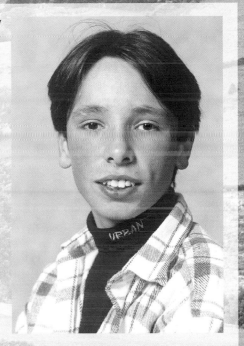

Terry Molloy 🍃 *Mike Tucker*

Terry studied music and drama at Liverpool University and played sax in a soul band in The Cavern alongside The Beatles. Terry decided to make his career in acting however and he started in the theatre working at the Birmingham Rep, the Belgrade in Coventry, The Victoria Theatre in Stoke-on-Trent and the Liverpool Playhouse. He took part in the national tour of *Godspell* and also toured extensively with the Prospect Theatre Company. His TV credits include *Crossroads, EastEnders, Bergerac, The Real Eddy English, Oliver Twist* and a number of one-off plays, including *The Exercise* and *Altogether Now*. He is also the face behind the mask of Davros, creator of the Daleks in *Dr Who* and a member of the hit squad for *Beadle's About*. Terry received the Pye Radio Award for Best Actor in 1981 for his role in Ron Hutchinson's *Risky City*, and he has hundreds of radio plays, documentaries and readings to his credit. He has been playing the part of irascible Mike Tucker in *The Archers* since 1972 and he is also a director of The Archers Addicts Fan Club. Terry lives in Birmingham with his wife, Heather, and their three children, Robert, Philip and Hannah.

Village Life

chapter five

It is in the painting of village life as a backdrop to the emotional lives of the central characters that much of the charm and originality of *The Archers* lies. While listeners may be hooked for a period of time on whether Tom Forrest will marry Pru, David will go for Sophie, or Sid and Kathy will buy The Bull, they come back and back because they like the sounds and the sights, the smell and the feel of the life that is Ambridge. There is something therapeutic in its ongoingness, in its ability to renew itself after damage, to affirm after denial. Ambridge is a cathartic experience - ultimately an optimistic place.

The village life of Ambridge is centred around its community life, its communal events and institutions, beginning,

Villagers on the steps of St Stephen's after the Sunday service in the 1960s.

Under Matthew Wreford, the bell-ringing team flourishes with Tom Forrest (Bob Arnold, left) at the helm.

some would say, with its Church life. The Parish Church of St Stephen's lies on the far side of Ambridge on the Waterley Cross road. It is built on the site of a 7th century St Augustan Church and the architecture is said to be a mixture of Saxon, Late Norman, Early English and Perpendicular styles. Church life centres around the ecclesiastical calendar and is galvanised, even today, by the personality of the resident priest.

Within nine months of the programme beginning, the first vicar of Ambridge, who is a likeable but rather old school scholar of Latin and Greek, leaves to take up a cathedral post and is replaced by John Ridley, a much younger and go-ahead man in his mid-thirties. John was wounded in Normandy during the war and so walks with a slight limp. He loves riding and fishing, encourages many community activities and is instrumental in setting up the Ambridge football team, the Ambridge Wanderers. The team thrive up until the late seventies when interest wanes in favour of cricket.

John Ridley appeals to all classes and types of people in Ambridge and he encourages a thriving congregation and strong choir. He is much missed in 1955 when he swaps places for a year with a priest from inner London called Norris Buckland. Norris is far too outspoken for Ambridge and many people boycott the church. John Ridley is welcomed back in 1956 with open arms.

In 1961 he is replaced by Matthew Wreford, who continues the tradition of energetic involvement in the community and plays a key role in supporting Jennifer Aldridge when she becomes pregnant by Paddy Redmond.

However, in many ways, Matthew is a very traditional man and it isn't until the arrival of David Latimer in 1968 that the Church really begins to reach out into the non-Church-going side of the community and invite them in. David is in favour of using the Church for secular activities during the week and he also organises local groups of people to come and tidy up the old tombstones in the graveyard and to visit the sick and entertain the senior citizens.

When Richard and Dorothy Adamson arrive, after David Latimer dies in 1973, Ambridge has its first experience of a working vicar's wife. The Adamsons have two children, Rachel and Michael, and it is difficult for

Richard Adamson (Richard Carrington).

them to manage on Richard's stipend, so Dorothy works, first for Carol Tregorran in her market garden, then in a boutique in Borchester, for a while in the village shop and finally as the doctor Matthew Thorogood's receptionist. Although she sometimes finds it difficult to juggle the necessary discretion required in being both doctor's receptionist and vicar's wife, in general her participation in the community is welcomed by all except the most conservative of parishioners. Richard is both a traditional and forward-looking priest; he runs the scout group and gives bell-ringing lessons but is not afraid to move with the times.

In 1975 the Church was beginning to divest itself of some of their older and bigger properties, which were becoming expensive to keep up and so in Ambridge too, the old vicarage and grounds are sold and the Adamsons move into a modern bungalow.

In 1979, the village is alive with gossip about whether the Church should marry Christine Archer and George Barford as George has been divorced. The subject of remarrying divorcees in Church was a hot topic throughout the country at the time and Richard plays a key role in the debate in Ambridge. The P.C.C. gets involved and comes out against the idea and even Phil, much to Christine's annoyance, votes against his sister. Richard's decision to go ahead with the marriage is a difficult and protracted one but it is based on considerable humanity as his conversation with Phil Archer shows.

When the Adamsons leave for County Durham in 1988, the village has an interregnum, during which the P.C.C. and the Church wardens play a considerable role in keeping Church life alive. It is at this time too that David Archer is married to Ruth Pritchard by the Reverend Carole Deedes, a visiting deacon. This certainly sets tongues wagging. Mrs Perkins, for one, takes Jill aside just before the ceremony and asks whether she really thinks the marriage will be legal!

VICAR	... You see, I was uniquely involved. If you cast your mind back to 1974, you will remember George Barford had a serious drink problem. And there was a suicide attempt. And when he signed himself out of hospital, there was every reason to fear that there'd be another attempt, and a recurrence of drinking.
PHIL	Wait a minute now... The Samaritans!
VICAR	Who work in total confidence... Ironic isn't it, that a man like George, who professed to have no time to talk to parsons, opened his soul to its very depths on the telephone to an unknown and anonymous stranger!
PHIL	And that stranger was...
VICAR	When a man has reached those depths: an unsatisfactory marriage, a change of profession, drink, depression – or rather despair – he has very little reserve left. He opens up completely. What has he got to lose? That anonymous stranger on the telephone heard from his own lips his regrets, his self-searching and self-criticism.
PHIL	So it's for George you're doing this. Not Chris!

In 1989, the radical Reverend Jerry Buckle arrives. He has a colourful past. He served as a lieutenant in the Grenadier Guards in Nairobi but suddenly resigned his commission when he became a pacifist. He then returned to England with his wife Frances who very soon afterwards died of cancer. Seeking a raison d'être, Jerry entered the Church. He certainly sets the cat among the pigeons when he comes to Ambridge, with his green views and political sermons. Tom Forrest is, once again, not amused, thinking the Reverend Buckle exceeds his brief. But Mrs Antrobus, who spent some years in Kenya herself, becomes extremely fond of him.

Jerry certainly practises what he preaches and almost as soon as he moves into the vicarage, he finds himself sharing it with Sharon Richards and Clive Horrobin. They desperately need a home while they wait for a council house. Sharon, only seventeen, is pregnant with Clive's child and Jerry is extremely concerned for her health and with the fact that she doesn't attend ante-natal classes and appears to smoke all the time. He brings out the best in Sharon, in spite of the many villagers who disapprove of his familiarity with the couple, and she even accepts his invitation to go to the harvest supper in October 1989. In many ways Jerry provides a father figure for her, both during the pregnancy and afterwards. It is Jerry who feeds the baby and Jerry, too, who supports Sharon when Clive walks out on her two months after the child is born. Mrs Antrobus, of course, warns him that after this, the village will not look kindly on Sharon continuing to live at the vicarage alone with the vicar but Jerry is determined not to throw Sharon out in spite of adverse comments from the P.C.C. and from locals like Eddie Grundy who simply wish to stir things.

Eventually, Pat Archer comes to the rescue with the offer of a caravan at Bridge Farm in return for some help in the dairy. But by this time the Reverend Buckle is feeling unsupported by the parish at large and decides to leave Ambridge to go on a missionary trip to Mozambique. There, eventually, he decides he will stay.

In 1991, Robin Stokes, complete with old English sheepdog, arrives at the village fête. Robin is a new type of vicar for Ambridge. He is a non-stipendiary minister and, as such, has another job to balance with his pastoral care: he is a part-time vet. The more conservative wing of the

The wedding of David and Ruth in St Stephen's on 15th December 1988.

Church also has to swallow the fact that Robin is divorced with two children, Sam and Oliver, who often come to stay with him in the school holidays. Sarah, his ex-wife, still lives in Kent and gossip soon fills in the gaps. Robin's dual role has often threatened to over-burden him and his dedication to his new-found calling, the Church, ultimately cost him his marriage, or so the rumour goes.

Robin's personal life in the five years he is in Ambridge is, inevitably, the subject of much village speculation, most especially when his name becomes romantically linked with bachelor girl Caroline Bone. Although Caroline is not a Church-goer, romance blossoms between them slowly in the first couple of years and it is further strengthened by the fact that Caroline gets on well with Robin's two children, making successful efforts to win around the elder, Sam, who at first resents her.

It isn't long before everyone in Ambridge thinks of Robin and Caroline as an item, but their confident social facade covers a complex and, at times, fragile relationship. Robin finds it difficult to come to terms with much of Caroline's past, particularly when, jealous, Brian Aldridge tells him of their affair. And Caroline, coping well with Robin's children and his busy schedule, nevertheless often battles with the strength of his religious belief.

However, by April they both propose to each other and by June the wedding date is set for 19th February 1994 to coincide with Sam and Oliver's half-term holidays.

Caroline (Sara Coward) and Robin (Tim Meats). Their confident social facade conceals a complex relationship.

But a cruel fate intervenes and Caroline's accident, only two days before her wedding, changes everything. At first confused and then blaming herself for Mark's death, she cannot accept what has happened nor the part, as she sees it, that Robin's God has played in it. Slowly the ever-present gap between the couple widens and after a holiday with her mother in the south of France, Caroline tells Robin that she cannot marry him.

The end of the relationship is a difficult and slow process for both of them. For a year, both Caroline and Robin manage, with dignity, to co-exist in the same small village, sometimes bumping into each other in the village shop or by the village green, the object of idle gossip or sympathy when they are seen together. When the new owner of the estate, Guy Pemberton, sets his eyes on Caroline, Robin decides that enough is enough and in August 1995 he moves back down south to be nearer to his children.

Robin's rather hasty departure means that the villagers once more have
to cope in an interregnum and the difficult business of finding a priest to
cover Ambridge begins again. The villagers organise their own services and
lay readers and clergy from the nearby parishes are invited to help out. One
of these is the new female vicar of Darrington. Janet Fisher is first heard in
Ambridge presiding over the funeral of Martha Woodford. As she says
herself, she wishes it was in happier circumstances, but everyone, including
friends of Martha's, Bert Fry and Tom Forrest, cannot help but be impressed
with the service and the care with which Janet speaks about Martha. It is Jill
Archer's real hope, therefore, when the bishop floats the idea of Ambridge
merging with Darrington, Edgeley and Penny Hassett under Janet Fisher,
that most parishioners will be in favour. Jill should have known better.
Opinion, as ever, in Ambridge, is fiercely divided, not only on the issue of
the merger, but most particularly on the business of accepting a woman
priest.

Eventually, in February 1996, an open meeting votes in favour of Janet
by a narrow margin as much because of lack of other options as because of
Janet's own record. The decision is endorsed by the P.C.C. the following
week and Janet is welcomed at a wine and
cheese party at the end of February. But she
knows she has a struggle ahead and will often
need to be better than many of the men who
held the post before her.

Along with Church matters, sport can
play a prominent role in the social life
of any village, and Ambridge is no exception.

Ambridge started with a football team,
introduced by the Reverend John Ridley in
1951. The football pitch was behind Mrs Perkins's
cottage in those days and the team was obviously
very successful because the continuity cards of 1953
tell us that they didn't lose a home match. In those
early years, the writers chose not to capitalise on the
sporting fixtures as a setting for major stories and the
programme seems to have contented itself with
reports of whether the team won or lost.

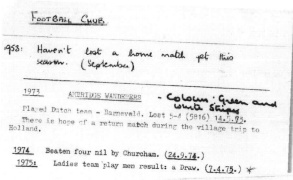

FOOTBALL CLUB.

1953:   Haven't lost a home match yet this
season. (September)

1973   AMBRIDGE WANDERERS   - Colours: Green and
Played Dutch team - Barneveld. Lost 5-4 (5816) 14.7.73.   white stripes
There is hope of a return match during the village trip to
Holland.

1974   Beaten four nil by Churcham. (24.9.74.)
1975:   Ladies team play men result: a Draw. (7.4.75.) ✳

LADIES FOOTBALL TEAM.

1975

Harry Booker asks Pat Archer to be Captain. (March)
Betty Tucker, Mary Pound & Polly Perks to play. (March)
Also Susan Harvey.   Christine Johnson (goalkeeper)
Jennifer is playing.   Also Barbara Drury.   & Jill Archer

A secret practice match is held on one of Brian Aldridge's
Fields. against Borchester Ladies. Result.
Borchester Ladies. 3. Ambridge Ladies. 2.
Referee. Brian Aldridge (3.4.75.)

Match against men ends in a draw. They used seven members
of the Borchester Ladies Team as substitutes. (7.4.75.)

However, in the seventies, there is clearly a burst of interest in football, presumably, if the nineties are anything to go by, reflecting the interests and passions of individual members of the writing team or production team of the time.

1975 and 1976 see the Ambridge Wanderers compete fairly successfully for the Crocker Memorial Shield. Much to captain, Harry Booker's chagrin, they don't win the shield but they do get as far as the fifth round.

In 1976 Harry is pressured by his wife into giving up the captaincy, and the team begins to fall apart. In April 1977, the Ambridge Wanderers play their last match.

Nothing much has been heard about football since that time. Scratch teams would have come and gone, of course, for some special occasion or other, but Ambridge obviously awaits another Harry Booker to bring back the action.

Cricket, on the other hand – always part of the fabric of Ambridge life – has flourished in recent years, in part due to the excessive enthusiasm of two of the writers Chris Thompson and Mick Martin. Listeners, beware if your Saturdays are spent playing in village teams with Chris or Mick, as you could find some of your shenanigans floating, thinly disguised, across the Am and into the country park where the cricket pitch now sits.

The original cricket pitch was on the Village Green, of course, and in 1951 Squire Lawson-Hope is president of the team with George Fairbrother and Dan Archer as vice presidents. Again, up until the early nineties, stories tended to revolve around fixtures listings and who won or lost.

It is in 1983 that Jack Woolley, then president of the club, pays for half the cost of a new cricket pavilion and has the pitch moved into the country park. By 1985, regular players

AMBRIDGE WANDERERS F.C.
FIXTURES LIST 1976 - 7

At the A.G.M. of the Ambridge F.C. it was decided not to enter the Crocker Memorial Shield Competition this season, on financial grounds. Harry Booker was re-elected team captain and coach, and Tony Archer was appointed as vice-captain.

1976

Sept.	11	Darrington	A	Won	1 - 0
	18	Loxley Barrett	H	Draw	2 - 2
	25	Felpersham	A	Lost	0 - 3
Oct.	2	Churcham	H	Won	2 - 0
	9	Rimford	H	Won	3 - 2
	16	Clayhampton	A	Draw	1 - 1
	23	Hungerton	A	Lost	0 - 4
	30	Ansley	A	Won	1 - 0
Nov.	7	Banthorpe	H	Won	3 - 2
	14	Lyttleton	H	Draw	3 - 3
	21	Edgecombe	A	Lost	2 - 3
	28	Glenbrook	A	Lost	0 - 2
Dec.	5	Ilton	H	Won	5 - 0
	12	Madeley	H	Draw	2 - 2
	19	Neesfield	A	Won	1 - 0
	26	Special Boxing Day Fixture against a Scratch team from Borchester. Abandoned after an hour's play because of the conditions of both teams.			

1977

Jan.	1	Darrington	H	Draw	2 - 2
	8	Loxley Barrett	A	Lost	0 - 3
	15	Felpersham	H	Lost	1 - 4
	22	Churcham	A	Lost	2 - 3
	29	Rimford	A	Won	4 - 3
Feb.	5	Clayhampton	H	Won	6 - 1
	12	Hungerton	H	Lost	1 - 2
	19	Ansley	H	Lost	0 - 4
	26	Banthorpe	A	Won	1 - 0
March	5	Lyttleton	A	Draw	2 - 2
	12	Edgecombe	H	Draw	0 - 0
	19	Glenbrook	H	Lost	0 - 1
	26	Ilton	A	Won	3 - 2
April	2	Madeley	A	Lost	0 - 4
	9	Neesfield	A	Lost	5 - 2
	16	to be arranged			

for Ambridge include David and Tony Archer, Brian Aldridge, Nelson Gabriel, Neil Carter, Mike Tucker and Sid Perks. In 1987 the team get an influx of talented new blood when Mark Hebden – former captain of Penny Hassett – joins and Robert Snell, recently moved into the area with his wife Lynda, offers his services as a particularly fine batsman.

In 1988, women are allowed into the cricket club dinner for the first time after a petition is organised by Mrs Antrobus, herself a keen cricket fan and resident scorer for the team. By 1988 too, Mark Hebden has taken over the captaincy and has instituted a new regime of hard training. Early morning three-mile runs nearly kill Matthew Thorogood and Kenton Archer to name but two. In 1990, Sid Perks takes over as captain and capitalises on the stronger team built up by Mark. Winning now becomes a very real possibility but Darrington often stand in their way.

Writers Chris Thompson and Mick Martin picking the seam out of a storyline.

By 1993, with a couple of relatively successful seasons behind them, Ambridge seriously aims to do well in the South Borset Village League. David, Mark, Robert Snell and Sid Perks are clearly players to be reckoned with, even if several of the others, including Tony, are there more to enjoy the fresh air and make up the numbers. But the single most obvious reason for the team's new-found potential is clearly the advent of the excellent batsman, Dr Richard Locke. This, coupled with the introduction of newcomer John Archer, who is a promising batsman and sound medium-pace bowler, means that the team has a solid core of six real cricketers out of eleven and Roy Tucker standing by in reserve and looking likely to be as good as John. Real skill suddenly means that the stakes are high and the drama can begin.

Tony Archer (Colin Skipp) at the crease.

It all starts, then, with a match against Darrington on 28th May. Suddenly, mid-game, Richard is called away to see a patient. Eddie Grundy, enthusiasm unlimited but with absolutely no ability, has to be drafted in as reserve and Ambridge, predictably, lose. When Richard returns, revealing that the call is a hoax, Mark Hebden is suspicious enough to investigate and finds out that Darrington has indeed stitched them up.

In May 1994 the annual single wicket competition is particularly moving as Shula Hebden presents the Mark Hebden Memorial Trophy for the first time to the winner, John Archer.

Later that year, Darrington's misdeeds are not forgotten and in July, Richard, with the help of cricket fan Nigel Pargetter, contrives a plan for Ambridge's revenge. Nigel is detailed to write a letter to Worcester County Cricket Club which would necessitate a reply. In that way he obtains some headed notepaper which he then proceeds to copy. A phoney letter, apparently from the Worcestershire selectors, is then sent out to three of Darrington's best players asking them to a try-out for Worcester on the day of their crucial match with Ambridge. Richard banks on pride getting the better of the Darrington members, who, of course, would forego the Ambridge match for the chance of greater things to come.

Sure enough, on 19th August, the day of the match, Chris Mills, the captain of Darrington, phones Sid to say that the pitch in Darrington is flooded by a burst water main and that the match will have to be cancelled. The Ambridge team smell a rat. They go across to inspect the pitch and it isn't long before they decide that the flooding is superficial and, on further inspection of the surrounding area, find a highly suspicious hosepipe hastily coiled up behind the pavilion. Towels and sponges are called for to mop up the pitch, and umpire Phil Archer declares that if it is dry by 4.30pm, the rules state that a limited over match can go ahead.

Unfortunately for Richard and Nigel, the resulting delay means that three furious Darrington players are able to arrive back from the non-event in Worcester to declare that they have been thoroughly set-up. The Darrington captain, Chris Mills, threatens to report Sid's team to the league and

John (Sam Barriscale, left) and Tony Archer (right) advise their captain, Sid Perks (Alan Devereux), as he leaves the pavilion.

Darrington then go on to beat Ambridge fair and square. The tension between the rival teams is stronger than ever.

Two years later, as June 1996 approaches the old rivalry between Ambridge and Darrington gathers momentum once more until the new female vicar, Janet Fisher, takes it upon herself to put paid to the whole thing by lecturing the teams from the pulpits of their respective churches on the theme of fair play. Darrington takes offence at the sermon as soon as they hear it, thinking that Janet has been put up to it by Ambridge. And it is only when Ambridge, hearing the same sermon directed at them one week later, decide to go to the pub at Darrington to complain too, that both teams are able to isolate the common enemy. It is obviously the vicar. A thoroughly good evening's drinking is then had by all as, for the first time in many years, they put aside their differences and vow to have nothing more to do with this 'meddlesome priest'. When rumour reaches Janet of their mutual outrage, she is simply able to smile and remember that sometimes 'God moves in mysterious ways'.

Robert Snell (Graham Blockey) catches John Archer out at the Single-Wicket Competition in 1996.

𝒩othing is more likely to show 'God moving in mysterious ways' through the highways and byways of Ambridge life than the many festivals, fairs and fêtes which have taken place over the years in the village. Such community events bring out the best and the worst in Ambridge residents as they join together to raise funds for good causes one minute and compete for aggrandisement in the latest competition the next.

Every year Ambridge has its Summer Fête, usually held between June and August, and its Flower and Produce Show in mid-September. Sometimes there are one-off activities like the Ambridge Spring Festival in May 1989 and the Rural Reminiscences Project organised by Jennifer Aldridge as part as the Town Twinning Ceremony in 1994.

Such key village activities occupy the energies of Ambridge residents for months and they can also attract star personalities, from time to time. In 1952 the annual Fête held on the last Saturday in June is opened by Gilbert Harding. On 6th July 1957, the day after Tom Forrest's release from prison, it is the turn of band leader, Humphrey Lyttleton, and in 1962, Ambridge welcomes filmstar Richard Todd, who has been filming nearby.

These days, the annual fête is a lower-key affair, usually opened by the owner of the estate or the vicar, but, carrying on a great historical tradition, Ambridge is still visited by famous personalities on occasion. In 1989, for example, Terry Wogan pops into Grey Gables for Jack Woolley's Celebrity Golfing Weekend, organised in conjunction with the Spring Festival and, in 1984, Ambridge's most famous visitor is Princess Margaret who attends the Borsetshire N.S.P.C.C. Centenary Fashion Show, also at Grey Gables. Anneka Rice arrives in 1993 to help with the project to refurbish the village hall, John Peel and Radio 1 host their annual Christmas dinner at Grey Gables in 1991 and Eddie Grundy and family win a competition to meet Britt Ekland backstage at her pantomime on 23rd December 1992.

In the 1970s, the fêtes are busy affairs, often with a competition for the Ambridge Beauty Queen. In 1977 the judges are Jack Woolley, Paul Johnson, Brian Aldridge and Colonel Danby, and Underwoods of Borchester

By Royal Appointment: Episode 8715 is recorded at Kensington Palace where HRH Princess Margaret becomes the first member of the royal family to join the cast of a soap opera. She plays a scene with Sara Coward (Caroline Bone) and Arnold Peters (Jack Woolley).

It's all smiles for William Grundy (Philip Molloy) as he meets filmstar Britt Ekland in December 1992.

Terry Wogan drops into Grey Gables in 1989 for Jack Woolley's golfing weekend.

Anneka Rice arrives to help Lynda Snell with her project to refurbish the Village Hall in 1993.

present the winner with an outfit. This proves a delightful surprise for young Neil Carter when his girlfriend, Ellen Padbury, wins. Somehow I don't think Pat or Ruth Archer would be too happy if a similar competition was held in 1997.

The Midsummer Festival, held at Home Farm in June 1996, in aid of the Dan Archer Memorial Playground, is typical of the large one-off events which villagers get involved in to raise funds. Having got Brian to donate a barn for the event, Jennifer Aldridge inevitably finds herself playing a key organisational role as catering co-ordinator. As usual, however, a full-time committee is set up, and while Usha Gupta arranges the barn dance and brings her professional experience as a solicitor to bear on all the licensing arrangements, Lynda Snell organises the publicity and Kathy Perks co-ordinates the talent competition. Many villagers help out, including Neil and Susan Carter, who organise a boules competition, and Roy Tucker and Kate Aldridge, who sell vegetarian food.

In 1994, Ambridge is twinned with Meyruelle, a French village in the Languedoc-Roussillon, and Jennifer Aldridge organises a rural reminiscences project timed to coincide with the first town-twinning ceremony and the visit of the French dignitaries led by the Mayor of Meyruelle, Henri Bergaud, and his wife Marie-Claire.

For several months before the visit, Jennifer tape records the memories of the older members of the community. War-time Ambridge proves particularly interesting and she decides to dramatise some individual moments of time in detail, using a narrator to skip from time to time and guide the audience through. Sometimes collecting source material first-hand proves frustrating, however, as people's memories differ and Jennifer finds herself in some confusion, for example, over the date of the arrival of the first tractor in Ambridge because Tom and Bert cannot agree. Ultimately, she has to consult wider sources, opt for her own scholarly decision and offend somebody.

Tom Forrest (Bob Arnold) puts his rural reminiscences on tape for Jennifer Aldridge (Angela Piper).

The great day soon arrives on 15th September and it begins with a twinning ceremony organised by Lynda Snell in which speeches of welcome are made to the visiting dignitaries. The town-twinning scrolls are exchanged and a presentation of a painting of St Stephen's by Caroline Bone is made to the Mayor of Meyruelle. All goes extremely well except when bell ringer Ernie Bennett drops his glasses while taking his jumper off just as Tom Forrest takes up his walkie-talkie to cue the bells. The bells, of course, are late. That evening at 7.30, also on the Village Green, Jennifer Archer's rural reminiscences begin with the end of an era. It is 1958 and Dan Archer, played by his grandson David, is remembering the time when his two beloved cart horses, Blossom and Boxer, drew the hay cart which took the Squire's lady, Lettie Lawson-Hope, to her final resting place in Ambridge churchyard. As the villagers file slowly behind the hay cart and coffin, Ambridge goes back in time.

The evening, directed in the end entirely by Pat Archer, who has to take over from Jennifer when Kate goes missing from Home Farm, proceeds very well, although Lynda surprises everyone at the last minute by insisting on translating key passages of Jill's narration into French. This does not, however, have the desired effect of making the French guests feel at home as they find Lynda's accent difficult to follow and rely instead on the universality of the visual picture clearly being presented in front of them.

The Ambridge Flower and Produce Show always takes place in September, although it did slide into August for some reason in the mid-eighties. There has always been a Flower and Produce Show Committee and in the sixties Committee members included Doris Archer, John and Carol Tregorran and Peggy Archer, while nowadays, Jill, Marjorie, Shula, Lynda and still Peggy take the helm. Of all the Ambridge community events, this is the one that seems to bring out the most rivalry between the villagers, probably because it centres around a series of competitions for home-made and home-grown produce. For years, Tom and Bert have slugged it out for who can grow the best strawberries, onions or runner beans, and in 1990, for example, when the show was judged by Jack Woolley and estate owner Cameron Fraser (the latter being, as far as residents knew at the time, an honourable man) Tom and Bert were sniping over the merits of the entries of their respective wives.

In recent years they have had something new to complain about, as Mike Tucker has begun to win some categories with produce grown in his new market garden. Tom and Bert both want the rules clarified to exclude professional growers. For many years Pru Forrest won category after category with her pickles, jams, chutneys and cakes but, since she has been in a nursing home, the winner in these categories is by no means certain. In 1994, William Grundy won the best onion competition which, as it was judged by Monsieur Bergaud, the French Mayor of Meyruelle, was considered to be a great honour. However, Tom Forrest didn't think the Mayor knew what he was talking about and went around reminding everyone that he was, after all, only a butcher by trade. Usha Gupta entered the show for the first time in 1995, causing Tom to complain that as Bert did her garden, the entry should have been in his name. And Lynda Snell, having been forced upon straitened times when her husband's computer business went bankrupt, is now growing her own vegetables, so the Flower and Produce Show in 1997 had better beware!

Hedli Niklaus 🍃 *Kathy Perks*

Hedli has played two other parts in *The Archers*, Libby Jones the milk recorder and German au-pair, Eva Lenz. But she came back to play the central role of Kathy Perks in 1983. Hedli studied drama at University in California and in Manchester and started her professional acting career with Brian Way's touring company, working in schools throughout Great Britain. Since then, she has played in rep all over the country and she met her husband, actor Leon Tanner, when they were both in the theatre in Torquay. Hedli has been in many radio and television plays and can be heard in countless voice overs ranging, as she proudly boasts, from the scream of a carnation suffocated by a branded weedkiller to the yowling voice of a cat outraged by the inferior quality of carpet on which it was sitting. She gives talks to all sorts of organisations and teaches presentational skills at her local asthma centre. *The Archers* now dominates much of Hedli's daily life as she is the managing director of Archers Addicts, the fan club run by members of the cast, and she is also one of the three co-authors of *The Book of The Archers*. Hedli lives in Warwickshire with Leon and their two children, Nick and Kate.

Norman Painting 🍃 *Philip Archer*

Norman joined the cast of *The Archers* to play the central role of Phil for the Midland pilot episodes in 1950 and is the only member of the cast to have played one part, without a break, since the beginning. Norman has also written nearly 1200 scripts for the programme, under the pen name of Bruno Milna. Norman left school at fifteen and spent three years working as a librarian where he saved enough money to see himself through Birmingham University, gaining a first class degree in English and a research scholarship to Christ Church College, Oxford. While at Oxford, he joined the Dramatic Society and got his first real taste of acting. But it was while pursuing a freelance career researching, writing and presenting programmes for the BBC that he was asked by Godfrey Baseley to join *The Archers'* cast. Over the years Norman has made regular appearances on many TV and radio programmes, including *Call My Bluff, On The Air, Stop the Week, Quote Unquote* and *The Gardening Quiz*. Norman is a life Governor of the Royal Agricultural Society of England and in 1976 was awarded the O.B.E. He lives in South Warwickshire.

Ian Pepperell ◙ *Roy Tucker*

Ian was born in 1970 in Oxford and trained at the Webber
Douglas Academy of Dramatic Art in London. His first
professional role was playing the lead in David Wood's U.K. tour
of *The Gingerbread Man* which was soon followed by a tour of
Italy as the lion in *The Wizard of Oz*. Ian has since played a wide
range of roles in the theatre, including Danny in *Playing by the
Rules* by Rod Dungate and Mole in *Toad of Toad Hall* at the
Birmingham Rep. His most recent TV appearances have been in
Pie in the Sky, EastEnders and *The Bill*. He joined the cast of *The
Archers* in 1995 to play Mike's bright but easily led son, Roy, and
was immediately plunged into a major storyline involving racist
attacks on the Asian solicitor, Usha Gupta. Ian lives in London
and one of his most recent theatre credits is the title role in a
production of Shakespeare's *Hamlet* which toured England.

Arnold Peters ◙ *Jack Woolley*

Arnold began his broadcasting career with a *Children's Hour*
programme called *Hastings of Bengal* in 1951. After serving in
the RAF he started acting at the Royal Theatre, Northampton
where he learnt his craft in five years of weekly and fortnightly
rep. In 1953 he joined *The Archers* for the first time to play
farmhand Len Thomas. In fact, Arnold is something of an *Archers*
veteran because when Len was written out he played the
Reverend David Latimer who became vicar of Ambridge in 1968
and when that character died in 1973, he took a break from
Ambridge, returning in 1988 to take over the part of
Jack Woolley. Arnold lives in the East Midlands with his wife
Beryl. He has one daughter Caroline and is the proud
grandfather of Abigail and Polly.

*B*ehind the *S*cenes

chapter six

The creation of the busy world of Ambridge on a daily basis is
a demanding and complex process and over the years it has
been achieved in different ways. In the fifties, control of the
script process was a fairly tight and relatively simple business
because up until 1962 every one of the nearly 3000 episodes of *The Archers*
was written by either Geoffrey Webb or Edward J. Mason. They worked in
close collaboration with editor Godfrey Baseley, who, although he had an
interest in amateur theatricals inherited from his parents, had no training in
drama and was therefore heavily reliant on the writers to blend his factual
farming material, so crucial to the programme in the fifties, into the
emotional and dramatic life of the village. Godfrey had a terrific instinct for
what was needed at the time, however, and, as he was an ex-staff speaker for
the Ministry of Information during the War, he was also well aware of the
power of propaganda emanating from the right hands. His instinct to
pursue Henry Burtt's idea of 'a farming *Dick Barton*' was inspired, even if
some of the jerkiness of early scripts showed that the team took a while to
integrate fully the drama, melodrama and factual farming information.

The acting was also of a variable nature since Godfrey used a mixture
of professional actors and 'real people', believing that the authenticity and
understanding of country life inherent in the real country characters made
up for, and sometimes even exceeded, the results of the technique applied
by the professional actors. Today one of our most popular characters, Tom
Forrest, comes from that stable. Bob Arnold, having literally learnt his craft
'on the job', now combines the best of 'real life' with the technique of the
experienced radio actor.

Occasionally in the fifties and sixties, Godfrey would also invite a
senior figure from the farming world to appear as himself on the
programme. In 1961, for example, Mr Richard Trehane, chairman of the
Milk Marketing Board, stayed with his wife as guests of Charles Grenville,
'Squire' of Ambridge, and his fiancée Carol Grey. He was to make a speech

to local Borsetshire N.F.U. members the following day. All this combined with the acting styles of the time, made the programme's pace and sound very different from today.

In 1950, the process of getting sound effects recorded and assembled fell to senior sound engineer, Tony Shryane. He spent many weeks out and about recording effects for the Whit Week trial on the Midlands Home Service. When the programme itself was eventually recorded, it was done on large record 'blanks' which meant that each episode had to be performed from start to finish as live and if a mistake was made, everyone had to go back to the beginning and start again. The playing in of sound effects had to be tightly timed, controlled and cued from the sound desk, which Tony himself operated. Microphones, too, were far less sophisticated than they

Charles Grenville (Michael Shaw, right) and fiancée Carol Grey (Anne Cullen, second from left) entertain Mr Trehane, chairman of the Milk Marketing Board (left) and his wife.

Producer Tony Shryane at the control panel recording a scene with Dan (Harry Oakes) and Doris (Gwen Berryman) in the fifties.

Tony Shryane (left) talks to Mr H. J. Dunkerley, controller of Midland Region, at The Archers' *2,000th party, 26th September 1958.*

are today and positioning of actors on microphone and for entrances and exits was crucial.

By the time *The Archers* went on air nationally on 1st January 1951, Tony was given the role of junior producer, on loan on a gentleman's agreement from his studio manager duties, and Godfrey's brief as editor was to be responsible for policy, acceptance of the scripts and 'any trouble that might arise'. Again, Godfrey was expected to cope with all this as well as his duties as a farming producer.

By the summer of 1951, Tony was appointed to work full-time on *The Archers*. Tony, Godfrey and both their secretaries shared one small office, which, if a little cramped, at least made communication easy. Tony's fuller role freed Godfrey to spend more time researching ideas for the storylines and it is clear from Godfrey's book, *The Archers – A Slice of My Life*, published in 1971, that he spent some time carrying out the kind of detailed research with farming and government advisory bodies which would now be done by one of the producers on our team. He details one example when a landowner he knew wanted to increase his gross profit margin by farming another 200 acres of his estate without incurring any further capital expenditure. To lay his hands on the land, the landowner wanted to edge out two of his older tenant farmers, who in his opinion, were neglecting their farms. Godfrey immediately saw strong possibilities for a potential storyline and checked out the landowner's point of view with the Country Landowners Association, the legal position with the Land Agents Association, the viability of the landowner's plan with the Government Agricultural Land Service and the National Agricultural Advisory Service, and finally he looked at the tenant farmers' position by consulting both national and local branches of the National Farmers Union. Only when all this work had been done, did he present the idea to the two script writers at one of their regular quarterly script meetings which were held to determine the exact storylining of the next thirteen weeks.

But Godfrey admits in his book, somewhat ruefully and magnanimously, to the fact that no amount of detailed research will prevent the odd mistake creeping through on a fast-turnaround daily programme. He remembers one scene particularly, in which Dan was dressing his corn fields with 2cwt of nitrogen to the acre in line with government advice of the time, designed to increase the yield on the crop. Instead of the 2cwt however, somehow the script mentioned two tonnes. Godfrey admits to failing to notice the error when checking the script prior to recording and so two tonnes was duly broadcast to the nation. Needless to say it brought a flood of correspondence from farmers pointing out the error – and some included cartoon drawings. Godfrey particularly remembers one of a farmer standing on a ladder with a pair of shears in his hands, trying to harvest the crop that had shot up towards the sky. Today, Godfrey would also have had to cope with a barrage of complaints from the environmentalists, the Organic Movement and those wedded to Integrated Crop Management.

As the team was so much smaller in the fifties, I am sure that it must have been easier than today for the two writers to meet the editor more regularly on an informal basis and this, coupled with the fact that each writer wrote one or even two months of scripts before handing over to the next, meant that quarterly formal meetings would have sufficed. Today, all eleven writers on the team meet every month. In those early days, however, the quarterly meeting was a top-heavy affair. The morning began with the editor and writers discussing and agreeing the story content for the next thirteen weeks.

After this producer Tony Shryane joined the meeting and plans were outlined to him so that he could begin to decide what new casting or sound effects would be needed and to organise the studios and facilities necessary. This could be quite complicated, particularly if last-minute topical inserts, such at the Royal Show or the results of the Annual Agricultural Price Review, were planned.

The second part of the day involved meeting the BBC hierarchy to outline the proposals, which Godfrey says were accepted without modification in most cases. However, there were times when new eyes saw more potential in the story or when an idea would clash with plans already made by another department to cover the same issue.

Matters of policy were also discussed as they related to the programme and in the late fifties, the team would have been concerned with how much news coverage *The Archers* should contain in view of the increasing news and current affairs programming which the BBC was undertaking. This would have been a conversation not unlike the one I was having with my current team in 1996 when BSE hit the farming community. The decision we make now, of course, is to tell the story from the point of view of how it affects our characters and not to disseminate information for its own sake. Interestingly, the role of *The Archers* as an information conduit for farmers – an inheritance from the brief of the programme in the fifties – came to an end in the early seventies and was, no doubt, much discussed at the quarterly meeting of that time.

In the fifties, Godfrey himself planned the programme in three phases. He worked five years ahead on broad research, keeping an eye on the latest information coming from scientists working on nutrition, biology and genetics; a year ahead on broadstrokes; and thirteen weeks ahead on detail. The fifties was a tremendous decade for *The Archers* and by 1958, Tony Shryane had set up magnificent systems for staying within budget, controlling studio time, the booking of actors and the regular recording of sound effects out on the farm.

The programme peaked on listening figures at an astonishing 20 million in 1955, before the advent of ITV and before television had really begun to bite. The 1960s, in comparison, was a much less certain time.

One of the key writers, Geoffrey Webb, became ill in 1961, and a young Birmingham-based playwright, David Turner, was brought in to write some of the scripts. Television was growing in popularity and was inevitably affecting audience figures.

When Geoffrey died in 1962, he was replaced some months later by playwright and novelist John Keir-Cross, a Scot living in the West Country and a friend of Ted Mason. At his first script conference, John was told, 'what we need is more humour, more sex, more drama ... and a strong carry over from the Friday to the Monday episode', not so very different from the advice we give writers today. Also in 1962, the BBC – not having the benefit of the wisdom of Michael Grade's theory that bold scheduling can make or break a show, and not having seen his astute stripping of *Neighbours* at tea-time some twenty years later - decided to move the Omnibus edition of

Tony Shryane, Godfrey Baseley, Edward J. Mason and Geoffrey Webb escape for a day in the country in the 1950s.

The Archers from the Light Programme to the Home Service. The Archers promptly lost half its listeners who remained tuned to the Light Programme for the music.

The team did not take this lying down, however, and more work went into the scripts. The evening episode was eventually given a lunchtime repeat on the Home Service, but by January 1965 television was snapping at its heels and the two editions were getting the same audience as a single evening edition had got in 1962. The total audience was now down to seven million. Writer Ted Mason wanted to be more provocative, to use stronger language and to have more sex in the programme, but permission from the BBC hierarchy, presumably at one of those quarterly meetings, was not granted.

By early 1967, *The Archers* was taken off the Light Programme altogether and was switched to the Home Service, which was, in time, to become Radio 4. Godfrey Baseley was now already two years beyond the official BBC retirement age of 60, and it was therefore decided to reshuffle programme responsibilities in a fundamental way. Tony, who, unbelievably, had been on contract since the programme began, was finally brought on to the staff and given full authority for 'every aspect of the programme, excluding script editing', while Godfrey was asked to carry on with a new contract as script editor, concentrating totally on the scripts and storylines.

When John Keir-Cross died, Norman Painting, the actor who plays Phil Archer, was brought in to replace both him and eventually David Turner, who was clearly not seeing eye to eye with Godfrey. And under the pen-name Bruno Milna, Norman went on to write 1198 scripts over the next thirteen years. In 1969, Ted Mason suffered a stroke and Brian Hayles, a writer, actor and sculptor who had been working with the team as a reserve writer for a while, was brought in full-time to replace Ted. But thankfully Ted recovered and was able to rejoin the team for a while the following year.

The second half of the sixties was therefore a period of change and instability, particularly in the writing team. Knocked hard by schedule changes imposed from above and by the inevitable inroads of television challenging its listeners' loyalty, *The Archers* came into the seventies shaken and bruised, but still, in radio terms, with a large audience.

Unfortunately, the first big story of the decade, that of the kidnapping of Jennifer's three- year-old-child, Adam, was not liked either by listeners or the BBC hierarchy. The general feeling seemed to be that such events did not happen in a country village and that, in any case, the story was handled

*Writer Brian Hayles
joined the team in 1969.*

in a melodramatic way. Certainly, the style of the programme had not
sufficiently moved with the times and it was beginning to sound
increasingly anachronistic to the modern ear. Simply putting more and
more dramatic storylines into the format would do little to alleviate the
problem if they were treated in an old-fashioned way.

I have always felt that *The Archers* can handle almost any subject if the
tone is right and in keeping with the times. If one or other of these factors
gets out of sync, problems arise.

By the end of 1970 there was a slight drop in audience figures in the
evening and an even bigger drop in the Omnibus listenership. By January
1971, morale was so low that there was no 20th anniversary party, although
the official line was that they were waiting to celebrate the 21st. In *A Slice of
My Life*, Godfrey astutely predicted many of the major changes ahead for
farmers and the countryside. He wrote about the acceleration of the pace of
change in farming, the increasing dominance of large-scale farms over the
small, the rise of convenience foods, the increased leisure and recreational
use of the countryside and the development of dormitory villages with the
problems of incomers.

He saw *The Archers* as being ready to tackle all this, but he also predicted nothing but canned, dried or frozen vegetables, a huge uptake of reconstituted milk and the fact that *The Archers* would have to sacrifice some of its nostalgia. The latter three predictions, I think, have been seen to be much less accurate.

By the end of 1971, Ted Mason died and Godfrey poignantly admits to feelings of isolation within *The Archers* structure. By this time Jock Gallagher had been appointed Head of Network Radio in Birmingham and was charged with revamping *The Archers* before, failing a marked improvement, it was taken off the air. One has only to read the various books and memos that were written at the time and since then to realise that Godfrey and Jock did not get on and, in the end, Godfrey eventually agreed to retire, making a gracious and diplomatic farewell appearance on television's *Late Night Line-Up*. However, by the beginning of 1972, he was in a less conciliatory mood. He did not attend the 21st birthday party and made it clear to the press that he had been dumped. In fact, almost twenty years later, Jock, in *The Archers Omnibus* of 1990, wrote an apologia for his treatment of Godfrey, admitting to a certain insensitivity to his position, occasioned by the arrogance of youth with a pressing job to be done. But he nevertheless sticks to his guns over the urgency of sorting out *The Archers* before it was 'rested' for ever. Certainly the two were magnanimous enough to make it up in public at *The Archers'* 10,000th birthday celebrations in 1989. I was invited to that glittering occasion and was delighted after the meal to participate in a richly deserved standing ovation for both Godfrey and Tony Shryane.

Charles Lefeaux became editor of The Archers *in 1973.*

It was Tony Shryane who continued to give the programme stability and continuity and, no doubt, helped ease the path for the period which followed, in which Malcolm Lynch from *Coronation Street* and then Charles Lefeaux, took the editor's chair. It was at this time too that Tony Parkin, then head of farming programmes for BBC in the Midlands, came on board as agricultural story adviser, as neither Malcolm nor Charles came from a farming background.

Malcolm got the writers down to writing one week at a time and introduced radically dramatic storylines. The audience figures began to revive. The scripts improved with better dialogue and, undoubtedly also as a result of Tony Parkin's influence, the farming material became better integrated into the programme. But there was also a feeling that the programme's pace was simply getting too fast and too many big events were happening in one week. In any case, after only a year with the programme, heart problems meant that Malcolm had to retire. In 1973, Charles Lefeaux took over the reins in what was supposed to be a stop-gap appointment but which lasted a successful five years. Charles was a city man through and through and he leaned heavily on Tony Parkin to provide and monitor the agricultural part of the programme. But his expertise in radio drama was much appreciated by both the writers and the cast. He tightened up on the writing schedules and greatly increased the writing team, bringing in Kerry Lee Crabbe, Keith Miles, William Smethurst and the programme's first woman writer, Tessa Diamond, to join Bruno Milna and Brian Hayles. By 1974, the listening figures were stable at a healthy three million.

1976, the year of the programme's 25th anniversary, saw a rush of books: Norman Painting's autobiographical history of the programme, *Forever Ambridge*, two novels, *Spring at Brookfield* by Brian Hayles and *An Ambridge Summer* by Keith Miles, the first *Who's Who of Ambridge* and a TV documentary inevitably titled *Underneath the Archers*. Norman Painting was awarded the O.B.E. in the New Year's Honours list and Gwen Berryman as Doris was voted Midlander of the Year. In 1977 further changes to the schedules meant that the evening episode was moved from 6.45 to 7.05, where it has remained ever since and the Omnibus was moved from Sunday morning to 6.15 on Sunday evening. However, listeners created such a fuss about the latter that a year later it was moved back to Sunday morning but at the later time of 10.15, and there it has remained.

When Charles Lefeaux retired in 1978, Jock invited William Smethurst to take over, and it was at this time too that I joined the programme as a producer, working both to William and Tony Shryane, directing the programme in the studio with responsibility for casting new characters and, when time allowed, producing other radio drama as well.

Between 1978 and 1986, William greatly raised the profile of the programme and exploited every marketing opportunity possible. He brought back the character of Caroline Bone, for which I recommended

William Smethurst flanked by Gwen Berryman (Doris) and Edgar Harrison (Dan), and members of the cast in the seventies.

actress Sara Coward, introduced Nigel Pargetter, for which I recommended Graham Seed, and he also brought in Kathy Perks, Mark Hebden, P.C. Dave Barry, and, of course, Eddie Grundy. I remember getting a strong idea of the kind of character Eddie was just by sitting and listening to William describe him for half an hour. I was delighted, then, to find local actor Trevor Harrison in the first round of auditions. As soon as he arrived in the studio I was sure that – although nervous and at that time inexperienced – we had a real winner. William agreed. In William's time too, Eddie got his own fan club and the programme developed a cult status. I designed T-shirts, for which I invented the slogan, 'Cultivate The Archers', and they sold like hot cakes. William wrote several books, including *The Archers Official Companion* and, under the pseudonym of Jennifer Aldridge and John Tregorran, *Ambridge: An English Village through the Ages*.

Between 1978 and 1980, William radically changed the writing team, which was, in any case, in some disarray when he joined: Keith Miles wanted to leave to do other things; Brian Hayles was retiring on health grounds and William himself could now no longer write for the programme. To join Bruno Milna, he brought in theatre writers Tim Rose-Price and James Robson, both writers with some radio experience, agricultural journalist Graham Harvey, for a while the novelist Susan Hill and eventually several relatively new writers including solicitor's clerk Helen

Leadbeater, her old school friend, Birmingham-based school teacher Mary
Cutler, Margaret Phelan and former production secretary on the programme
Joanna Toye. He finally added Alan Bower, Debbie Cook and Julian
Spilsbury. The programme had never had so many writers.

William also changed the writing pattern. He wanted writers to write
six months on and six months off in two teams of four. He believed that
writing the programme constantly without a break was not good for any
writer and that periods away to recharge the batteries and do other work
was crucial. Joanna Toye agrees but remembers that the junction between
the two six-monthly stints was a bit of a nightmare for the writers. They
were all sent the previous months' scripts and storylines just before they
rejoined the programme and were, of course, expected to have listened in
the interim. There was a lot of material to absorb. However, she goes on to
say that continuity within each writing month was eased by the fact that
writers were not writing simultaneously; they could look at the
previous scripts before they wrote the bulk of their own scripts
and William encouraged writers to be inventive with smaller
stories, usually comedy-based plots, which did not necessarily
need picking up the following week. At this time too the concept
of rewrites within the system did not exist. Writers were
expected to get the script right first time and if any rewrites were
felt necessary, they were done by the editor.

By the early eighties, then, the programme was on top form
again but with the emphasis firmly on social comedy. It was not
a time for strong dramatic storylines, great passions, or
reflections on the more difficult side of life. It was a time for fun
and mischief in the programme, some of which caught the
attention of the press. The
programme's profile was
strong. But it was a time also
when the cluster of older-
aged characters was
beginning to show. The first
Jack Woolley – actor Philip
Garston-Jones – died and so
did Norman Shelley, who
played the wonderful Colonel

HOW AMBRIDGE IS HOTTING UP!

Shula's kiss makes history

THIS is the breathtaking moment every follower of everyday life in Ambridge has been waiting for—the first true kiss broadcast on the Archers.

That business of kissing the back of their hands to provide a sound effect, is a thing of the past.

And it was fitting that popular village beauty Shula Archer should be deeply entwined in the history-making moment.

When Shula dallied with hot-blooded Nick Waring in his sports coupe this week the kiss that listeners heard was genuine.

Worse (or better) may follow. Tomorrow evening, Nick (played by 26-year-old Gareth Johnson) tries to seduce Shula (Judy Bennett—a young 35) in front of an open fire.

Real kiss . . . by Judy and Gareth

EVENING NEWS L 9

the hand

Now those Archers kisses are for real

EXTRA REALISM has come to The Archers, that long-running every day story of country folk.

For 28 years the cast of the Birmingham-made BBC radio serial have kissed the backs of their hands when they wanted to convey passion.

Now, when you hear a kiss that is exactly what has happened inside the Pebble Mill studios.

Director Vanessa Whitburn,

EVENING NEWS REPORTER

said: "It's the normal thing in radio drama. When the script calls for a kiss then the actors kiss each other just as they would on TV.

"But The Archers is such a well-established programme that any changes there happen more slowly.

"When we told the cast

there was some laughter, but I think they enjoy the new method.

"We have quite a young, attractive cast. They react to any new challenge.

PROVOCATIVE

"Of course, some of the older members aren't called upon to kiss very often, though Doris did have her bottom pinched recently. That caused quite a scandal.

"And we've recorded a

scene in which Nick seduces a girl in a car outside Brookfield.

"That will be coming up on the air soon. It's not too provocative though. We leave a lot to the imagination."

In spite of the switch in the traditional time slot, The Archers still has a regular audience of around 1,500,000.

Miss Whitburn said: "We hope that will go up. We want to attract new listeners while keeping the older ones.

Danby. The actor playing Walter Gabriel, Chris Gittins, was very ill for a while, but thankfully recovered. And on 27th October 1980, Doris Archer had to die because the actress Gwen Berryman, who was by then in a nursing home in Torquay, could no longer get to the studio for recordings.

In 1986, William resigned to take up an offer to try to breathe new life into the ailing TV series *Crossroads* and Jock Gallagher appointed Liz Rigbey, a young *Farming Today* producer, as his successor. By this time, I was next door to the editor's office, working as a senior producer in radio drama and, apart from the odd foray into studio and helping out as a director, I had not been significantly involved with the programme since 1983. I had, however, remained an avid listener. I was intrigued by the new appointment, both because I didn't know who Liz was and because I knew that, as William had effectively asset-stripped the programme by taking most of the writers and a few of the actors off to *Crossroads* with him, it would not be an easy job for his successor.

When I was first introduced to Liz in the BBC canteen I must admit to wondering how this seemingly gentle and rather shy young person would cope. How wrong can you be! Jock was right – she was terrific. She immediately set about rebuilding the devastated writing team by luring

Gwen Berryman outside Buckingham Palace proudly displaying her M.B.E., 10th February 1981.

Liz Rigbey took over as editor of The Archers *in 1986.*

Rob Gittins away from *EastEnders*, taking on local writer Sam Jacobs, newcomer Tony Bagley and TV writer Eric Saweard. Eventually, too, she was able to attract one or two of the old regulars, Mary Cutler, Graham Harvey and Simon Frith, back into the fold as they became disenchanted with the choppier waters of TV. Liz's time was a tempestuous one. She remembers inheriting an unhappy cast who felt themselves too often ruled by fear – and morale was obviously low since the rumours spread about the depletion of the writing team.

One of William's last gestures before leaving the programme was to kill off the character of Dan Archer and no-one was really sure what direction the programme might take. Immediately Liz set about placing more emphasis on the agricultural storylining as well as on the more serious domestic issues. Feeling that the programme had strayed too far from its roots into "Grundyland", she was determined to bring it back to its heart, centring it on the Archers at Brookfield. She was particularly interested in David's ambitions to have more say in the running of the farm and the parallels that this would draw out with Phil's early attempts at influencing his own father, Dan, in the fifties and sixties. She dispensed with David's funny but dizzy girlfriend Sophie and brought in a new and far more likely love interest in agricultural student, Ruth Pritchard. She looked at Pat Archer's feminism from a more serious perspective and introduced considerably more complex issues around the organic Bridge Farm.

One of William's last gestures before leaving the programme was to kill off the character of Dan Archer. Here he rehearses the scene with Frank Middlemass (Dan), Alison Dowling (Elizabeth) and sound-recordist, Steve Portnoi.

Angela Piper ❧ *Jennifer Aldridge*

Angela was born and brought up in Derbyshire before training at the Royal Academy of Music where she took a teaching course in Speech and Drama, gained her Dip.Ed and won the broadcasting prize. She went on to work in rep and with the Open Air Shakespeare Company and to become a presenter of BBC2's *Playschool*. She joined *The Archers* as rebellious young schoolgirl, Jennifer Archer, in 1963 and 33 years later finds her character now trying to cope with an equally rebellious daughter, in Kate. As well as her role in *The Archers*, Angela regularly reads letters on BBC TV's *Points of View* and could be seen in Yorkshire TV's *Life Begins at Forty* and *Third Time Lucky*. In 1962 Angela married BBC announcer Peter Bolgar. They have three children – all now adults with diverse and successful careers and the family home is in Essex where Angela and Peter are surrounded by dogs, cats, hens and ducks. One of her greatest pleasures is in cooking for friends and family and in 1995 Angela wrote *Jennifer Aldridge's Archers Cookbook* which proved a huge success with cooks and fans alike.

Graham Roberts ❧ *George Barford*

Graham joined *The Archers* in 1973 to play gamekeeper George Barford. He went to Manchester and Bristol Universities before studying drama at the Bristol Old Vic Theatre School. His National Service was spent in the Royal Navy before he went on to his first professional engagement with the Arena Theatre touring out of Birmingham. He has appeared in rep all over Great Britain and among favourite theatre jobs were the world premiere of Eric Linklater's *Breakspear in Gascony* at the Edinburgh Festival, the Old Vic production of Ben Jonson's *The Alchemist* with which he toured Italy, and the West End plays *Samson, The Wild Duck* and *Bristow*. His television credits include *Z Cars, Lizzie Dripping* and *Adam Smith,* and on film he has been seen in *The Sporting Life, A Taste of Honey* and *A Touch of Brass*. On radio he has been heard in countless plays for Radio 3 and 4 and introduced *Your Concert Choice* on Radio 3. For many years Graham was a continuity announcer for Yorkshire Television and he is married to the soprano, Yvonne Robert.

Lesley Saweard ❧ *Christine Barford*

Lesley was working as a teacher in 1953 when she met the late Denis Folwell, who played Jack Archer and he remarked on how similar her voice was to that of Pamela Mant, the girl who was then playing Christine. Lesley, who was trained as an actress, jokingly said that if Pamela left, he should let her know. Little did she realise, at the time, how that chance remark was to change her life, because Pamela did leave the programme shortly afterwards and Lesley was called to Birmingham for an audition.

She got the part and the voice match with Pamela was so complete that hardly anyone noticed the change and she's been playing Christine ever since. Lesley met her husband, Geoffrey Lewis, in *The Archers* when he was playing the role of Dr Cavendish. They have one daughter, Sarah, who like Christine, is a qualified riding instructor. Alongside *The Archers*, Lesley's radio work has included *Morning Story* and *Points of View*.

Graham Seed ❧ *Nigel Pargetter*

Graham was educated at Charterhouse and trained as an actor at RADA. He made his professional debut with Sir John Clement's Chichester Festival Company in 1972 and from there went on to play many roles in rep. His first London appearance was in 1973 at the Bankside Globe and he followed this with two classical seasons at Greenwich directed by Jonathan Miller. His most recent theatre work includes a tour of Alan Ayckbourn's *Relatively Speaking* directed by Penelope Keith. Graham's television credits include *Edward VII*, *Bergerac*, *Brideshead Revisited*, *Crossroads*, *Brookside* and *Madson*. He has been seen in many films including *Gandhi* and *Little Dorrit*. Graham is married to Clare Colvin, an archivist for the English National Opera and lives in London with his two children, Toby and Nicola.

The Archers *cast collecting the Sony Radio Gold Award, presented to the longest-running daily serial, in May 1987.*

She increased the number of storylines running at any one time and streamlined the system so that all four writers in any one month wrote at once. She also introduced the idea of the synopsis in the writing schedule, which we are still using today and which considerably enhances the editorial control of both storylining and continuity. By the time she left in 1989, she had fully computerised *The Archers'* office and the writers were delivering their scripts on disc.

Those early days were tough though, as she herself admits. She was doing a lot of her learning 'on air' and inevitably some of her stronger storylines drew criticism from a few of the old guard among the listeners who preferred their *Archers* frothier and thinner. A car dealer in London started a campaign to get her removed and even the *Guardian* called for her resignation. But she stuck with her instincts, enduring the slings and arrows of outrageous fortune which also, sadly, included the suicides of two of her cast, Fiona Mathieson who played Clarrie Grundy and Ted Moult who was retired Derbyshire farmer, Bill Insley. Within a year, her tenacity began to pay off, however, as the serious newspapers started to devote column inches to many of the issues being raised in the programme and respected reviewers, like Gillian Reynolds and Paul Donovan, analysed and commented on the storylines.

The funnier side, so well built up by William, was not forgotten either, as the Grundys still maintained their high profile and Liz launched professional countrywoman, Lynda Snell, onto the Ambridge scene. Lynda's meeting with her Australian counterpart, Dame Edna Everage, will go down as a golden moment in *Archers*' history.

Tempestuous times returned in 1987, however, when, after a lunch given to celebrate *The Archers* winning the prestigious Sony Gold Award, four of the actors, the assistant producer and Liz herself went down with hepatitis. Eventually it became clear that several other guests had also gone down with the virus and although Liz heroically refused to give in to the debilitating symptoms for a long time, eventually I was drafted in to help rearrange recording sessions and cope with some of the rewrites and studio direction.

In fact Liz was off for remarkably little time and even at her lowest was directing operations from her bed. By late 1987, she was back in harness and able to enjoy some of the programme's new-found prestige. But stormy waters did not stop there. Liz then had to cope with the death of two of the older cast members, Chris Gittins (Walter Gabriel) and Ballard Berkeley (Colonel Danby), before learning that her own father was also seriously ill. In 1988 she made the difficult decision to take a six month sabbatical to spend time helping to nurse him and when he died in 1989, seeing that the programme was in good heart and good shape, she decided to call it a day. She wanted to write a novel; she wanted to diversify. Jock Gallagher received her resignation with sadness, but in the certain knowledge that he still had a successful programme on his hands.

In 1989, just in time for the programme's 10,000th edition, Jock appointed Ruth Patterson, who, at 28, was the programme's youngest ever editor. She had a background in radio features and had spent a year working on *Countryfile*, the Sunday lunchtime television programme which also comes from Pebble Mill. Ruth continued to build on Liz's stronger storylining, introducing, particularly, more environmental issues and bringing in Sharon the single mum who ended up living in the caravan at Bridge Farm with her daughter Kylie. Sharon allowed *The Archers* to look at issues involving homelessness and poverty in the countryside and to focus, too, on some of the prejudices which local inhabitants displayed towards incomers from the bottom of the pile. Ruth also brought in new writers Caroline Harrington, Paul Burns and Sally Wainwright and focused strongly on Shula Archer and her overwhelming desire to have a child. When this desire seemed to be thwarted, Shula went through a period of acute depression, which put a huge strain on her marriage to Mark. She also started her IVF treatment which provided me with a ready made situation to develop when I arrived as editor in 1991.

I have spoken elsewhere in this book about the rich mix which is essential in plotting *Archers* storylines. But what I have tried to do in the nineties is to add a stronger focus to the central stories. If we are with Shula and Simon for a few weeks or months, we are with them in a big way. I am convinced that *The Archers* of the late nineties needs to tell good stories. We do this, I hope, by providing a balance of gentle, humorous and agricultural storylines along with some strong, deep emotional stories at the centre of the programme. Most of our lives, after all, are much more emotionally complex than we would care to admit over the sherry.

Ambridge has grown over the last 46 years as the present core cast of 48 characters shows, to say nothing of the many silent characters who also enrich the landscape. We visit Ambridge for fifteen minutes each weekday. We are not, in that time, about the business of covering lives. We are about the business of telling stories and to tell our most important story at any one time, I imagine a satellite camera circling high above the village looking down upon it. Every so often the camera focuses in on one family, one corner of The Bull, one happily or unhappily married couple or on one individual. The camera closes in and comes to rest and lets us gently and sometimes deeply enter the life or lives of some of those villagers we have come to know and treasure over the years.

The Bull in Ambridge is modelled on this real-life pub, The Old Bull, in Inkberrow, Worcestershire.

The writers and production team in 1996. Front row, left to right: Caroline Harrington, Peter Kerry, Vanessa Whitburn, Graham Harvey, Mary Cutler. Back row, left to right: Tony Parkin, Simon Frith, Chris Thompson, Louise Page, Sam Boardman-Jacobs, Keri Davies, David Ian Neville, Peter Leslie Wild, Louise Gifford.

These days we run as many as eight or ten stories in any one week. The structure is complex and the focus all important. Our listeners are a sophisticated bunch. They enjoy speculating on the stories, second guessing where writers are going to move and twitching the metaphoric lace curtain to see what is going on out on the village green.

One of the biggest changes I initiated when I came back, this time as editor, was to ask that the writing team came to all the storyline meetings, whether they were writing that month or not. There was no doubt that the regular monthly storyline meetings which I had chaired at *Brookside* from 1988 to 1990, had benefited from the continued presence of all the writers; a real team feeling and memory existed and each writer, helping to create every storyline, had a vested interest in the overall shape and direction of the programme. Six years on, this has given *The Archers* a really solid foundation.

Today the tight team of eleven writers comprises old hands Mary Cutler, Simon Frith, Graham Harvey, Sam Boardman-Jacobs, Caroline Harrington (who was brought in by Ruth Patterson), Louise Page (who came in when I arrived in 1991), Mick Martin (who joined in 1992), Janey Preger (1993) and Chris Thompson and Peter Kerry in 1994. Chris Hawes arrived in 1996 and wrote his first scripts in January 1997. Writers know their *Archers'* schedule a year ahead, which allows them to juggle their other writing work around the demands of the programme, and, touch wood, the system seems to run very smoothly.

New blood bringing a fresh perspective is important from time to time, of course, and I am contacted often by people who want to write for *The Archers*. But every writer, no matter how experienced, has to leap successfully through several hoops before they are invited on to the team. First they are asked to write a trial script from a trial storyline and then, if we are interested, we will place them on a reserve list and ask them to keep in touch with us.

Mick Martin was on this list for over a year but luckily for us, was still available and interested when a space came up around the table. When a writer gets invited on to the team, they participate in the script meetings but do not write for several months. This way they are able to catch up on the storyline from what they have been hearing as a listener to what the team are currently planning, which is three months ahead. They are also able to absorb the feeling of the team towards the characters and begin to make the world of Ambridge as real as they will need to be able to write it accurately and fast.

Eventually they put pen to paper for their first set of scripts. Peter Kerry remembers limbering up for that daunting experience by doing a trial run. He prepared a parallel set of synopses a month before he was due to write. The synopsis is an outline of the 30-35 scenes in a writer's week. It has to be done in four days after receipt of the storylines and Peter recalls paper and panic everywhere. His practice run paid off, however, and the feeling of panic was considerably reduced when he came to do his first real synopsis. In fact, the other writers are a supportive bunch and are happy to give advice to newcomers or simply to share problems.

It is difficult to get on to the team precisely because the team is kept to a minimum. A group of nine to eleven regular writers at a meeting provide an excellent dynamic range of opinion. Altogether, with a production team of six, there are up to seventeen people around the table, including the agricultural story editor. It seems to me to be the perfect number. Small enough for a collective consciousness and responsibility yet big enough for a diversity of opinion and a good argument if necessary. I wouldn't want to make the team any bigger; I wouldn't want to cut, too often, into the stability of its make-up. In 1997 I am extremely proud of the writing team which I believe is stronger now than ever before.

I am proud, too, of the production team. Keri Davies is the senior producer with special responsibility for the press and PR profile of the programme. He also co-ordinates the various marketing initiatives which are submitted to us, directs in the studio and, if necessary in an emergency, can do just about any job in *The Archers* production team. Being something of a musician in his spare time, he also wrote Eddie Grundy's latest single 'A Pint of Shires' and played accordion on it. Producers Peter Leslie Wild and David Ian Neville have been with us for about two years and share the responsibilities of script editing, casting and researching the storylines. Both of them get into studio and direct on a regular basis and both play a key role in writing up the storylines after the regular monthly eight-hour script meeting. Peter, David or I will chair the script meeting and the ultimate responsibility for the storyline and just about anything else connected with the programme rests with me. When time permits I get into studio to direct too which is still, after all these years, one of my favourite parts of the job.

Senior producer, Keri Davies, records little Daniel Mark Hebden for posterity.

Archivist Camilla Fisher puts all the contemporary continuity details onto a computer. She is also slowly transferring 43 years of Archers' continuity cards, in the green boxes behind her, onto the Ambridge database too.

Louise Gifford, our programme assistant, supervises the digital editing of the programme and the compilation of the weekly omnibus, if necessary cutting the final few seconds or minutes to bring each programme down to time. Louise's job also involves checking for continuity, providing information ranging from the price of a pint in The Bull to details of the latest films on release in the Borsetshire area, and she also helps the producers with storyline research. When she is not busy with all this, Louise can be found out and about recording special sound effects for the programme, which include the many gurgles and giggles from the children of Ambridge – particularly, recently, those belonging to Pip Archer, Daniel Hebden and Jamie Perks.

Production assistants Jane Froggatt, Sarah Andrews and Sue Nicholls, are the lynchpins of the office, ensuring that the regular monthly casting is done on schedule and that scripts are printed up and sent out to the actors and technicians on time. They also deal with all the correspondence which each day tumbles into the production office, making sure that producers get to see and reply to all the letters. Jane Froggatt, the senior production assistant, has her hands full tracking the finances of the programme.

And last but not least, Camilla Fisher, our archivist, now places our modern continuity notes directly on to computer and is carefully and

The Archers in 1996

Back Row (left to right): Moir Leslie (Janet Fisher), Patricia Gallimore (Pat Archer), William Gaminara (Richard Locke), Souad Faress (Usha Gupta), Alan Devereux (Sid Perks), Hedli Niklaus (Kathy Perks), Lesley Saweard (Christine Barford), Graham Roberts (George Barford).

Fourth Row (left to right): Carole Boyd (Lynda Snell), Graham Blockey (Robert Snell), Colin Skipp (Tony Archer), Sam Barriscale (John Archer), Sara Coward (Caroline Pemberton), Peter Wingfield (Simon Pemberton), Hugh Dickson (Guy Pemberton), Vanessa Whitburn (Editor), Brian Hewlett (Neil Carter), Arnold Peters (Jack Woolley), Charlotte Martin (Susan Carter), Yves Aubert (Jean-Paul), Terry Molloy (Mike Tucker), Pamela Craig (Betty Tucker).

Third Row (left to right): Trevor Harrison (Eddie Grundy), Lucy Davis (Hayley Jordan), Graham Seed (Nigel Pargetter), Judy Bennett (Shula Hebden), June Spencer (Peggy Woolley), Timothy Bentinck (David Archer), Charles Collingwood (Brian Aldridge), Ian Pepperell (Roy Tucker).

Second Row (left to right): Edward Kelsey (Joe Grundy), Philip Molloy (William Grundy), Mary Wimbush (Julia Pargetter), Alison Dowling (Elizabeth Pargetter), Patricia Greene (Jill Archer), Felicity Finch (Ruth Archer), Angela Piper (Jennifer Aldridge), Kellie Bright (Kate Aldridge), Tamsin Greig (Debbie Aldridge).

Standing Front Row (left to right): Rosalind Adams (Clarrie Grundy).

Seated Front Row (left to right): Margot Boyd (Mrs Antrobus), Bob Arnold (Tom Forrest), Norman Painting (Phil Archer), Jack May (Nelson Gabriel), Roger Hume (Bert Fry).

gradually compiling details from 43 years of old continuity cards on to the database too. Her careful cataloguing is, of course, constantly interrupted by requests from any one of the writers for archive information, or by questions from the production team, or from the many phone calls and letters which pour into the office asking for information for anything from a pub quiz to an edition of *Panorama.*

These days *The Archers* runs on a four weekly cycle. Week one begins with the script meeting and preparation and dissemination of the storylines. In week two the writers' synopses, based on those storylines, arrive and are edited by the script editor for continuity and tone, and to double check that the line of the stories are held and developed across the month. Week three in some ways can feel like the busiest week because that is the studio week and we are in studio for six days recording a month's worth of scripts. The office is usually alive in week three, with actors popping in between studios wanting to catch up on their bookings, pick up a script or see a member of the production team. It is a fun time. Everyone likes having the actors around. Meanwhile too, Louise Gifford, has begun editing the programme almost as soon as the raw material has come out of studio.

In week four main research is done for the storyline pack, which will go out to the writers at the weekend and will inform the script meeting the following week. In week four too, scripts arrive from that month's four writers, and whoever is script editing will bury themselves, probably at home, for two or three days to edit the scripts and decide what rewrites, if any, will be required. These days the writers do their own rewrites. If I haven't done the script editing myself, I will read the edited scripts over the following weekend and meet with the producer

Marjorie Antrobus (Margot Boyd) made a grand entrance with her Afghans at The Archers' 45th birthday party in London, January 1996.

Former Home Secretary, Michael Howard, chats to Norman Painting at The Archers' 45th birthday party.

Charles Collingwood (Brian Aldridge), Patricia Greene (Jill Archer), the author and Trevor Harrison (Eddie Grundy) at The Archers' 42nd birthday party at the Botanical Gardens in Birmingham.

to outline any rewrites I still require on the Monday morning. Then we are into the next script meeting and the whole process starts again. Time flies when you are in *The Archers'* production team.

This book has really been about the storylines and the production process and so I have not been able to spend much time writing about the actors who, every month, breathe life into the scripts with their talent and their craft. Even regular core characters only come into studio for two or three days per month and most of our cast juggle working in *The Archers* with other acting jobs. Many work in theatre and television as well as radio drama. I am constantly in admiration of their ability to pick up their characters month by month, sometimes after longish gaps, as if they have never let them go. And yet, many of our cast are so busy with other work that they have played several different roles in the interim.

The Archers is normally recorded during the day and so if an actor is working at night in the theatre, he or she can still take part. I remember Ian Pepperell coming in to play Roy in the middle of a very complex story, which involved him in the racist attacks on Usha Gupta, while he was playing Mole in *Toad of Toad Hall* at the Birmingham Repertory Theatre at night. I had seen the production and was always expecting Roy to begin to sound like Mole, at least in rehearsal. But he never did. His ability to portray the subtle shifts and changes in Roy's psyche as he slowly came to the realisation of the true horror of what he was involved in, filled me with admiration. This kind of skill is duplicated again and again among our splendid cast. The directors hang on to the continuity of the events; the actor is first base in hanging on to the continuity of the portrayal of character. All of them do a great job.

Others who contribute to the programme's success are, of course, the loyal four million listeners. Over 100 letters arrive in *The Archers'* office every month, to say nothing of the constant flow of phone calls and e-mails.

Big stories, of course, engender big reactions. When Simon Pemberton hit Shula, I was surprised at how many fans wanted Shula to give him a second chance. A listener from Middlesborough wrote:

> No, Shula was not right and yes, most certainly she should have given Simon a second chance. When Simon struck her he was desperate to explain, but she would not give him the chance. He was an idiot two-timing her, but this Harriet seems to have been pestering him mercilessly.

And another from Kent:

> Please could we have a dramatic reconciliation?
> I do think that one slap on the cheek, whilst unacceptable,
> does not really constitute domestic violence.

There's a world of debate in that statement alone, I would have thought. Of course the strong stories are at their most potent when they also stimulate debate outside the storyline. 1995's story about the racist attacks on Usha Gupta signalled considerable interest in rural racism in the press, for example.

And the death of Mark Hebden in February 1994 provoked a wide response. From a listener in Plymouth:

Angst in Ambridge: Souad Saress, who plays Usha Gupta in 'The Archers', fictional victim of an all-too-real rural racism./Photograph by David Mansell.

1995's storyline about racist attacks on Usha Gupta (Souad Faress) caught the attention of the media. The Observer joined the debate on 9th April 1995.

> I felt that I must write and tell you how beautifully you presented such a poignant and tender situation. I am an ardent follower of The Archers and I mourn with all the characters as if I know them personally.

On the other hand, from a listener in the Midlands:

> Do you really believe that we the audience want a fatal death and a comatose bride? Yes, I know that the real world is cruel, but aren't I entitled to a bit of make-believe after a hard day at work?

We also had many letters complaining about the leak of the storyline in the *Daily Telegraph*. A listener from Cumbria wrote:

> Why on earth is it felt necessary to leak news of impending doom to the press? I assume that the leaks must come from high up in The Archers' hierarchy, but for the life of me I can't understand what purpose they serve - a programme as successful as The Archers doesn't need to stoop to such tactics!

Let me set the record straight here. It is quite clear from the many letters and calls we receive when a storyline does leak, that our listeners, unlike the viewers of many of the TV soaps, hate to know what is going to happen in advance. I can assure fans therefore that the leaks do not come from anyone in *The Archers'* hierarchy. In fact, we had been discussing the story of Mark's death, in one way or another, for about nine months, so the scriptwriters and production team had successfully kept the story quiet, as they do many others, for a considerable time. The leak was a most unfortunate one. It happens from time to time and it ruins our pleasure in creating the story as much as the listeners' in hearing it.

Meeting the listeners is one of the most interesting parts of the job. Nothing can beat feedback from the fans and these days the actors and production team get to meet them in a variety of ways. From birthday party celebrations at the Birmingham Botanical Gardens and London's Livery Club, through book launches in Harrods and Waterstones to the launch of the latest Eddie Grundy CD in a pub on the outskirts of London. From touring some of the major theatres of the country with *An Evening with the Archers*, a two-hour performance designed to take audiences behind the scenes to show how the programme is put together, to *The Archers: From Roots to Radio*, the slimmed down 90-minute version for colleges, universities and arts festivals, the Archers seem to be everywhere!

The fan club too, run by the cast, organises bi-annual conventions, cruises on some of the most famous cruise liners in the world and residential weekends in Ambridge country. In recent years, Archers Addicts conventions have been held in the Pebble Mill studios, where fans were able to meet actors and members of the production team for informal chats, see the studio where *The Archers* is recorded and watch a scene being put together. Some even found themselves acting alongside their favourite characters!

Ambridge goes to Osterley in 1995.

In 1994, a convention was held in the heart of *Archers'* country at Malvern in Worcestershire, where the Ambridge Fair was opened by actress Wendy Richard. Hedli Niklaus who, as managing director of Addicts, was organising the event, remembers a hair-raising half-hour as everyone anxiously waited for Wendy to turn up. Arnold Peters (Jack Woolley) was standing by alongside the chairman of

Malvern Council to take over if necessary. But fans were expecting the *EastEnders* star, one of Ambridge's most loyal supporters, and Hedli didn't want to let them down. At the eleventh hour, Wendy rushed in, full of apologies. She'd been stuck in a motorway traffic jam. Crisis averted, the rest of the day went off like clockwork. The fancy dress parade boasted some proud Ambridge vegetables and fans were able to browse at leisure through Nelson's antiques, Jill's WI cake stall, play Scrabble with Peggy and guess the weight of the pig with John Archer. Outside the barn, Lynda Snell took her turn in the stocks and you could take a pot-shot with a sponge while the Grundys invited you to a wellie-wanging competition. The festivities went on late into the evening with a barn dance called by Jack Woolley, featuring the dulcet tones of the hit of the Borsetshire C&W scene, Eddie Grundy.

Wendy Richard takes her revenge on Lynda Snell (Carole Boyd) at the Archers Addicts Malvern convention in 1994. For more information about Archers Addicts call 0121 773 0111.

In 1995, Archers Addicts went up-market with a garden party and hat parade in the grounds of Osterley Park in London. Osterley provided a delightful double for Grey Gables and Jack Woolley, in elegant panama and white linen suit, was in top form as host. Legions of fans, including Jenny Webb of the 'Free Susan Carter' campaign, arrived wearing elegant summer hats. They ranged from one built entirely of wine corks, dedicated to Nelson's Wine Bar, to the delightful identical hats created for Jill Archer and Lynda Snell by milliner Bridget Bailey.

On the day, Hedli remembers one fan telling her that she had been about to leave her job because she was not happy with her boss, until one lunchtime she came upon him listening to *The Archers*. They started to talk about the programme and found out that they were both avid listeners, and from that moment onwards their relationship improved. Now she's no longer thinking of leaving. Then there was the fan who recounted a tale of arriving, laden down with goods, at the checkout of a large supermarket only to find that she had forgotten to bring her credit card. On frantically searching through her purse, she found that her Archers Addicts card was all she had with her.

Wendy with the Ambridge vegetables in the fancy dress competition at Malvern.

'Don't worry,' said the assistant. 'I can take that as a guarantee.'

I remember the sun shining down upon us all day. Sat listening to the Hollerton Town Band, drinking champagne and eating our cream teas, we really were the essence of good English country living. Most of the production team were at the festival, and the events on the bandstand were co-ordinated and directed by Hedli and producer Peter Leslie Wild.

The cast of The Ambridge Pageant, organised by Archers Addicts. Arnold Peters (Jack Woolley), Charlotte Martin (Susan Carter), Trevor Harrison (Eddie Grundy), Patricia Greene (Jill Archer), Hedli Niklaus (Kathy Perks) and Graeme Kirk (Kenton Archer).

Over the years, there have been many marketing ideas surrounding *The Archers*. As well as the inevitable array of mugs, T-shirts, pens, badges, key rings and photos, the BBC Audio Collection has released three double cassettes of archive recordings, you can buy an Eddie Grundy CD, a Jennifer Aldridge cookbook, an Ambridge map, a model of The Bull, and a dictionary of every character that has ever been heard in the programme. Not every idea comes to fruition, of course, and in the late eighties there was even an abortive attempt to build an Ambridge theme park!

Recently, the most successful 'live' ventures have been the two theatre tours organised by Archers Addicts. *The Ambridge Pageant*, written by Ted Kelsey (Joe Grundy) toured theatres nationwide in 1991 and *Murder at Ambridge Hall* often played to audiences of over a thousand in 1993. Hedli remembers *Murder at Ambridge Hall* was a success essentially because it was aimed at family entertainment. The fan club got many letters that year thanking the company for a show which, at last, they felt able to take the whole family to see. She remembers too an evening in Hull when, after the show, a group of women fans, burly truck-driver husbands in tow, came up to speak to the cast. Hedli and Paddy joked with the men about being dragged out by their wives to see the show, only to realise that it was they who were the fans and the wives who had been coerced into the visit. Never take an *Archers* fan for granted. They may just surprise you.

*B*ut what of the future? Running *The Archers* inevitably involves thinking long term and planning ahead. Godfrey Baseley had his five-year, one-year and thirteen-week strategy and we have our regular monthly script meetings, and two long term per year. Godfrey's five-year plan, inevitably, was a rather speculative affair and so, of course, it should have been. Trying to pin things down too far in advance leads to oversimplification at best, inaccuracy at worst. And it would be a sure way of frustrating the creative potential of the contemporary team. However, it is important to be abreast of current trends; to realise, for example, that all farmers, whether they be organic or simply interested in fertiliser control, are becoming more and more conscious of the larger environmental issues which will become increasingly important in the next century. And those that hang behind will, eventually, when they see the inevitable reciprocity of interest, get involved. It is important, too, to speculate on how long a subsidised culture in farming can last and for the team to concern themselves with the debate currently raging in farming circles about whether removing subsidies altogether would produce a fairer system for all.

Then of course there are the characters. Will Shula ever find anyone who matches up to her memory of Mark? Will Phil ever really let David take over responsibility for Brookfield? Is Brian looking to Debbie to take over at Home Farm when he retires? Will Nigel and Lizzie turn the business around at Lower Loxley and see their ancestral home begin to make a profit? Will Lizzie ever have a child?

While we are crystal ball gazing, lets look·still further into the future. What will Philippa Rose Archer be doing in 2011 when she is eighteen? Will she take after her mum and want to be a farmer or will she do something altogether different? Daniel Mark Hebden will be seventeen. Will he be a farmer like his grandfather and namesake Dan Archer or will he, perhaps, take after his own father and become a solicitor?

So many questions. Such fun in store for someone to guide a team to work out the answers. And who knows who will be the guiding hand and write the words and speak the lines when that year comes? For it is a salutary thought for all of us involved in *The Archers* that, like so many of our enduring works of art, the whole is somehow greater than the sum of its parts. And all editors, after all, are but caretakers for the future. And if we do take care, in the nurturing and growing of this unique programme, I am sure that, as we roll on into our 48th year, there will be many a glass raised in celebration and in anticipation of the big one - 50 golden years of *The Archers of Ambridge* in 2001. I hope to see you at the celebrations.

The author, Vanessa Whitburn, with Godfrey Baseley, creator and first editor of The Archers who died on 2 February 1997.

Colin Skipp ✿ *Tony Archer*

Colin started writing scripts with actor, Victor Maddern, while working as an office boy with the Rank Organisation and he was determined, eventually, to earn his living in the theatre. But first he had to do National Service as a private in the Army Pay Corps. It was after this that he won a scholarship to the Royal Academy of Dramatic Art and worked his way through washing dishes at the Lyons Corner House in Oxford Street. After winning the RADA fencing prize and the BBC drama student prize, he went into rep and it was while doing a summer season in Guernsey in 1968 that he met his wife to be, actress Lisa Davies. By then, Colin had been playing Tony for about a year. He is several years older than the character and one newspaper, confusing his age with that of Tony, reported that Lisa was marrying an eighteen-year-old. Colin remarks that all her friends thought she was cradle snatching. Away from *The Archers*, Colin enjoys working as a director as well as an actor. He and Lisa have one daughter who is an actress.

June Spencer ✿ *Peggy Archer*

June is the only other member of the current *Archers* cast, along with Norman Painting, to have played in the pilot episode in 1950 as well as the first national episode broadcast on 1 January 1951. From the beginning she played the part of Peggy, Dan and Doris's daughter-in-law, also doubling in 1951 as the flighty Irish girl, Rita Flyne. In 1953 she took a break from the programme when she and her husband Roger adopted two children. She was back in Ambridge a year later playing Rita again, and she resumed playing Peggy in 1962 when Thelma Rogers left the programme. June studied drama at Stockwin Music College and began her career doing comic monologues, many of which she wrote herself, on the after-dinner circuit. June has worked extensively in radio on everything from *Children's Hour* to radio plays, from pantomime to poetry readings. She has also worked on *The Archers'* predecessor *Dick Barton* and its one time rival, *Mrs Dale's Diary*. Two books of her comedy sketches and a one act play have been published and she wrote a series of three satirical feature programmes for the BBC as well as a number of Odd Odes for Cyril Fletcher. In 1991 June was made an O.B.E. She lives with her husband, Roger, in Surrey.

Mary Wimbush *Julia Pargetter*

Mary joined *The Archers* in 1992 to play Nigel's monstrous mother Julia, crowning a long and successful career in theatre, television and radio. Her theatre credits include *The Prime of Miss Jean Brodie* at the Royal Exchange, Manchester, *Butley* in the West End, and *Richard III* and *The Wild Duck* at the National Theatre. Her favourite film role was in *Oh What a Lovely War* directed by Richard Attenborough. Her recent TV credits include *Wycliffe*, *Miss Pym's Day Out* and *Jeeves and Wooster*. Mary has also been a familiar voice in BBC radio drama for over 50 years and in 1991 she won the Sony Radio Award for Best Actress. In 1993 she played Lady Edith in *The Governor's Consort*, a part especially written for her by Peter Tinniswood.

Peter Wingfield *Simon Pemberton*

Peter joined *The Archers* in 1995 to play Simon Pemberton. He was born in Cardiff and like Graham Blockey (Robert Snell) originally studied medicine. But it wasn't long before Peter decided that his true vocation lay in drama and since then he has worked extensively in television, radio and film. TV credits include *Martin Chuzzlewit*, *Over There*, *Crocodile Shoes*, *Highlander* and *Death and Beauty*. On film he has appeared in *Uncovered* and on radio played leading roles in H.E. Bates's *Fair Stood the Winds for France* and Barbara Vine's *Going Wrong*.

Index